MYNDERSE LIBRARY

Seneca Falls, N.Y.

TWANGED

Also by Carol Higgins Clark

DECKED
SNAGGED
ICED

TWANGED

CAROL HIGGINS CLARK

WARNER BOOKS

A Time Warner Company

This book is a work of fiction. Names, characters, places and incidents are either the product of the author's imagination or are used fictitiously, and any resemblance to actual persons, living or dead, events, or locales is entirely coincidental.

Warner Books, Inc., 1271 Avenue of the Americas, New York, NY 10020
Visit our Web site at http://warnerbooks.com

 A Time Warner Company

Printed in the United States of America
First Printing: March 1998

ISBN 0-446-51763-1

For Maureen Egen and Larry Kirshbaum,
my good friends.
And Regan Reilly's too!
With love and thanks.

*"Music oft have such a charm
To make bad good, and good provoke to harm."*

William Shakespeare, Measure for Measure

TWANGED

1

The thick sweet scent of turf burning in the chimney of Malachy Sheerin's one-hundred-and-fifty-year-old stone cottage, set back from the road yet not too far from the rugged coastline of the West of Ireland, always made him feel at peace. He lived in a little town called Ballyford, just south of the Ring of Kerry. It was practically the westernmost point in all of Europe.

Outside, the weather was deliciously foul. Even though the calendar said June, the cold rain and lashing wind made the inside feel that much cozier. It was the kind of night when a cup of hot tea or a slug of whiskey never tasted better.

Malachy's one and only door didn't quite meet the jamb. It probably never had. As a consequence the gusty wind whistled shrilly through it and under it, creating its own night music and causing the door to shudder and shake.

Malachy didn't seem to notice. He was well into one of his lengthy oral discourses, expounding into his tape recorder. . . . "You can see why they used to call the fiddle the 'dance of the devil' or the 'devil's box.' It's associated with dancing and drinking. Actually, I see it as one of the first great stress relievers. It helped people let loose after a hard day's work on the land." He lit his pipe again. This was what he loved: sitting in his favorite chair by the fire, inhaling the pungent aroma he cherished, and hearing himself talk.

Old Grizzly, he took to calling himself. His weathered appearance made him look as though he'd done a lot of hard living in the midst of frequent inclement weather. At seventy-four years of age his face was deeply lined, his shaggy hair was gray with dark streaks running through it, and a protruding belly hung over his favorite turquoise belt buckle.

"Music is people's release around here, even more than the rest of Ireland. Always has been. Out in the middle of nowhere like this, there's nothing more brilliant than gathering in the evening in a neighbor's parlor and telling tall tales around the fire. Nothing too small to hang your hat on, God knows. Anything at all that comes to mind is ripe for discussion. Talk of weather, ghosts. Old Granny McBride could talk the hind legs off a donkey with her stories of fairies and leprechauns. But then"—Malachy paused as if to savor the memory— "when the time was right, I'd bring out my magic fiddle and start to play. That moment was always grand. Before you knew it, toes were tapping, arms were raised, and the cares of the day were forgotten as even the most timid got out of their chairs and started to move to the music. Six days ago I bequeathed you the legendary fiddle, my pet, so now it's your turn to let the magic come alive and play on! Play on, Brigid! Ignore what they're saying about its curse. It's a bunch of blarney." He paused. "Now, this fiddle here . . ."

Malachy Sheerin, the former all-Ireland fiddle champion and notorious traveling storyteller, laid his pipe on the hearth next to his whiskey. After taking a hearty swig he leaned over to pick up the fiddle that was propped against the side of the chair, but the effort was great. With his arthritic fingers he grasped the bow and the fiddle and rested them in his lap.

"I'll just close my eyes for a minute," he said. A moment later he was asleep.

The tape recorder next to him whirred on.

Within seconds the door opened and the drenched stranger who had been observing him from the window quickly made his move. He stealthily extricated the fiddle and the bow from Malachy's lap and placed them in the case he had noticed in the corner of the room. His eyes brightened when he saw the tape recorder. Hurriedly he took off his raincoat, grabbed the little machine, and wrapped the coat around his stash for further protection from the elements.

He didn't notice the receipt that fell out of his pocket. It fluttered onto the floor, landing between the heap of Malachy's old newspapers and the fireplace.

Malachy was now snoring gently, but the increasing momentum of the snores made the stranger nervous. One good snort and Malachy would wake himself up. The intruder stole a final glance around the room, grabbed the whiskey bottle for a quick gulp, and slipped out the shaky door to his waiting car. He wanted to make as quick an escape as possible on the dangerous and winding coastal roads. Roads that hugged magnificent cliffs and overlooked the angry roaring waves of the Atlantic Ocean, the same body of water that lapped at shores nearly three thousand miles away on the South Fork of Long Island, on the famous beaches known simply as the Hamptons.

2

Chappy Tinka frowned at the sun from a cushioned lounge chair perched next to his swimming pool with the big black musical note he'd had painted on the bottom to show everyone his interest in the arts. His gams felt sweaty, particularly behind his pudgy knees. He had drowsed for several minutes hugging his legs to him, and now droplets of perspiration were forming miniature puddles on the cushion. The straw hat with the logo for the Melting Pot Music Festival was starting to itch around his ears, and strands of his salt-and-pepper hair poked out from under the brim. The Sunday papers were in disarray around him, and whenever a breeze blew up from the beach they would begin to flap, threatening to scatter hither and yon. In general a great sense of irritability was settling into every fiber of his privileged being.

He sipped his now watery iced tea and reflected on the fact that he hadn't heard a thing all day regarding the bloody fiddle he wanted so badly. A fiddle he needed so desperately! A fiddle that belonged on the grounds of the Tinka homestead, which, after Mother died, he had dubbed Chappy's Compound, future home of Chappy's Theatre by the Sea—if they could ever get started with the construction!

Chappy fished the lemon out of his glass and sucked on it. His face puckered, although to the untrained eye there was no discernible difference in his countenance. It seemed to be a family trait. Most of his ancestors, though generally a friendly lot, looked as if they were born not with a silver spoon in their mouths but a slice of lemon. Premature frown lines appeared on the visages of many a Tinka, and numerous winces were captured on old black-and-white photos that were hung in the hallway.

As his tongue ran around the lemon, one thought ran around Chappy's head. That idiot Duke had better get the fiddle for him!

To think that he, Chaplain Wickham Tinka, had been in Ireland just last Sunday morning with his wife, Bettina, and they'd stumbled across that stupid pub in Ballyford on the last day of touring the castles in the West. The pub had been a mess: cigarette butts, dirty dishes, and a tired bartender who'd opened the door and waved them into a room smelling of stale beer. "Big celebration last night," he'd said. "It was grand. Just got here to start the cleanup."

Chappy had been disgusted enough to want to leave immediately, but Bettina had complained that her blood sugar was very low and insisted they stay and have something quick.

The bartender had started to yak with Chappy when Bettina went to the ladies' room. He droned on about the birthday party they'd had the night before for a young American girl named Brigid who was on her way to becoming a country music star. Her mother's family lived in town and they had all been in attendance. Brigid had performed several duets with the famous all-Ireland fiddle champion Malachy Sheerin; he, of course, had played his legendary Fiddle of the Cliffs.

"Why legendary?" Chappy asked.

The bartender's eyes widened. "Why, lad, it was fashioned from the wood of a fairy tree. There's a blessing on it. Whoever owns it will always have good luck and get his heart's desire."

Chappy's ears perked up. He believed in good-luck charms. Maybe if he owned the fiddle, he could be a musical-comedy star after all.

"How can I make arrangements to buy it?" he asked.

The bartender looked at him as though he were nuts. "That's a laugh. Out of the question. It's an Irish fiddle that will stay with the Irish."

When Bettina returned, he served them some dreadful leftovers. Then when Chappy handed over his credit card while Bettina headed out to the car, the bartender's eyes widened again.

"Chappy Tinka," he said with gusto. "CT. Those are the initials carved into the fiddle. Theories abound, but no one knows what they stand for."

Chappy Tinka, they stand for, you moron! Chappy wanted to cry out. Now he knew he had to have it! It was meant to be! Somehow or other he had to get it.

Slapping the bill in front of Chappy, the bartender continued, "Malachy Sheerin has had that fiddle for over sixty years now. It was given to him when he was a lad. He's carried it all over the countryside with him, going around playing and telling his stories. More Irishmen have heard that fiddle . . ."

Chappy could barely listen. For him to hear someone tell him there was something he couldn't have was very provoking. Throughout his fifty-four years of life, what Chappy wanted, Chappy got. Usually, anyway. The Tinka name was recognized everywhere. His grandfather had made a fortune in the thumbtack business, and Tinka Tacks was about as respected a company as you could get. Unfortunately for Chappy, people on the A-list for parties in the Hamptons didn't get too excited about thumbtacks. But Bettina was working tirelessly to get them on that list.

So was Chappy, actually. In the fall he'd finally be building a little theatre in the compound, a theatre where he could produce plays and maybe even star in a few himself. Who cares if he had, just last year, been encouraged to drop the improvisational acting class he had signed up for with such enthusiasm? Who needs it anyway? he'd decided. Some of the best actors in the world had never taken a lesson. The teacher was just envious of him, he was sure of it. To say that his range seemed to be limited due to his upbringing! What nerve!

Chappy had come away from that class with one bit of unintentional advice from the teacher, which he planned to heed.

If you want to work as an actor, you'd better build your own theatre.

Amen, Chappy thought. So be it.

And to have the magical fiddle! He would eventually mount a production of *Fiddler on the Roof* and cast himself in the lead. He'd keep the fiddle under the stage for good luck when he wasn't playing his heart out. The feng shui specialist brought in by the architect of the theatre to rearrange furniture so their life would be more harmonious also believed in the power of special objects. "Put a crystal in the wealth-and-power corner of the room, which is the far left," he'd said. "You'll be wealthier, happier, and more famous." Chappy had thought he was full of bull, but when he'd found out about the fiddle, he couldn't help imagining what the legendary fiddle would do for him if it were placed *stage left* in Chappy's Theatre by the Sea. Chappy nearly trembled at the thought. His plays would win awards and he would show off to all the Hamptons swells what an artistic and talented man he was.

Why, the 1910 picture of Grandma and Grandpa Tinka's wedding party hanging in the hallway had three or four fiddlers flanking the happy couple! Clearly it was time to bring fiddling back to the Tinka homestead.

So in that little pub in Ireland, Chappy had decided that no matter what, that fiddle would be his. Who cared if it was supposed to stay with the Irish? Chappy wasn't Irish at all. The thumbtack clan dated far back in this country, but not as far back as they would have liked. The *Mayflower* had been pulling out of the dock in Plymouth, England, when Chappy's forefathers had arrived late, screaming for its return. Too late. They had literally missed the boat and been forced to wait for the next pilgrimage. Ever since that day, the Tinka descendants had been neurotic about punctuality.

Chappy couldn't steal it himself, of course. There was no time and he couldn't let Bettina in on his plans. But when he got home he'd dispatched his idiot employee, Duke, to go to Ireland and bring it back. And for days now Chappy had had no choice but to wait and worry.

Of course he'd gotten phone calls from Duke, with nothing but the usual bumbling excuses. "I went to the wrong cottage." "He had guests who stayed late and I had jet lag, so I went back to my hotel." "He got drunk at a party and stayed over at his friend's house in the village." You'd think he was asking him to unload a Brinks truck! How hard could it be to steal a fiddle from a cottage in rural Ireland? There probably wasn't even a lock on the door.

Chucking the lemon into the pool, Chappy got up and went into the house, entering through the sliding glass door with the trumpet-shaped handle. A few notes of "When the Saints Go Marchin' In" played every time the door opened.

Constance, the beady-eyed fortyish housekeeper who always looked confused, came running. She was wearing a denim skirt, and a bottle of window cleaner was fastened to a holster around her scrawny hips. She had just finished spraying a glass display case of harmonicas that Chappy had installed about the same time he'd had the musical note painted at the bottom of the pool. "Mr. Tinka," she asked breathlessly, "is there something else I can get for you?"

"No. Nothing!" he shouted. "Nothing. Where is my number one sweetheart?" he asked, referring, of course, to his wife, Bettina. In actuality, she was sweetheart numbers one and two. They'd married each other twenty-five years ago, after Bettina had graduated with honors from charm school at age twenty-one. But since the course of true love was never rock-free, and charm school training only goes so far, and Chappy's mother, who had never approved of the match, had done her best to break them up, they'd divorced.

"I've never seen a gold digger with a bigger shovel," his mama had said.

But the story had a happy ending. Bettina, just separated from a husband she couldn't stand talking about, had called Chappy to express her condolences when she'd learned of Chappy's mother's passing. So what if she'd only heard a couple of years *after* Hilda Tinka's demise?

"I've just heard the terrible news," she'd said. "We've lost Mother."

Funny, Chappy had thought at the time. Bettina had never called her anything but "that old bat" during their marriage. But Chappy had realized that maturity brought forgiveness and understanding to Bettina. They'd been reunited and in September would celebrate the one-year anniversary of their second go at marriage. Now they divided their time between a sprawling Park Avenue apartment and their castle in Southampton.

"She's getting ready for a session with Peace Man in the meditation room. The ladies have all arrived," Constance said breathlessly.

"Very well," he grunted as he charged down the hallway, past the old family snapshots of his parents and grandparents in their Sunday best sitting in the sand under the broiling hot sun. Framed pictures of celebrities in the grips of his and Bettina's arms also adorned the walls. Most of the celebrities wore the expression of deer staring into headlights, having been pounced on by Bettina at the moment of recognition.

A blown-up picture of a miniature Chappy smiling out from his baby buggy was Chappy's favorite.

He kept walking. At the other end of his gargantuan summer home was a turreted room with floor-to-ceiling windows that looked out on the Atlantic. Peace Man was Bettina's new guru, and he liked to lead his chanting sessions in there.

"We are close to the sea and the salty air. We are close to the source of life. Peace Man likes it in here," he'd said, as usual referring to himself in the third person.

Chappy stood in the hallway and watched as ladies from other expensive houses, who had been scrounged up by Bettina, sat down in yoga position on the floor and shut their eyes. Peace Man was busying himself plugging in his lava lamp. Bettina was sitting right up front, anxious to soak up every scrap of New Age garbage that Peace Man would offer. It really bugged Chappy to see her so mesmerized by a weird guy with a shaved head who wore a light green outfit that looked as it it had been issued by the state.

Finally, Peace Man spread out his hands to the assemblage. "My sisters, are you ready to get in touch with your inner child?"

"Yes, Peace Man," they answered in hushed tones.

"Are you sure?"

"Yes, Peace Man."

"Now I want you all to relax. We need to open ourselves up. To be available to what the universe sends us. To pick up its energy and heal ourselves. To see the light. Have any of you, my sisters, had a near-death experience?"

"YES! I did, Peace Man!" a platinum-haired twig called out with her eyes still shut tight.

"Tell Peace Man about it," he said in a soothing tone.

"My husband cut up my American Express card."

Gasps rippled through the room. "That's worse than death," a nasal voice honked from the corner.

"Sisters, sisters, hush now. Material goods are not what we seek. Spirituality is something that money can't buy. . . ."

Chappy turned away. "Then what do you do with all that money you collect from me?" he grumbled to himself.

"Mr. Tinka, oh, Mr. Tinka," Constance called, breathless again, as she came running toward him, practically skidding in her cowboy boots on the slick mahogany floor. Chappy liked it when the staff wore western-style clothing.

"What now?" God, what a day, he thought.

"Duke is back. He's looking for you."

"He's back! He didn't call first. Well, where is he? Where? Where? Where?" he asked, spitting out the words.

Constance gestured dramatically. "I told him to wait in your study and I'd find you. This house is so big and I feel old today."

Chappy didn't run very often, never really exercised much because he was out of shape and it was so hard to start, but this occasion deserved a bit of a sprint on his part. He reached the double doors of his study and frantically pushed them open.

Duke, grinning like the Cheshire cat, sat in the studded leather wingback chair, holding on to the fiddle case. "I've got it, boss!" he cried, raising it up in the air as if he had just won Wimbledon.

Fumbling, Chappy closed the doors behind him. "Give me that," he blurted, grabbing the treasure and laying it out on his antique desk. Carefully he unbuckled it. "I'll have to replace this cheap case."

He pulled out the fiddle, examined it as Duke sat there smiling, and suddenly screamed, "I ALWAYS KNEW YOU WERE AN IDIOT! THIS ISN'T IT! WHERE ARE MY INITIALS?"

Duke, an aspiring actor himself, who had devoted the last ten of his thirty-five years to working as Chappy's assistant when he wasn't chasing down a part or memorizing lines from plays, frowned at the employer he'd actually met in an acting class a decade before. Chappy had had to secretly sign up for it because his mother was still alive: She disapproved of Chappy's thespian aspirations almost as much as she disapproved of Bettina. "What are you talking about? You can always get it monogrammed."

"THE MAGICAL FIDDLE I WANTED HAD MY INITIALS ON IT! THIS ISN'T THE RIGHT FIDDLE! WHOSE IS IT?" he screamed.

Duke stared blankly, something that he did many times a day. He ran his hands through his wavy, shoulder-length blond hair and shrugged his broad shoulders. "I don't know, man. I snuck into Malachy's house, risking my butt, and took the fiddle he was playing with. I saw him playing it! I stuck it in the case and never looked at it again until now!"

"Well, this isn't the fiddle I need for *Fiddler on the Roof!*" Chappy stomped his foot and sat down.

"Fiddler on the Roof?" Duke repeated. "Did you get a part in something and not tell me?"

"NO! For the Chappy Theatre, stupid. And I also need it for feng shui when the theatre is built."

"Is that a new play?"

"NO! It's the Chinese art of placing special objects around the home so things go better. Rearranging the furniture and such."

"I get it."

"Well, thank God. Now, you didn't see any other fiddle in his house?"

Duke stared into space and scrunched up his nose, the only indication he ever gave of being deep in thought. "No, man, he lived in a one-room cottage. Wow, it was small. Not too much furniture to arrange there. I didn't see any other fiddle. Hmmm," he uttered. "Hmmmm. Hmmmmm."

"WHAT ARE YOU HMMMMMING ABOUT?"

"I stole a tape recorder he'd been talking into."

Chappy looked at him, appalled by what he had just heard. "Why did you do that?"

"Mine broke before I left. Maybe we should hear what he was talking about." As he reached into his carry-on bag, Duke said, "It was really weird. I thought the old dude was just talking to himself when I was watching him from the window. But when I went inside I saw this . . . ." He placed the small machine on the desk.

"HURRY UP!" Chappy yelled.

"Chill, man, chill," Duke urged. He rewound the tape and pressed play.

The two men listened intently as Malachy blathered on about fiddles and storytelling. Finally they got to the good part.

"HE GAVE IT AWAY!" Chappy moaned as he pounded his desk. "BUT TO WHOM?"

"Play on, Brigid!" Malachy said.

"BRIGID?" Chappy cried. "Ignore the curse? What was he talking about?"

"Listen," Duke said, his ear cocked. The sound of a door opening and the wind whistling came through the tinny machine. "That's my entrance," he noted excitedly.

"You are an idiot," Chappy said as he scratched his face. "Brigid. Brigid was the name of the girl he was playing with at the pub. The bartender said she's about to become a real star."

Duke sighed. "Lucky duck."

"We've got to find her. Somehow we've got to find her. Maybe you should go back to Ireland."

"But I'm tired right now," Duke complained. "And I've got a suitcase of dirty laundry."

"Tomorrow, then." Chappy leaned over his desk and growled at his employee and fellow thespian. "Don't forget. I'm doing this for Chappy's Theatre by the Sea, and you know what that means."

"You'll hire no directors who won't cast both of us."

"That's right, you moron. Now go do your wash. Tomorrow you're headed back to Shamrocksville so we can find Brigid and that cursed fiddle once and for all!"

That night Chappy lay in bed with the big fluffy quilt pulled up around his chin for comfort, one hand exposed just enough so the ever-present remote control could be aimed at the big-screen television opposite the king-sized bed. The cavernous boudoir was designed with every creature comfort as yet thought-up by man. Ocean breezes blew through the large window, and if nature couldn't be depended on to lower the temperature in the room to a pleasant sixty-five degrees, an electronic cooler kicked in. The place was built to look like a castle but behave like the starship *Enterprise*.

Bettina was in the bathroom, nearly a city block away, engaged in her nightly ritual of applying creams and potions, anything on the market that laid any claim whatsoever to staving off the aging process. It was at this time every night that Chappy would lie there, the remote control in his hand giving him a heady sense of power, and zap from one station to the next. Most of the images went by in a blur. His limited attention span presented a particular challenge to broadcasters. If he wasn't enticed within seconds, like a child with a new toy, the program on the screen was passed over for the next offering.

Tonight he felt positively peevish. Peevish and restless. "And miles to go before I sleep," he kept thinking. "And miles to go before I sleep." I won't rest until I have that fiddle, he thought. I know I won't.

Normally he enjoyed the nice feel of his Brooks Brothers pajamas and "one hundred and ten" percent cotton sheets, as he liked to call them. But all he could think about was the stick of wood from a dead tree back in Ireland that was enjoying its incarnation as the Fiddle of the Cliffs. It intrigued him that not only did it bring good luck, but it also carried some kind of curse. It only made him want it more.

Zap! went the remote control. "Good evening. On werewolf hour we have as our special guest—"

Zap! ". . . To find out about your hidden potential, call our operators at 1-800- . . ."

Zap! ". . . When I found out he liked to wear my nightgowns around the house, I must admit I got a little worried. . . ."

"How distasteful," Chappy muttered. But it was the next zap that changed Chappy's life. At least temporarily.

". . . Country Music Cable is here in Nashville, and we're talking to Brigid O'Neill, who with a heated performance won the fiddling contest at Fan Fair just yesterday. Brigid, tell us how that feels."

"Oh, it's just the greatest, Vern. My mentor in Ireland gave me his fiddle. He'd won the all-Ireland fiddling contest over there with it. It's a very old, magical instrument, and when I got up there at the contest yesterday, I felt like I was being swept away by its power. Legend has it that this was made from the wood of a special tree. . . ." As the bubbly redheaded chanteuse held up the fiddle for the camera, Chappy let out an ungodly moan.

"I'll be right there," Bettina yelled from the bathroom. "Every year this takes longer and longer."

Chappy sprang from his bed as the initials CT jumped out at him from the fiddle on his enormous-screen TV. With trembling fingers he quickly pressed the record button on his ever-ready VCR. "This is it," he mumbled. "This is it!"

"We've heard that this fiddle is supposed to have a curse on it if it leaves Ireland," the interviewer said to Brigid.

"Well, isn't that the silliest thing, Vern? I just won the Fan Fair fiddling contest with it. If that's a curse, then I want to be cursed out all the time. . . ."

Vern laughed. "I suppose you're right, Brigid."

When the brief interview, which in his excitement he had barely focused on, was over, Chappy yanked the tape out of the machine and ran like a man possessed from his room and into the hotel-sized hallway, nearly bumping into a table that had been moved by the feng shui expert. In a blur he raced to the wing where Duke was now dead to the world, resting up in his room for the trip to Ireland he would no longer have to take.

3

*H*e stared down at the little article in USA Today *that heralded the addition of Brigid O'Neill to the Melting Pot Music Festival in the Hamptons on July the Fourth.*

Nervously he slurped his coffee. "Hey, waitress," he called in a squeaky voice. "How about another cup of joe? I'm running low here."

"No prob," she called back as she added up the check she was about to plunk on the counter where another lone diner had just partaken of his breakfast. Scooping up the coffeepot without even looking, she walked to the booth and started to pour. "So, hon, can I take these dishes away for you?" she asked.

"Not done yet," he said.

She looked down at the thick white dinner plate, practically licked clean except for the thinnest coating of egg yolk she'd ever seen in her twenty-odd years of slinging hash. He'd mopped it mighty hard with his English muffin. It didn't faze her, though. She'd seen it all in this job. Especially on the late-night shift. "Another muffin?" she asked.

"Nope," he answered as he slurped his freshly refilled cup.

"Holler if you need me." She walked off, her white rubber-soled shoes squeaking slightly on the grimy floor.

He stared down at the paper again. The Melting Pot Music Festival in the Hamptons. Melting Pot, my foot, he thought. You're allowed in the Melting Pot only if you've got a lot of gold to throw in with you.

But Brigid O'Neill was coming to the Hamptons with her fiddle. That's all that counted. Right after he was so rudely thrown in jail, her hit song, "If I'da Known You Were in Jail (I Wouldn'ta Felt So Bad about You Not Callin')," had come on the radio. It was the first time he had heard it. He was sure she was sending a message to him.

Now he was in love with her. If he could just get the chance to be alone with her, he was sure she would feel the same way about him. Like in the movie The Sheik, *which his mother liked to watch. Rudolph Valentino had kidnapped the girl and carried her off to his tent in the desert, and she fell in love with him. Why couldn't that happen to him with Brigid? He hadn't been able to get close to her at Fan Fair or in Branson, where he'd camped out in the woods. But she was coming to the Hamptons, where he lived in a shack off the beaten path. Another sign from her! He would find a way to get to her there!*

Time to get back on the road and head home. He'd done enough wandering around this week.

4

Regan Reilly sat at the scarred wooden desk in her perfectly adequate office on the fourth floor of an old building on Hollywood Avenue in Los Angeles—home to her private investigative agency. Battered files lined the opposite wall, old-fashioned black-and-white tiles covered the ancient floor, and a small window offered a somewhat limited view of the Hollywood Hills.

To Regan it was the perfect home office—actually the only office of her one-woman operation. She had contacts all over the country to help her out when she needed it, and her handy computer with all its databases to find out everything you wanted to know about who were checking out and were probably right in being afraid to ask.

Investigating suspects' past, uncovering their present, and maybe altering their future gave Regan great delight. Her parents, Nora and Luke Reilly, concluded that the choice of occupations of their thirty-one-year-old only child could be attributed to equal parts nature and nurture. "You were born with an antenna for gossip," Nora always said. Since Nora wrote suspense novels and Luke owned three funeral homes in Summit, New Jersey, Regan's formative years were spent listening to numerous conversations about crimes and cause of death.

Regan poured a second cup of coffee from the thermos on her desk. Lately she'd decided that making a pot of coffee when she woke up and bringing the remains with her to work made sense. The sole drawback was that it didn't fill the room with the wonderful scent that only a coffeepot gives off, but the old-building smell that permeated her office, nothing antiseptic about it, made Regan happy.

Outside, the California sun was shining mercilessly, it being unseasonably hot for the month of June. On days like this, Regan loved to hole up in her office and become absorbed by her work. But today was Friday, and Regan was really there just to tie up loose ends. In the evening she was flying out on the "red eye" to Newark. A car would pick her up and take her to her parents' house, then in the afternoon they'd all drive to the vacation home in the Hamptons that Luke and Nora had bought just last year.

The Hamptons, a collection of beachside villages on the South Fork of Long Island, were about a two-hour drive from New York City, depending, of course, on the traffic. Sometimes called "Hollywood East," the South Fork was considered a high-profile stage because of all the celebrities it attracted during the summer months. With its tip jutting out as far as eighty miles into the Atlantic Ocean, the Hamptons were renowned for an almost-magical light that illuminated the flat picturesque landscape. People flocked there to see and be seen and to enjoy not only all that nature had to offer but also the parties and socializing that went full steam ahead between Memorial and Labor Days.

Regan's Fourth of July week would be spent going back and forth between her parents' home in Bridgehampton and the group house that her best friend, Kit, an insurance agent from Hartford, Connecticut, had unexpectedly joined out there. Group houses in the Hamptons consisted mostly of singles from the New York City area who rented houses together in pursuit of sun, fun, and that elusive someone who might be found at any of the parties that took place in the more than fifty-mile stretch of towns from Westhampton to Montauk. It was like a big game of hide-and-seek for adults.

Regan and Kit had just gotten back from vacationing in Ireland a few weeks earlier. And here I am leaving again, Regan thought. But she and Kit always planned an adventure together every year, and this time it had been Ireland in June. Now that her parents had the house in Bridgehampton, the week of the Fourth of July seemed to be a good time to take her other vacation of the summer.

Regan sipped her coffee and stared at the framed prints depicting the coats of arms of both the Regan and Reilly families, which had recently been added to her eclectic collection of wall hangings. Regan had bought them on the bus tour she and Kit had taken of the Ring of Kerry, a tour that made frequent stops at the souvenir shops that had sprung up around just about every bend of what was otherwise a most rural Irish route. The prints were hung next to the window; Regan felt it an appropriate spot, since the Regan family motto was "The hills forever," and under the Reilly crest, black lettering urged "With fortitude and prudence."

The phone next to her began to ring, jarring her back into the present. Quickly she grabbed it.

"Regan Reilly," she practically chirped, leaning back slightly in her orthopedically correct chair, a chair that tilted and swayed and was guaranteed to maneuver in almost any direction as it conformed to her body. Regan thought that, considering what she'd paid for it, it should also take her to lunch.

"Ah, Regan, it's Austin. How're ye keepin'?"

Regan smiled. It was her young Irish neighbor. He'd moved into her apartment complex six months before, coming to Los Angeles from Ireland to pursue a career in comedy. When he found out that Regan was going to vacation in Ireland, he'd insisted she visit the West and attend the birthday party his family was having for his American cousin "Brigid the singer" at the local pub in their little village. "I'm still adjusting to being back from Ireland, Austin. Your family was so great. They sure know how to throw a party. Thanks again."

"Ah, they enjoyed having you there, Regan. That's actually why I'm calling."

"Really?"

Austin cleared his throat. "You haven't heard anything about what's been going on with Brigid this week?"

"No, I haven't," Regan said quickly, picturing the beautiful green-eyed, redheaded dynamo whose singing and fiddle-playing at her party got everyone dancing, including some on the bar. Regan knew that after her birthday bash Brigid had been going directly back to Nashville to get ready for the tour to launch her debut album. Austin had said her record company was pulling out the stops; after her hit single, they were expecting the album to take off.

But Austin's tone sounded worried.

"Well, first of all, she was at Fan Fair last week."

"What's Fan Fair?" Regan asked.

"An annual five-day celebration in Nashville. Country music singers meet their fans," he explained hurriedly. "Mobs of people there. There are concerts and parties. The stars sign autographs for hours. On the last day they have a big fiddling contest." Austin paused, then announced with pride, "Brigid won."

"That's fantastic," Regan said. "I'm not surprised. When she and Malachy played together at her party, it was incredible."

"Well, she won the contest with Malachy's famous fiddle," Austin informed her.

"Malachy's fiddle?"

"He decided to give it to her for her twenty-fifth birthday. The day after the party."

"Wow," Regan said slowly, thinking of all the talk at the party about the celebrated fiddle. "He gave it to her for keeps?"

"Yes. He said he was getting old and she should have it now."

"So Brigid won with it. Talk about a lucky fiddle!"

"Well," Austin elaborated, "lucky and unlucky. A few things have happened since."

"What?"

"A journalist in Ireland looking for a story is making a big stink, saying the fiddle should have never left the country. He's blowing it up to being a national treasure. He unearthed this whole story about there being a curse on it if it leaves Ireland. But get this, Regan. Someone walked right into Malachy's home last Saturday night when he was sleeping. They stole a fiddle off his very lap, probably thinking it was the famous one. Actually, it was Brigid's. She insisted on swapping when Malachy gave his to her."

"Talk about a thief with bad timing."

"Indeed. Now everyone back at home is arguing about the fiddle and the curse, and she's starting to get incredible publicity here in the States about the whole business."

"Well, her album is coming out. That can only help the sales," Regan said practically.

"True. Now the latest is she's been invited with her band to play at the Melting Pot Music Festival on July Fourth in Southampton. Have you heard of it?"

"Of course!" Regan replied. "It's a benefit they've had for the last couple of years at a college in the Hamptons. It's quite a scene."

"Well, it just came up. Some guy in the Hamptons saw her on TV. He's involved with the festival and he's loaded. He got in touch with Brigid and invited her and the band to come up for the week, all expenses paid, to stay at his guest house and perform at the festival."

"That's a great festival for a new band. It gets a lot of hype," Regan said.

"That's what Brigid figured. The guys in the band agreed to it and are bringing their golf clubs. It'll be a nice little break before they start their tour, which will be fairly grueling."

"Brigid must be pretty happy," Regan responded.

"Indeed. But there is a problem. That fiddle is getting so much attention, it's like she's traveling with the crown jewels."

"And fame always attracts weirdos."

"Exactly. She called me the other night and read me a threatening letter that had been left for her at Fan Fair, which shook me up quite a bit. I told her, between that and someone stealing the fiddle from Malachy, things were getting a little scary."

"Is Brigid upset by it?" Regan asked.

"Yes, but not as much as we are. She's too excited about going on tour to give it much thought." He paused. "We were wondering, would you have any interest in taking on the job of being her body-guard out there for the week? She liked you, and I know you're headed there anyway. My family is a bit concerned and would like to have the peace of mind that someone was looking after her. Brigid didn't want to ask you herself. She feels a bit silly about the whole thing and knows that you're going out there to be on vacation. . . ."

Regan hesitated, then thought of how much fun Brigid had been the night of her party. This would certainly be an adventure. "I've always wanted to be a groupie, Austin. Maybe this is my chance."

Austin laughed. "Thanks, Regan. This will make us feel so much better."

"I'm glad," Regan said, remembering Brigid's mother, the fiftyish blonde glowing with pride when Brigid had sung at the party. "Should I call Brigid, then?"

"I'd like you to speak to her manager, Roy, to make the financial arrangements. Let me give you Brigid's number so you can give her a call, too. She's on the tour bus on the way to New York from Branson, Missouri."

"What was she doing in Branson?"

"Her band did a couple nights of shows there, replacing someone who had to cancel concerts. They figured they might as well take the job, since they were traveling anyway. Brigid's pretty ambitious. She's willing to work as hard as she needs to in order to make this album fly."

"Good for her. By the way, where is this guy's house we'll be staying at?"

"Oh, yes. Let's see. I wrote it down right here. Chappy's Compound in Southampton."

"Chappy's Compound!" Regan exclaimed. "That's where Kit's house is. Apparently there are old servants' quarters he's renting out to her group. I'd be spending time there anyway!"

Austin laughed. "Perfect, then! I guess it's Mr. Chappy who invited them. He sounds like a good fellow . . . so generous . . . very different from the usual sort you find about."

"Right," Regan answered. But somewhere in the back of her mind she recalled Kit saying something about the whole setup being a little bit strange. "Mr. Chappy certainly sounds unusual," she said with conviction.

5

As the tour bus rumbled onto the Long Island Expressway, Brigid O'Neill looked out the window and smiled. It was great to be back in her home state, near where she'd grown up. And she was headed for the ocean, where she had spent many a summer day in her childhood.

Raised in Brooklyn, Brigid and her parents used to go to Rockaway Beach in the summertime. They'd loved to ride the rough waves onto the shore, feeling the salt water washing over their bodies and pulling them in. Then they'd laugh over the unbelievable loads of sand that somehow found its way into every inch of their bathing suits. At night they'd go to Playland and ride the roller coaster and the bumper cars and eat cotton candy. Her father had usually ended up carrying a sleepy, sunburned Brigid back to the car. On these and other family trips Brigid and her father used to sing together. They'd make up crazy songs as they drove along.

They were Brigid's happiest memories.

Sometimes it didn't seem like that long ago, and other times it felt like another lifetime.

Her father had died when she was thirteen. Her mother had decided that the best thing for them would be to go to Ireland for the summer and spend it with her family. They'd ended up going there every summer, leaving as soon as Brigid got out of school and her mother finished teaching the third grade. It was when and why Brigid had gotten to know Malachy so well.

Brigid sighed. Daddy, I wish you were here to see me sing, she thought wistfully. On a big stage with an audience—not in the car! Smiling, she picked up the guitar next to her and started strumming. He had such a sense of humor, she was sure he'd have gotten a kick out of the lyrics to "If I'da Known You Were in Jail." Or the song she'd written about one of her old boyfriends: "I miss you, baby," she began to sing. "I miss the burned toast you served me in the morning. I miss the cheap wine you poured me at night. You had a way of blocking my vision so I couldn't tell left from right. Oh yeah, baby . . ."

Jeez, Brigid thought as she plucked on her guitar. In the seven years she'd been in this music business, she'd run into all kinds of nuts. She'd had to put up with so many sleazes, schemers, and con artists, when all she wanted to do was sing and play!

Fueled by a desire to make music that was practically a life force for her, she had sung wherever she could get her hands on a microphone. She'd warbled at firemen's picnics, in people's garages, in bowling alleys, and in what seemed like every little pizza-and-beer joint within one hundred miles of civilization.

And now people were lining up to buy tickets to her show!

She patted the case on the seat next to her. The case that held the fiddle, the case that she kept close by at all times. I've got to keep my eye on this, she thought. It's not everyone who gets her mitts on a legendary fiddle that helps her win contests. And after the theft at Malachy's cottage, it's obvious at least one person is out to get it. Brigid's body shivered ever so slightly.

Thank you, my man Malachy, she thought. Ever since she'd gone on the air with the fiddle after the contest at Fan Fair, things were popping. Ticket sales for the tour had picked up, radio stations were playing her hit single more frequently, and she'd been invited to the Melting Pot Music Festival. Publicity was begetting publicity. It was the kind of boost every entertainer dreams about!

But deep down inside she had a little bundle of nerves that jumped around when she thought too much about having in her possession a piece of wood that attracted so much attention. Then there was that Irish journalist who was creating such a stink about the curse and how it shouldn't have left Ireland. Unfortunately Brigid was Irish enough that she couldn't dismiss the curse completely.

It's okay, she thought as she strummed on her guitar. I've got Regan Reilly coming along to keep an eye on things this week.

Farther east on the same highway, Regan Reilly woke up in the backseat of her parents' car. She sat up and rubbed her eyes. "I guess I was really out," she said.

Nora Reilly, a petite blonde, turned around from the front seat. "Welcome to East Coast time, darling."

Silver-haired, six-foot-five Luke, his eyes on the road as he drove, smiled. "I got home from the parlor, you woke up from your nap, got in the back of the car, and fell asleep again. So, how have you been?"

Regan laughed. "Fine, Dad."

Luke grabbed the newspaper on the seat next to him and handed it back to Regan.

"What's this?" she asked.

"I was just showing your mother. We get the *Irish Tablet* at work because we advertise in it."

"I thought you only advertised in the church bulletin. Isn't the *Tablet* printed in New York?"

"Death is everywhere," Luke declared. "This newspaper has a big readership among the Irish community in the entire New York area. I picked it up this morning and look what I found on the front page."

Regan quickly read the article that named Brigid O'Neill as being the recipient of a treasured, mythical fiddle that should do nothing but help her burgeoning musical career.

However, it also hinted at potential trouble ahead for Brigid:

Legend has it that it was made in the last century from the wood of an enchanted tree that was especially dear to the fairies and was cut down by mistake. The fairies were angry but were placated when the wood from the tree was used to make this fiddle and they could enjoy its music. They said they'd place a curse on anyone who took it away from their Emerald Isle, thereby depriving them of its music. Any such person would have an accident or face death.

But whatever the legend, Miss O'Neill now has many people who are angry at her. There's a call for her to honor her Irish heritage and pass it on to a musician in Ireland. Needless to say, she should guard that fiddle with her life. There are more than a few people who would like to get their hands on it.

Regan looked up. "You'd think she had run off with the Blarney Stone."

Nora frowned. "An accident or face death? Maybe she should give it back."

"Mom, it's a superstition. As Brigid said to me on the phone, Malachy called her and wants her to keep it. He said that it was his to give, and she's about as Irish as you can get, even if she wasn't born there. He just wants her to be careful."

Nora sighed. "That's where you come in."

Regan nodded. "That's why she wants me around with her this week. Between the fiddle and the letter, it's better if there's someone looking after her. Besides, we'll have fun."

"I suppose," Nora said hesitantly. "You know, Regan, it actually works out that you're not staying with us this week."

"What do you mean?" Regan asked as she folded the newspaper.

"Now maybe you can stay next week instead. When you're finished your job."

"Mom, why does it work out that I'm not staying with you this week?"

"Well, you'll never guess who's coming out for a few days."

"Cousin Lou?"

"No."

"Cousin Pete and the munchkins?"

"No."

"Louisa Washburn and her boring husband, Herbert?"

"How did you guess?"

"MOM! They're America's houseguests."

"But they're both so bright," Nora said earnestly.

"That's your adjective for everyone who's boring."

"She called the other night to set up a dinner date and mentioned they were staying in the City over the holiday week. They're looking forward to seeing you, Regan. Louisa's decided to write an article about the Hamptons. She's done so much fact-checking for magazines over the years, she decided to try a little writing herself."

"I like them," Regan said. "But not for days on end. Once they arrive, they do tend to stay. And stay and stay and stay."

Luke looked in the rearview mirror and winked at his daughter.

An hour later they exited the Long Island Expressway, took Route 111 to Route 27, and eventually found themselves driving through Main Street in Southampton. They kept going and finally located the Chappy Compound, whose backdrop was the sparkling waters of the Atlantic Ocean.

Luke pulled between the opening in the hedges and through the gates where a sign greeted them:

WELCOME TO CHAPPY'S COMPOUND
GROUNDBREAKING WAS BEFORE YOU WERE BORN

"Good to know," Regan commented after reading the sign aloud.

Luke drove slowly as the three of them looked leftward and took in the sight of the mammoth mansion perched in a spot overlooking the sea at the end of the long driveway. It was obviously built to resemble a castle, but it looked like the kind you'd see in an amusement park.

"My God, how . . . vulgar," Nora whispered, letting out her breath.

"Not exactly a shanty in old shanty town," Luke observed.

"Or a little cottage by the sea, by the sea, by the beautiful sea," Regan offered.

"I like the idea of a castle, but this one looks so new and fake," Nora said.

"It takes a few hundred years for castles to develop the lived-in look," Regan noted. "Kit told me that Chappy built the castle a couple of years ago on the foundation of his mother's old house, which he tore down after she died. He then renamed the place Chappy's Compound."

"His poor mother," Nora said.

Regan looked around at the grounds, which included a circular drive in front of the castle, an expansive, probably sodded front lawn all set up for a game of croquet, and, along the sweeping right side of the property, an attractive rambling cottage that was more traditional—a weathered, shingled number that looked as though it would have made a sea captain happy. Farther out by the water was what looked to be a guest house.

"Kit said she's in the cottage here."

Luke veered to the right and pulled the car up to the front door. "Should I honk?" he asked his daughter.

"No, Dad. Please. They only do that in the movies. Here comes Kit anyway."

Dressed in a bathing suit cover-up, her blond hair wet and combed back, Kit hurried down the steps of a wraparound porch. "Hi, everybody," she called.

As Nora, Luke, and Regan got out of the car, a horn blared behind them, making them all jump.

"I thought they did that only in the movies," Luke remarked, his eyes crinkling. They turned as a huge bus with wheels the size of circular picnic tables crunched through the open gates. Still honking, it rumbled past them and swerved around the circular driveway, swiping the Rolls-Royce parked in front of the castle.

The front door of the castle flew open and a middle-aged man came running out.

"Welcome, welcome!" he shrieked, then stopped, obviously taking in the altered state of his Rolls. It did not deter his exuberance. "No need to worry about the dent!" he yelled to the bus driver. "No need at all. That's how auto body shops make a living."

"That's Chappy, the thumbtack king," Kit said. "The word's out that he's so happy Brigid is staying here, he's on the verge of a stroke."

"If I had a Rolls and someone smashed into it, I'd have the stroke," Luke commented. "He must sell a hell of a lot of thumbtacks."

He may be crazy, Regan thought, but at least this place looks as if it will give Brigid plenty of privacy. She turned to her mother. "Would you like to meet the Lord of the Manor?"

Nora nodded. "I wouldn't miss it for the world."

As they all walked across the sprawling property, Brigid emerged from the bus and almost stepped into the arms of the ecstatic Chappy.

"Brigid, Brigid, Brigid!" he cried. "A hundred thousand welcomes, as you Irish say. I'd like to say 'a million welcomes.' At the very least!"

Regan could see the startled look on Brigid's face, but then Brigid smiled warmly. "Now that's a lot of welcomes, Mr. Tinka."

"Chappy," he interrupted, his voice rising with every syllable. "I INSIST you call me CHAPPY."

"All right. All right," Brigid said hastily. "Chappy it is." She took a deep breath and appreciatively sniffed the air. "When we lived in Brooklyn, we were near the water. By God, I love the scent of the sea."

"Brooklyn!" Chappy exclaimed. "I keep forgetting that you weren't nurtured on the Emerald Isle. With all the talk of the fiddle, I see you in my mind as Irish."

Regan decided to try to rescue Brigid. "How about another welcome?" she asked.

Brigid turned. "Regan! Kit! It's so good to see you." As she hugged them she murmured, "What's with this guy?"

"Very hospitable." Regan grinned.

"And so forgiving," Kit whispered. "Did you see what the bus did to his car?"

"Sweet Jesus," Brigid muttered as she looked at the Rolls. "It's a wonder he didn't boot us out of here."

Regan managed to introduce Brigid to Nora and Luke before Chappy jumped in. It didn't take him more than an instant to realize that Nora was Nora Regan Reilly and very much on the A-list in the Hamptons. "Oh, how my Bettina will thrill to meet you," he said. "Oh my, what a happy day." He pointed at the three young women. "You all know each other?" he asked with what sounded like a hint of anxiety.

"Sure do," Brigid said. "Kit's in your group house here, and Regan is a friend of mine who'll be staying with me." She turned and winked at Regan. "We plan to have fun this week."

Regan had warned Brigid not to say anything about her acting as a bodyguard. When someone invites you to be their houseguest, it might be considered insulting to show up with your own security force. What would Miss Manners say about that one? Probably better to keep your mouth shut.

"Hello, Mr. Tinka," Kit said. "We haven't met yet. This is my first weekend at the house."

"Good good good," Chappy replied distractedly. He seemed to Regan like the human version of a washing machine on the spin cycle. His hands fluttered and he looked from side to side. "Mr. Reilly," he said, "Mrs. Reilly . . . are you staying at the Chappy Compound, too?"

Luke's eyes almost popped out of his head. "No," he blurted. Then, in a calmer voice, he said, "We have a house in Bridgehampton." He turned to Nora. "As a matter of fact, the Washburns will be there soon. We'd better get going."

Chappy jumped in. "Do come back tonight. I'm having a little cocktail party. Just a small group I've thrown together. We'll have drinks on the deck. Drinks and hors d'oeuvres. A little buffet. You must come back. . . ."

"We'd love to," Nora said. "But we have houseguests coming."

"Bring them along," Chappy insisted.

Brigid's band members finally emerged from the bus. In unison all three reached up and tilted their cowboy hats, for all the world reminding Regan of "Bonanza" reruns. Adam, Little Joe, and Hoss tilted their hats the same way, she thought. Clad in blue jeans and cowboy boots, Brigid's band members walked the walk of country musicians.

Brigid did the honors. "Everybody, I'd like you to meet Teddy, Hank, and Kieran."

Regan had trained herself to try to get names straight the first time she was introduced to anyone. These three would be easy to remember. Teddy was clearly the youngest. He couldn't have been more than twenty and had reddish brown hair, freckles, a baby face, and a long, skinny frame. The other two looked to be in their late twenties or early thirties. Hank was stocky, with curly dark blond hair, basset hound-brown eyes, and a handlebar mustache. Kieran had dark hair, twinkling blue eyes, and a warm smile. He was, Regan thought, what they termed in country music magazines a hunk-a-billy.

"And here comes Kieran's girlfriend, Pammy," Brigid said.

"It figures," Kit murmured to Regan.

Regan smiled. Had Brigid's tone been a bit less warm? she wondered. Interesting.

Pammy, a petite baby-doll type, clad in blue jeans and a halter top, threw back her waist-length, honey-colored hair as she looked around and smiled at everyone. "Kieran and I have been looking forward to being here and meeting you all," she said in a singsongy voice. She grabbed his arm and stroked it lovingly. "Right, honey?"

"Right, baby," he said quickly.

Regan thought he looked embarrassed.

Chappy's hands started fluttering. "Indeed, indeed. Welcome one and all. Welcome . . ."

Here we go again, Regan thought.

". . . Why doesn't everyone get settled, then?" Chappy continued. "I'll get my assistant to help you with your bags. Duke!" Chappy bellowed. "DUKE!"

Regan refrained from putting her fingers in her ears. But his bellowing worked. From inside the house, someone yelled, "Yo!"

"Yo," Nora murmured to Regan. "Is that butler talk?"

Regan smiled and shrugged her shoulders.

"GET OUT HERE!" Chappy hollered, and then he spun back around to his guests. "Yes . . . uh . . . yes . . . After everyone enjoys a bit of relaxation, perhaps a little swim, we all can meet for cocktails at six P.M. How does that sound?"

Regan turned to Nora. "Will you come back?"

"If Louisa and Herbert are willing . . ."

Regan turned to Chappy. "They'll be back."

"Wonderful!" he cried. "The start of a beautiful week! Wonderful!"

The bus driver sheepishly appeared from around the back of his vehicle as the group started to break up.

"This here is Rudy," Brigid said with a smile.

Forget a hundred thousand welcomes. Not even one measly "hello" came from Chappy for this newcomer. "Are you staying here?" he sniffed.

"Nah," Rudy said with a wave of his hand. He was small and slight with graying hair. "Someone is picking me up. I'll be back Friday night so we can hit the road after the concert. Where do you want me to stick the bus?"

That's a loaded question, Regan thought.

"Oh yes yes! Around the side of the house. Over there!" Chappy pointed as Rudy lit up a cigarette.

Upstairs, her tanned body clad in a leopard leotard, her teased, bleached blond hair pulled up in a scrunchie, Bettina stared out the window in horror as she did her bends and stretches. Her white toy poodle, Tootsie, yapped at her heels.

That tour bus looks like it escaped from Ringling Brothers, she thought grouchily. But she couldn't even complain about it, since Chappy had begrudgingly allowed Peace Man to set up camp in his RV on the side of the house for the summer season.

"We have our own on-site guru," Bettina had said. "Don't you think that looks impressive?"

Reluctantly Chappy had agreed and Bettina had been pleased. But a tour bus! Next thing you know, Bettina thought, we'll have an ice cream truck parked outside. Or a yellow-umbrella hot dog stand.

It was so hard to get things just right. To do things the way they should be done. To give the right impression to the right people.

But Bettina kept trying.

She was working hard to fit in, but it wasn't easy being a new wife in Southampton after all these years. She was certainly glad that she and Chappy had gotten back together. Her in-between husband was so broke, he couldn't afford a night out at Chucky Cheese's. There was no way she could endure that lifestyle until death did them part.

After her final stretch, Bettina grabbed her oversized T-shirt and walked out of the room, Tootsie following close behind.

"Mama has to get ready for our party tonight," she said, smiling down at her dog. She passed a portrait of Chappy's mother and stuck her tongue out at it. "I've got your son and your jewelry, you old bat."

6

In the greenhouse in the backyard of his cottage in Sag Harbor, retired master fiddle-maker Ernie Enders sat hunched over his workbench. He was surrounded by his prized tomatoes, but they did little to distract him. Thanks to the hounding of Chappy Tinka, Ernie had emerged from his retirement as a master fiddle-maker. Tinka had driven past Ernie's music shop many times over the years but had never darkened its doorstep. Now that Ernie had closed those doors for good, Chappy tracked him down at his home and begged him for his help.

"A masterpiece he wants," Ernie grumbled. "A masterpiece. In no time at all, I'm supposed to create a masterpiece. Tsk. Tsk. Tsk. Disgraceful."

Ernie looked up from the plywood mold with the golden maple sides and squinted at the blown-up pictures of the model fiddle propped up in front of him. "How am I supposed to make a fiddle look old in less than a week?!" he shouted. "How?"

He looked back down at his work in progress and sighed. These rich people want what they want when they want and it's always right now, he thought. I'm sick to my stomach. Sick sick sick. I haven't built a fiddle since retiring seven years ago and now I'm told to do it in a rush. And he wants me to carve this CT on the side just like it is in the picture.

Gingerly he picked up the unfinished hunk of wood and held it up to the pictures. Pictures taken off a television set. Ridiculous. I guess I shouldn't complain, Ernie thought as he studied the pictures. He's paying me a lot of money. Then again, he should. Ernie compared the stain on the fiddle to the one in the picture.

The door of the greenhouse opened and he turned to see Pearl, his wife of fifty years, wearing a housedress over her skinny frame and carrying a tray of lemonade and ginger snaps. "You must eat something to keep up your strength," she said. "How's it going?"

"Slow. Real slow. Tinka wants it to be exactly like the one in the picture. But how can I do that? I need to hold the original and examine it."

"Drink up, Ernie. It's hot in here." Pearl poured him a glass of the lemonade and placed the tray on his workbench. "Ernie, don't worry. You were the best in the business. Do you want me to pack your wool socks for the trip?"

"Ach," he said. "Why not?"

Having lived in the charming village of Sag Harbor their whole lives, they'd become increasingly distressed by how crowded the Hamptons now got during the summer. Especially Ernie.

"Too much too much too much," he complained to Pearl.

This year they'd planned to dodge the tourists by getting out of town for six weeks. On Wednesday they were leaving for their grandniece's wedding in Pennsylvania. After that they'd drive west.

"Some places it might get cold, you know. Maybe it is a good idea to bring your wool socks. They're a little heavier and I know how you get when your feet are cold. Nothing worse than having cold feet." Pearl sat down and stared at him.

"The only person we have to worry about getting cold feet is the groom," Ernie grumbled. He turned to Pearl. "Pearl, you know I can't work with you staring like that."

"I feel lonesome inside. I have no one to argue with. I'm not used to you working."

"With what I make on this we can take a trip to Florida this winter." He turned back to the fiddle.

"Two trips in one year. You're the last of the big spenders." Pearl laughed and got up. She leaned over to give Ernie a kiss on his bald head. Startled, he jerked and knocked the pitcher of lemonade all over the freshly stained wood.

"Pearl!"

"I'm sorry, Ernie. I'll run and get some paper towels!"

Ernie picked up the damp wood and shook his head. "More delays," he said to himself. Talking to himself was a habit he'd picked up in childhood, and it had only gotten worse when he started his solitary business of building fiddles. "More delays. I'm going to have to strip and revarnish." Ah nuts, he thought. I just hope that Chappy Tinka doesn't show up and start bugging me again. What a pest!

7

When Nora and Luke pulled into the driveway of their Bridgehampton home, they found Louisa and Herbert Washburn sitting on the front steps waiting for them.

Louisa jumped up as if she had just won Lotto. "We made wonderful time getting out here!" she exulted.

Ten minutes later they were accepting cool glasses of Chardonnay from Luke and plopping themselves onto a couch in the rear "living space" that ran the length of Luke and Nora's airy home. Pine floors, white couches and chairs, a blond wood dining room table off the open kitchen area, and large windows that overlooked an expansive grassy yard complete with a pool and large trees bordering the property—all combined to give a feeling of elegant simplicity.

"I've heard of that thumbtack family you know, *hnnnnnn*," Louisa said. It never took long for a new acquaintance of Louisa's to realize that many of her statements were punctuated with a nasal exhale and, if someone was close enough, a grab and shake of their elbow. As a result, many a drink had been spilled at cocktail parties.

Louisa turned to Herbert, a nondescript man whose expression was like Switzerland—always neutral. After forty years of marriage he didn't seem to notice Louisa's grunts and grabs anymore. A vague look in his watery blue eyes often made people wonder if the lights were on but nobody was home. "Lambie," she said.

"Yes, dear." Herbert was thin and mostly bald, a gray band of hair forming a horseshoe from ear to ear. He was a head shorter than Louisa, who was often seen affectionately smoothing out his little wisps on top.

"Years ago. Didn't we meet Hilda Tinka, this chap Chappy's mother?" she asked, stricken by a sudden urge to attend to her own hair. Someone had once told her she looked good in an upsweep: then and there it had become her permanent hairdo. Right now she strained to tuck in any stray dyed brown strands that had managed to escape from the bun. Between shampoo days her maintenance consisted of sticking in more and more pins, to the point where she couldn't make it through an airport X-ray machine without setting off the buzzer. But she was an attractive woman with soft features and warm brown eyes. "Didn't we?" she continued. *"Hnnnnnn?"*

Herbert scrunched up his mouth and blew out. His eyes remained in a fixed stare in the direction of the coffee table. Finally he answered thoughtfully, "Could be."

"That's what I thought. *Hnnnn.*" She turned to Luke and Nora. "I'm going to have to research that. I've put the information from all my datebooks for the past twenty-five years on my laptop computer. My life is in there. Names, places, parties, numbers."

"Half the people in it are dead," Herbert remarked.

"Lambie, not half!" Louisa said, grabbing his bony knee and giving it a good jiggle. "Nora, I'm the Queen of the Internet. It's where I do all my research. I'll teach you all about it this week."

Week, Nora thought. She didn't dare look at Luke. She had told him they were staying for three days at the most. In reply she managed to croak, "That would be very interesting."

"Tonight should be interesting," Louisa pronounced. "I love to get a feel for other people's homes."

You don't say, Nora thought. "Well, you won't be disappointed in this place," she said politely. "Not only did Chappy Tinka build himself a castle, but he's also going to renovate the servants' quarters and build a small theatre for his personal use."

Luke sipped his wine. "Like the Mouseketeers."

Louisa laughed. "Summer stock! How glorious!" she said, gesturing grandly with her free hand. "For my article on the Hamptons I'll have to include a little section on Chappy Tinka and his wife. Here is someone building a theatre in his own backyard! That's a long way from the days when people came out here and found nothing but a quiet farming place where people fished for excitement. I'll write about how the reasons people come out here have changed. Some people like the Hollywood feel out here, others don't." She paused slightly, emitting an exceptionally charged *hnnnnn.* "Tonight provides me with a wonderful opportunity to do some background research for my article, doesn't it, Lambie?"

"Wonderful."

Luke looked at his watch and turned to Nora. "Honey, it's four-thirty. I want to unpack the rest of the car and take a quick shower. If we're going to this party, we should leave here soon. The traffic gets pretty bad at this time of day."

"Oh, does it ever!" Louisa agreed heartily. "I'll have to put that in the article, too. 'From tractors to Mercedes-Benzes' . . ."

Nora smiled. "Why don't you two relax while we unload the rest of our things from the car and get ready?"

Louisa smoothed out the folds in her caftan. "Lambie and I will sit here and enjoy this nice view. Oh, I can't wait to see Regan. She's such a darling. I'm so sorry she won't be staying here with us."

"Duty calls," Nora said. "I think she'll have some fun on this job, though."

"Oh yes! God bless the young people! I'll certainly want to chat at length with Brigid O'Neill and get a good look at that fiddle I've been hearing so much about!"

"She seems like a lovely girl," Nora said, escaping through the front door and out to where Luke was leaning against the car and massaging his temples.

"Do you think they'd notice if we never went back inside?" he asked.

"She's always a little wound-up when she first arrives. She'll calm down. I hope." Nora leaned against her husband, enjoying the scent of his skin and his clothes, as he put his arms around her. The street was calm and quiet except for an occasional bird wanting to make its presence known with a chirp or a caw.

"Maybe she'll want to stay at the Chappy Compound to do her research," Luke said hopefully.

"Regan would kill us." Nora chuckled. "I just wonder who she'll latch on to at the party tonight."

"She's bound to rile some poor soul."

Little did he know just how riled.

8

This place is something, huh, guys?" Brigid called from her perch at the guest house's kitchen table as her band members came ambling down the stairs in their bathing suits. Before they could answer, the phone began to ring. "That's got to be my manager, Roy," she said as she ran to pick up the cordless phone that was plugged into the wall of the pantry.

After they had settled in, Regan and Brigid and Kit had congregated in the kitchen to catch up with each other.

Chappy and Duke had helped them shlep in their bags. "I hope these quarters will suffice!" Chappy had cried. "I've never had any complaints! But if you do, you must speak up and your needs will be attended to!"

After assurances were uttered over and over that indeed this was a most delightful, charming place to stay, with such an incredible view of the water, Chappy had, to the relief of them all, retreated to his castle to prepare for the party.

Upstairs were six bedrooms. Regan's room faced the road and Kit's house. Brigid's room was right across the hall and had a view of the ocean. They were furnished in typical old-beach-house style: floral wallpaper, wooden dressers circa who knows when, and beds somewhere in between twin-sized and full that very well might have been passed down by Chappy's Pilgrim ancestors. The bedspreads were the knotty white kind that Regan never ever saw for sale anywhere but always seemed to come across in people's vacation homes, particularly if they were near the water.

"What style would you call this decorating?" Regan had asked Kit while surveying her room.

"Early leftovers," Kit had answered. "Our house is much the same. I must say it's been a long time since I've seen a TV with rabbit ears."

"That's what I like about these kind of joints," Regan had said. "They take you back."

"To the Dark Ages. I feel as if our place is a set for a fifties television show, and Father Knows Best is going to walk in any minute," Kit had said while putting Regan's bag down on the hooked rug and studying the sheer white curtains blowing in the breeze. "I will say this: It's got that good beachy smell."

"Early mildew?" Regan had asked.

They were barely seated at the table when the call from Roy came in.

A few minutes later Brigid walked across the room, winding up the conversation. "Keep calling with good news. I'll talk to you tomorrow, Roy." She clicked off, laid the phone on the table, reached for the soda she had abandoned, and smiled at them benevolently.

Regan smiled back. "Good news?"

Brigid shook her head. "I can't believe how much has happened since I met you two in Ireland! This whole fiddle business is unbelievable! A couple of guys who started a country music station out here want me on their show on Monday. They're hosting the music festival." She put her feet up on the wicker chair next to her and glanced out at the water, as though to assure herself that she was so close to the Atlantic Ocean.

"Can I borrow the fiddle next time I go on a date?" Kit asked.

"Only if I go as your bodyguard," Regan answered.

"I'll take a pass."

Brigid laughed. "It's great to see you two again."

"You too, Brigid," Regan said. "Now that we have a quiet moment, would you mind showing me the letter that Austin spoke about?"

Brigid's face turned serious. "He's such a worrywart. I read it to him on the phone the other night, and he got all nervous and called my mother. I'm glad you're here, Regan, but I didn't feel that threatened by it. I know a lot of people in the public eye get nasty letters."

"I understand," Regan said. "But after the theft at Malachy's cottage, we've got to be extra cautious. So can I see it?"

Brigid swung her legs down off the chair. "Why not? Time for show-and-tell."

"By the way," Regan said as Brigid got up, "where is the fiddle?"

"Under my bed." She arched one eyebrow. "Where no one would think to look."

The nice part about being in a private place like this, Regan thought, is not having to worry about leaving the fiddle in a hotel room or lugging it around everywhere.

"As a matter of fact," Brigid said, "Chappy asked if I would bring the fiddle over tonight and play a little."

"Do you mind?" Regan asked, knowing that many performers resent being asked to entertain when they're invited to parties.

"Not at all. I'll ask the guys if they want to play, too. Let me get the letter."

A few minutes later she returned, carrying a white envelope in one hand and lugging a heavy plastic bag in the other. She dumped the contents of the sack, which included letters and postcards and little presents that people had left for her at Fan Fair, onto the table.

"Wow," Kit said, impressed. "Those are all for you?"

Brigid nodded happily. "To think that just last year I was playing to a bunch of empty chairs in the biggest dumps around. I read every one of these letters riding that bus. They are all pretty nice and normal except for this one." She handed the white envelope to Regan.

Regan took it from her and pulled out the single sheet of plain white paper. The angry black lettering gave her a chill. Someone had clearly attempted to disguise their handwriting. She read it aloud.

DEAR BRIGID,

YOU'VE TAKEN SOMETHING THAT DOESN'T BELONG TO YOU. AND I DON'T WANT TO HEAR YOU SINGING THAT SONG ABOUT JAIL ANYMORE. IF YOU DON'T HEED MY WARNING, I'LL HAVE TO TAKE FURTHER ACTION.

"Nice, huh?" Brigid said.

Regan sighed. "So someone left this last week at Fan Fair?"

Brigid nodded.

"The curse on the fiddle isn't mentioned, but the writer seems to know about it," Regan observed.

"What is this about the curse?" Kit asked.

Brigid rolled her eyes. "Oh, it's the blarney, as we say. The Irish have a history of superstitions." She explained it all to Kit, concluding with a half-smile. "The fairies like music, you see, and they don't want to be deprived of it. They never leave Ireland, so apparently the fiddle mustn't, either. Or else you'll have an accident or face death." She managed to laugh. "In my opinion the worst part of that letter is that the person who wrote it doesn't want to hear me play my hit song!"

Regan folded the letter and put it back in the envelope. "You don't mind if I hold on to this?" she asked Brigid.

"I don't want it," Brigid said.

"A lot of nuts write letters like this," Regan said. "But most of them are cowards who would be afraid to do anything in person."

"That's right," Brigid replied. "I have friends with albums out who get hate mail. And they've been fine."

"Absolutely," Regan agreed, the letter in her hand, the theft of one fiddle and the curse on this one weighing heavily on her mind. An accident or face death. Not if I can help it, she thought.

9

*H*e drove and drove, heading home, listening to his radio the whole time and thinking of Brigid. He liked to sing along to the music. Whenever the news came on, he switched channels.

So Brigid was in the Hamptons for the Fourth of July. When he was a kid, he liked that holiday. Not anymore. He hadn't been invited to a picnic in years. And he was scared of firecrackers. Ever since the owner of that chicken coop tried to shoot him, he didn't like any type of loud noises.

Now he'd have another chance to try and get to her. And be alone with her. Fan Fair had been impossible. Branson had been impossible.

He'd make it happen in the Hamptons.

10

Brad Petroni and Chuck Dumbrell had both loved country music from the time they'd been kids growing up next door to each other in Hicksville, Long Island. Their favorite game had been to dress up as cowboys, and instead of building a standard treehouse, like most young boys, they'd nailed together a little structure called Dumboni's Saloon, hand-painting the name over its makeshift swinging doors. Since neither one of them had access to horses, the family dogs were often called in as stand-ins, getting hitched to the post outside their establishment for thirsty cowboys.

At night in the summer, they'd arrange rocks in a circle and pretend they were sitting around a campfire, imagining themselves to be Roy Rogers.

When their friends had started listening to rock music, they'd put on their headphones and tuned in to Gene Autry and Johnny Cash and Patsy Cline. Now their selections included Garth Brooks and Clint Black and Dwight Yoakum and Reba McEntire and Mary Chapin Carpenter and the teenage sensation LeAnn Rimes. Their dream had always been to start a country music station in the New York area, which wouldn't be easy.

They never gave up the dream.

Now, both aged thirty-five and divorced, lonesome cowboys, as they called themselves, they'd pooled their limited resources, gotten a couple of loans, and bought a small, faded station in Southampton. They'd gone on the air Memorial Day weekend and were still working out the kinks, but their biggest break was not only to be named as the esteemed hosts of the Melting Pot Music Festival on July Fourth but also to obtain the broadcast rights. People would be driving in their cars to parties and listening to their radios at home. Everyone knew about the festival: maybe they'd tune in to listen to all the action and then leave their dial on Country 113.

One of their missions in life was to spread the word about country music. The other was to make a living at it.

Seven mornings a week they were on the air together. Sometimes at night, too.

Off the air they spent time dreaming up ideas for contests and promotions. Anything to get people to listen. Recently they'd been discussing how they could do some sort of tie-in to the music festival.

Right now they were both working quietly at their desks, doing catch-up work.

Chuck scratched his scalp and pushed his granny glasses farther back onto his pointy nose. He'd been thumbing through newspapers, looking for anything that might spark an idea for an on-air discussion when he'd come across the item in the *Irish Tablet* about Brigid O'Neill and her fiddle. Since much of country music had its roots in the rhythms and strings of the music Irish immigrants had brought across the sea with them, Chuck took out a subscription to the *Tablet*. It was a place they should advertise, he thought. Everybody these days wanted to get back to their roots. People who read the *Tablet* should be brought up to speed on how their ancestors' music had such an influence on country music today. "Let's leave no stone unturned, partner," he often said to Brad.

As Chuck read, he tugged on his strawberry blond hair, pulled back in the obligatory ponytail. He was a long and lanky type who always managed to look as if he had a couple days' worth of whiskers on his face. A toothpick hung from his mouth, its end decorated with blue foil. Slowly he looked up from the paper. "Ya know what?" he asked.

"Nope," Brad answered absentmindedly. He was busy poking around his desk, gathering papers together. A short, dark-haired man with rounded features and wild eyebrows, he was driven by a great desire to pay the bills. He never wanted to go back to working for somebody else.

"I feel a wind blowin'. It's brainstorm time."

"Shoot."

"I think I know how we can plug the Melting Pot Festival. . . . This article here talks about Brigid O'Neill and that fiddle of hers. We're going to have her on the show next week."

"Monday," Brad declared. He walloped the head of a stapler with his palm, and the three pieces of paper he had gathered together were now an official document. "Gotcha!" he said with satisfaction.

"The initials CT are carved into it. Why don't we have a contest to see who can come up with the best explanation for the initials? We'll give out VIP tickets to the concert for the most creative answer. And a copy of her new album that she can autograph in person at the concert."

Brad looked over at his partner, naked admiration in his eyes. He held up an imaginary gun in the air and fired the trigger. "Good brainstorm, Kemo Sabe. What kind of things do you think people will come up with?"

Chuck caressed his stubble. "My brainstorm didn't get that far. But the pot is stewing on the campfire. The fiddle is supposed to be cursed if it leaves Ireland. I guess Brigid O'Neill doesn't care. I hope she's right. Why don't we also talk about that and other Irish superstitions on the show with her?"

"You think she'd mind?"

"Nah. It's a hot story. We'll get everyone talking about the initials and the curse. And any other good curse stories we can dig up."

"What other famous curses are there? Besides the Hope Diamond?" Brad asked, referring to the diamond that always seemed to bring bad luck to its owners. Some of them, like Marie Antoinette, had been beheaded.

Chuck leaned back in his chair and chewed on his toothpick for inspiration. "Lava rock in Hawaii. If you take any home with you, the gods get real upset. Brings bad luck."

Brad started to get excited. "This is good," he said, his barrel chest heaving up and down and his rangy eyebrows furling and unfurling. He looked at the calendar up on the wall. "The concert is Friday. Let's announce the winner of the initial contest Thursday." He paused. "This is our big chance to get in the saddle, isn't it, partner?" he asked.

"You said it, buckaroo. It's our chance to kick up a little dust and raise some hell."

With that, the phone rang. Chuck took the call. Brad couldn't get the gist of the conversation because it was a lot of "yups," "nopes," and "good enoughs."

When Chuck hung up, he yelled, "Yeehaw!"

"What is it, partner?" Brad asked.

"Because we're the esteemed hosts of the Melting Pot Music Festival, we just got ourselves an invitation to ride over and dine with Miss Brigid O'Neill tonight at the Chappy Compound."

They leaned together and high-fived each other across the desk.

11

Get downstairs and help them out!" Chappy yelled to Duke's closed door as he pounded on it. He was dressed in white pants, blue blazer, and white buck shoes. People were due to arrive any moment and he was frantic.

The door opened. Duke was standing there with a can of hair spray in his hand. He looked at Chappy's flyaway locks. "Want some?" he asked.

"NO! Now let's get going!"

"Okay, okay." Duke took one last look at himself in his full-length mirror, put down the hair spray, picked up a bottle of cologne, and gave himself a good spritz. "Want some?" he asked again.

"NO! NO, I don't! I can't believe how long you take to get ready! Let's go!"

Duke, clad in crisp khaki pants and freshly washed blue-and-white striped shirt, had enjoyed a workout an hour before in the exercise room. He lifted weights, rowed a stationary boat, and did stretches. Now he closed his bedroom door behind him. "Are any casting directors coming?"

"What are you asking me that for?"

"But you said—"

"FORGET what I said. This party is so we can get Brigid to trust us. So we can get close to her. So at the end of the week we can switch the fiddle. That's what I'm worried about." Chappy stopped in the middle of the hallway to point his finger at Duke. "Got it?"

Duke saluted. "Roger."

"Ugh!" Chappy cried as he led the way down the grand stairway and across the foyer into the monstrous-sized kitchen where Bettina, dressed in a gold jumpsuit and spike heels, was harassing the help about the hors d'oeuvres.

"I told ya I wanted more healthy choices," Bettina crowed at Constance, who was in the process of preparing pigs in a blanket. Two waiters, dressed in the standard uniform of caterers at Hamptons parties—black pants and white shirts—were struggling with a pastry bag at the two-hundred-square-foot kitchen table.

Constance squinted her beady eyes at Bettina. "These pigs are Mr. Tinka's favorite."

"Did you make Peace Man's recipe?"

"The ingredients for that can only be found in the rain forest," Constance replied. "And I didn't have time to book a flight."

Chappy cleared his throat. Duke, following his cue, coughed.

"Hello hello," Chappy sang. "How is everything coming along?"

Bettina turned to him, plastering a big smile on her heavily made-up face. "Hi, poopy. Constance made you your pigs in a blanket. I was just thinking that some of the others might prefer a few more healthy choices."

"Oh"—Chappy waved his hand—"put out some wheat germ. And peel a few carrots. That'll keep them happy. Constance, did we set up a Mexican station out on the deck with tortilla chips and hot sauce?"

Constance looked up from rolling a piece of dough around a minia-ture hot dog and smiled. She was dressed in a starched gray dress that brought to mind the servants one might see on a PBS special. Chappy liked western wear during the day but Old English dress when they entertained. "Yes, sir. And that's where we'll put out the ice cream, sprinkles, and choice of toppings after dinner."

"Oh good!" Duke said.

The doorbell rang. It was actually made to sound like a gong.

"Hear ye! Hear ye!" Chappy cried. Slapping Duke's hand, which was picking at a tray of mushroom quiche, he ran out of the kitchen.

At the front door, which was the size of a jumbo wall unit, he composed himself and pulled it open. There stood Peace Man in what looked like a pair of gray pajamas with beads around his neck.

"Greetings," Peace Man said somberly.

Chappy turned away. "Bettina!" he screamed. He turned back. "Come on in," he said begrudgingly.

"Is Peace Man the first to arrive?" Peace Man asked.

Chappy looked at him. "Not a surprise. You only had to travel from the side of the house."

"Peace Man is very happy there. The ions from the ocean soothe. Only two problems. One is you don't have enough trees. Peace Man likes to hug a different tree every day. Number two is that big bus is blocking my sunlight."

Chappy was about to reach over and strangle him when Bettina came into the foyer.

"Sister," Peace Man said with a bow of his head.

"Peace Man," Bettina said with a slight curtsy. "Welcome to our humble home. Can I get you a drink?"

"Scotch on the rocks."

"Scotch on the rocks, coming right up."

"With a twist."

"With a twist, coming right up."

Together they ambled through the foyer, headed in the direction of the deck outside, where a bar had been set up. "Peace Man, I invited some of your other followers, but since this was planned at the last minute, they had already committed to other important parties and such," Bettina was heard saying.

"Peace Man understands. Will they be here for the special enlightenment session tomorrow?"

"They wouldn't miss it for the world!"

Chappy wanted to throw up but luckily he was diverted by the sight of the architect for the theatre, Claudia Snookfuss, and her boyfriend, Ned Alingham, the feng shui specialist, getting out of their brand-new Range Rover, bought from the proceeds of their work together. She drew up the plans for houses and whatever buildings people wanted to erect, and Ned told her where to place objects such as the banisters. "Don't put them by the front of the house," he always told her. "Or else the energy flows right out when the door opens."

Unfortunately for Ned, a lot of people didn't buy the idea of feng shui and wanted no part of him or his fees. Claudia worked alone on those jobs.

Together they came up the steps. Claudia, with a little button nose and straight chin-length blond hair held perfectly in place with a pink headband, looked as if nothing in her life could possibly be out of order. She had on a pair of striped pink-and-green canvas shoes to match her pink skirt and green top. Ned, average-sized with perfectly parted brown hair and owlish glasses, had a certain nervous intensity. He wore the expression of a child about to burst into tears. His relentless pursuit of harmony in his surroundings apparently did not apply to what he hung in his closet. He was wearing a pair of blue-jean Bermuda shorts, a multicolored iridescent floral shirt, white socks, and sandals. A camera hung around his neck.

"How do you do? How do you do?" Chappy asked as they stepped inside. He tapped Ned's camera. "I see you're planning to take a few pictures."

"Actually I've decided to self-publish a how-to picture book on feng shui. If you don't mind, I'd like to take a few preliminary snaps of the work I did here."

"Well then, shoot! Shoot away! And how are you, Miss Claudia?"

"Purr-fect," she replied, smiling her little smile. Not too broad, but friendly, as her mother had always told her.

"How are our plans for the theatre?"

"As ready as they were months ago!" she said. "We'll be raring to go with the bulldozer when you get rid of your tenants in September. But we have to talk. The seats are going to cost more than we thought."

"More money for the seats?" Chappy exclaimed. "Well, just as long as they're comfy."

"Oh, they are," Claudia assured him.

"And they'll be facing west," Ned added. "A better position for entertainment and relaxation."

"Oh good," Chappy said, but he felt momentarily irritated. The longer it takes to get this theatre started, he thought, the more it seems to cost. God, how I'll need that fiddle. The Tinka thumbtack fortune was not, as he would have liked, a bottomless pit. The castle had already put enough of a dent in it. Chappy slapped Ned on the back of his shimmering shirt and pushed them on through. "Get yourself a drink. Yes, yes, here come some more guests. . . ."

Regan and Kit and Brigid had been sitting for a long time at the table when they realized it was getting late. When Kit went back to her house, and Brigid headed for the shower, Regan put on her bathing suit and took a quick walk around Chappy's property to check out how secure it was. The compound seemed private enough, but anybody who really wanted to break in wouldn't have much of a problem, she thought.

Starting to drag a little as she felt the aftereffects of her all-night flight, she took a dip in the ocean, hoping the cool water would give her a jolt. I can't be out of it for the evening's festivities, she thought. You never know what might happen.

As the brisk water washed over her, it did the job. Feeling more alive, she hurried back into the guest house, which now had an abandoned feel to it. The late afternoon light gave a peaceful glow to the all-purpose room overlooking the water. It was the time of day when people compared their tan lines.

Everyone must be in their rooms getting ready, Regan thought. She walked over to check out something unusual she had noticed before. The wall had what looked like a door built into it, but it had no handle. That's so strange, she thought. Does it lead to the basement? She took a quick survey of the rest of the ground floor. There was no other door that would lead to the basement.

She went back outside and bent down at the well of one of the tiny basement windows. She rubbed the dirt off the window with her fist and peered inside. From what she could tell it was your typical gray cinder-block basement. There was nothing in it. The floor was bare. I guess that's why they don't need a door, she thought.

Regan shrugged, stood up, and went back in the house. She showered and changed into a short sleeveless black dress and sandals. Thank God for black, she thought. You can wear it anywhere and not have to worry. She fastened the fanny pack that held her .38 pistol around her waist. She'd gotten a permit to travel with her gun to New York. The rayon fanny pack with Velcro snaps was the perfect way to pack a gun without people noticing. If anything, she thought, wearing this thing makes me look like a nerd.

When Regan came out of her room, Brigid was standing in the hallway with Pammy, who was holding a skirt in her hands.

"I'm so sorry I burned your skirt," Pammy said to her. "That iron is so old."

"Don't worry," Brigid replied. "It was sweet of you to offer to press it for me in the first place. I have another one I'll throw on."

"I feel terrible," Pammy insisted.

"It's okay. Really," Brigid said.

A few moments later they all gathered downstairs. Brigid was now ready to party, dressed in a calf-length flowing skirt, white short-sleeved shirt, and vest. With her fiddle case in hand, she looked the part of the funky musician, ready to play. Teddy, Hank, and Kieran were all in their black jeans; the cases with their guitars, mandolin, and banjo lay on the floor by the door. Pammy, clad in a skimpy halter dress, was checking her makeup in a compact mirror, and Kit was knocking at the door. A group of eight people from her house stood out in the driveway waiting.

"They're anxious to meet you, Brigid," she said.

Introductions were made and they all ambled over to chez Chappy.

"Welcome! Welcome! Welcome!" he began again, barely letting the group get inside the door as he effusively greeted Brigid. "One hundred thousand and one welcomes." He chuckled.

"I think he's determined to say it a hundred thousand and one times," Regan whispered to Kit.

"Brigid, I hope you don't mind," Chappy said. "I invited a few members of the press to meet you. The two young men from the country music station in town are here, and a couple others from the local papers." In a stage whisper he added, "It's good publicity for the festival."

"That's fine," Brigid responded, smiling. "My manager already booked me on that radio show."

"Yes, I know. They've been advertising your appearance. And since they're hosting the festival, I thought I'd invite them! I see you brought that fiddle of yours! How wonderful!"

Between the coverage in the newspapers and on the radio, Regan thought, everyone will know where to find her.

"Hello hello to the rest of you," he said. "Come in, come in."

A voice from behind called out to Regan as she was inching her way in the door. "Regan! Oh, Regan!" She turned, and there was Louisa, resplendent in a red-and-white floral caftan, with a matching flower in her hair, jumping out of the car that Luke hadn't yet brought to a complete stop.

Here we go, Regan thought, answering with a warm "Louisa, how good to see you."

"*Hnnnnnn*. You too," Louisa responded, racing over and giving Regan a big hug. "This is such fun. Herbert! Come say hello to Regan."

Fifteen minutes later, everyone was gathered out on the deck, drinks in hand. Chappy had called everyone together for a toast. Brad Petroni and Chuck Dumbrell, the owners of the radio station, had already made a beeline for Brigid, while Louisa was making her presence and her intention to write an article about the Hamptons known to everyone. Regan, with one eye on Brigid as she leaned against the railing, liked to observe the dynamics of a group as people gathered for a party. She had the fiddle case by her side.

One of the guys from Kit's summer house, Garrett, had already tried to sell her stocks. One of the girls, Angela, dressed in a tight shirt that showed off her curvaceous figure, was hanging by the bar, flirting with Duke as he made the drinks.

Kit walked over and stood next to her. "Did you get a load of the guy with the shaved head and gray pajamas?"

Regan laughed. "I haven't met him, but I heard someone say he's Bettina's resident guru."

"Can I have everyone's attention?" Chappy shouted. "Thank you . . . thank you."

The crowd quieted, everyone turning to look at Chappy, who had one arm around Brigid, the other around Bettina.

That's some diamond necklace Bettina is sporting, Regan thought. And that rock on her finger could compete for size with some of the seashells on the beach.

"Welcome to Chappy's Compound. My wife, Bettina, and I are so honored to have Brigid O'Neill and her band as our guests this week.

We're also honored to have Nora Regan Reilly with us, and her husband, Luke."

Nora raised her glass and smiled.

"Hnnnn," sounded from the crowd.

"We're very pleased," Bettina said with a big smile. "Chappy and I are very, very pleased to host you all this evening."

Sounds like a canned response, Regan thought.

Chappy kissed her on the cheek and continued. "I want to welcome everyone else here tonight. I hope you'll all get to be friends." He paused, somewhat soulfully, Regan thought, as speakers always do before they say something they think is meaningful. Chappy did not disappoint. ". . . I have always been interested in music, especially country music, and I could think of no better way to enhance the Melting Pot Festival than to invite Brigid, a daughter of Ireland, to participate."

He waited as people attempted to applaud while holding their drinks. "As you might know, I am building a theatre right on this property that will be up and operating next summer. I intend to play my part in contributing to the arts in the Hamptons by producing plays that my invited guests will enjoy on summer evenings. But right now I urge you all to enjoy yourselves. Eat, drink, and be merry!"

"Hnnn," Louisa grunted approvingly. A few feet from Regan, she turned to Peace Man, who was right next to her.

"I'm Louisa Washburn. I didn't catch your name," she said to him.

"Peace Man."

"Peace to you, too. And your name is?"

"Peace Man. That's a name."

"How interesting," Louisa said. "What is it you do?"

"Peace Man opens the door to inner peace for others."

"Uh-huh." Louisa took a quick sip of her tropical drink and patted the flower in her hair. "I'm a fact-checker and I do research," she said as she started to invade his seventeen inches of personal space. "Facts facts facts. I'm writing an article on the Hamptons, and I would love to interview you."

Regan watched as Chappy escorted Brigid from group to group. She turned to Kit. "The people from your house seem nice. Although Garrett did ask me about my stock portfolio already."

"Oh, I know," Kit said. "I told him that when it comes to my investments, he should save his breath." They both looked over to the group by the window, where the tall, rangy, brown-haired Garrett, dressed in khaki pants, short-sleeved Lacoste shirt, and loafers with no socks, stood holding a vodka and tonic. He was deep in discussion with the guys from the radio station, who, dressed in blue jeans, cowboy boots, and spangly shirts, provided a marked contrast to his appearance.

"Let's join them," Regan said.

As they said hello, Louisa came up behind them. "So many good-looking young men at this party! And who are you?" When she found out that Brad and Chuck ran the radio station she was, as usual, ecstatic. "I know that station! No one could ever make a go of it. But I'm sure you will. It's a tough, tough business. I do research and fact-checking so I know how many radio stations fail—"

"Research?" Chuck interrupted. "Maybe you can do some work for us."

"I'd love to." Louisa beamed.

Regan and Kit retreated to the bar, where the amply busted Angela had planted herself. Her streaked blond hair was pulled up on her head, with just enough strands hanging down to look sexy. "Being an actor must be so interesting," she was saying as she leaned over to talk to Duke. "I was asked to pose nude once, but I thought my grandmother would have a cow."

Kit whispered into Regan's ear: "She's determined to find a husband this summer."

Duke looked at them. "What'll you have?"

"White wine," they both answered.

He seems amiable, Regan thought. Is he serious about acting? she wondered. With his muscular build and blond hair, he looked as if he could go up for a remake of *Beach Blanket Bingo*.

They took their glasses and followed Chappy and Brigid into the house, where some of the others were gathered. This kind of bodyguarding—to keep a watch on someone while not making it obvious and at the same time giving them space—wasn't easy. This was supposed to be a relaxing week for Brigid.

Luke appeared from around the corner.

"Hi, Dad. Where's Mom?"

"On a tour of the house with Bettina. I'm hungry. I hope they serve dinner soon."

Regan nodded her head. "Me too. Louisa is interviewing everyone at this party. Oh, here she comes."

"This is the most wonderful party. I'm having such a good time," Louisa pronounced as she joined them and started crunching on an ice cube. "Hello," she said to a couple walking by, their glasses empty. "And you are?"

"Claudia, and this is my boyfriend, Ned," Claudia replied perkily.

"How do you know the Tinkas?" Louisa asked gaily.

"I'm designing the theatre he's building, and Ned helps me with the placement of objects. He practices feng shui."

"Oh yes! I've read articles about that. I'm a fact-checker and do research, and I'd love to interview you for this article I'm doing." She drifted outside with them, in the direction of the bar.

"Chow time!" Chappy roared as he clenched Brigid's hand. "Yes, yes, grab a plate, everyone, and help yourselves. Brigid, you must sit with me. We have a special table . . ."

Brigid glanced at Regan, rolled her eyes, and smiled. She's so good-natured, Regan thought. Chappy is killing her with kindness.

Regan and Kit and Luke filled their plates with chicken and rice and salad and sat down in the cathedral-ceilinged living room, which could have been rented out for wedding receptions, Regan thought. Round tables for six were set up with white tablecloths, and large faux brightly colored thumbtacks the size of portobello mushrooms acted as center-pieces.

Within a few minutes Nora arrived with her plate, Herbert resurfaced with a piece of driftwood in tow, and Louisa made her entrance carrying two plates of food. "Lambie, there you are!" she cried.

As they ate, Louisa filled them in on all the interesting people she had met at the party. "I make it a point to say hello to as many people as possible at every party I attend. And in this case, I think I've covered everyone, and we're just starting dinner. Lambie, is that enough chicken for you?"

Herbert was busy chewing. He nodded his head.

Regan looked around and surveyed the rest of the tables. She noticed that Bettina was sitting with Garrett and Peace Man and Duke and Angela. Brigid was at the "media" table with Chappy and the radio station guys and two reporters from the local papers. Everyone at that table looked as if they were trying to be polite, listening as Chappy's hands flapped about. He's obviously in the middle of a story, Regan thought.

As all the guests seemed to be finishing up, Regan excused herself and walked over to Brigid.

"Sit sit sit, Regan," Chappy said to her. "Brigid was just telling us about the fiddle. . . ."

Another chair was instantly produced by one of the waiters, and Regan squeezed in next to Chappy.

". . . You know my theatre is opening next summer?" he asked Regan.

"Yes," she said, noticing that the two reporters who had their pads out and their pens poised had stopped writing when Chappy began to speak.

"Brigid, are you afraid of the curse on the fiddle?" the elegant seventyish woman who was the society reporter from the *Southampton Sun* asked in a well-bred voice. She sat ramrod straight and looked to be of the old guard.

Brigid laughed. "Oh no."

"But facing an accident or death is a pretty scary superstition," the young cub reporter from the *Hamptons News* said with enthusiasm.

He looks like he really wants to play that up, Regan thought.

"It's the Irish," Brigid answered, looking to Regan as if she were getting tired. "We've always been a superstitious lot."

Brad Petroni, ever anxious to plug his radio station, jumped in. "Brigid's agreed to talk about that with us on our radio show Monday. We'll be discussing curses and superstitions and the fiddle. Right, Brigid?"

"Right." She managed a smile.

Later, after dinner, the crowd gathered with their ice cream sundaes in the drawing room, where an eight-foot portrait of Alvin Conrad Tinka, founder of the Tinka thumbtack fortune, was hung near the portrait of his beloved wife, Agneta. Positioned between them on the wall was the baby portrait of their only grandchild, Chappy, in all his rosy-cheeked and ringlet-haired glory.

Chappy sat in a thronelike chair directly beneath his likeness of over fifty years ago. Bettina sat at his feet.

To Regan, who had taken a place in the back by one of the doors, where she could keep an eye on the crowd, he couldn't have looked happier.

"Let's see that fiddle!" he urged her. "Play the fiddle for us, Brigid," he said.

"Okay," Brigid responded. "I'll play a song with the fiddle, and then I want my band here to join me." She picked up the fiddle with an almost reverent feeling, Regan thought, balanced it on her shoulder, closed her eyes for a brief moment, then started to play. Lively music filled the room and Regan watched as Brigid's eyes started to sparkle and her body began to move. Her fatigue seemed to be swept away by the music.

She loves what she does, Regan thought. She's coming alive. It's as if playing the music is all that counts.

After the first song, Brigid said, "Come on, guys, I want you to play with me."

"Play your hit song," Brad urged.

"Coming right up," Brigid answered with a chuckle.

Kieran stood next to her, and Teddy and Hank took their places in the background as they went into a spirited rendition of the song that was making her famous. "If I'da known you were in jail," she began. Brigid's voice sounded so clear and young and fresh. The guys sang backup, with Kieran having a couple lines of his own, singing the part of the unfortunate inmate professing his undying love.

They're really good, Regan thought. They're going to make it. At that moment Regan realized something was bothering her. She looked over and noticed that Herbert was nervously glancing back at the door every few seconds.

Louisa was not there.

She hadn't been there for any of the music.

She wouldn't miss this, Regan thought anxiously. She hurried out of the room and down the hall to the two guest bathrooms. Both doors were open. They were empty.

Running farther down the hall, she glanced into the living room, where the waiters were folding the tables.

No Louisa.

Maybe she went outside, Regan thought frantically. Maybe she needed some air.

She hurried through the dining room and poked her head in the kitchen door, where the housekeeper was washing dishes at the other end of the room. Not wanting to waste time asking questions, Regan ran out onto the deck, where the containers of ice cream were slowly melting.

"Louisa?" she called into the darkness.

The only sound she heard was the breaking of the waves on the beach.

Oh God, she thought. Those drinks Louisa had were strong.

Taking the steps off the deck two at a time, she raced toward the water and then turned around. She wouldn't have gone near the ocean, Regan thought. Let me check the pool. Maybe she wanted to sit outside.

Regan's sandals were becoming weighed down with sand. She kicked them off and ran to the side of the house where the pool was. Everything seemed still, but when she raced up the steps, the sight of Louisa in her red-and-white caftan floating facedown in the pool sickened her.

"LOUISA!" Regan shrieked at the top of her lungs as she unfastened her fanny pack, dropped it to the ground, and quickly dove in.

12

When he saw she was being rescued, he turned and ran.

*A*fter arriving back in the Hamptons and enjoying his late afternoon meal of "poached eggs on toast, none of that gooky hollandaise sauce, miz, a side order of French fries, and a Dr Pepper," he'd driven over and parked his car down the street from the Chappy Compound. He'd known Brigid was there, and he had to be near her. He couldn't approach her yet, but just being in the same vicinity was very exciting.

What had his mother told him when he'd started to get crushes on movie stars?

She'd said, "Get a life."

That had hurt him very badly. She was the one who loved to watch old movies. Especially The Shiek. He had no father to go to. He'd disappeared so long ago he couldn't even remember him. Brigid had lost her father, too. He'd read that. So they had something in common and could talk about it when they finally were together. If he could just get the chance to carry Brigid off, she'd fall in love with him, too. He was sure of it.

That night he spent in jail he'd heard her hit song and knew that she was sending a message to him. Over the radio. Just to him. He didn't want her singing it to anyone else.

After parking his car, he'd walked onto the beach and down to the water in front of the Chappy Compound. He'd wanted to get a look at the setup. Because people were out for a stroll on the beach, he'd been able to blend in, but still he'd taken care to stay far enough away to not be noticed.

He decided he'd better keep moving, so he walked down past several of the big houses, then turned around and come back. That was when he saw two guys and a lady setting up food and a bar on the deck of the big house at Chappy's Compound. He decided to take a chance. When the coast was clear, he ran under the deck and hid.

They were going to have a party! How perfect!

When the crowd had gathered, he could hear them all laughing and talking above. Brigid was standing right over his head! He heard her answering questions about her music. She was going to be on the country radio station on Monday. She was looking forward to the concert. She was staying in the guest house by the pool.

Then they all went inside to eat. He felt so left out. But he had to make the best of it.

The sand under the deck started to feel damp. But he didn't want to leave. He squiggled to get into a more comfortable position and waited. He could hear the waiters moving around over him. He peeled the hard-boiled egg he had in his pocket and ate it.

Then everyone came outside to get ice cream. Some klutz knocked over a bowlful of sprinkles, and some of them fell through the cracks in the wood. He managed to catch a few in his palm. Slowly he licked them off with his tongue.

He could hear them talking about going back inside to listen to Brigid play. Time to go look at the house where Brigid was staying, he thought. It was dark now, and he could creep over there. After they all went back inside, he waited a little longer and then crawled out from under the deck, trying to brush off the sand messing up his Buster Brown haircut. What a pain.

He sneaked past the pool area and then picked up speed, feverishly heading across to the guest house where his Brigid was staying.

That was when he heard the noise—someone coming out of the big house and walking to the pool, making a funny grunting sound. He ran to the side of the cottage so he wouldn't be seen. When he'd positioned himself where he could take a good look without being noticed, he could see a woman leaning over the pool by the diving board.

When she fell in and made that splash, he was sure he'd seen a figure running away, even though the area was poorly lit.

She had been pushed! He didn't know what to do. Then someone came out yelling a name, found her in the pool, screamed, and dove in.

There was no way he could be found here. They couldn't think that he was the one who pushed her.

People came running out of the house. He turned and ran. What was going on in that place anyhow? Was Brigid in danger?

Brigid, I'll be back, he thought. I will be back.

13

Regan awoke early. With all the excitement, she'd slept fitfully. Turning on her side, she stared at the window, whose shade was flapping slightly.

What a night! she thought. A perfectly pleasant evening capped off with Louisa nearly drowning.

Regan sighed, thinking back on the chain of events. She'd hauled Louisa down to the shallow end of the pool; the radio station twosome had jumped in and helped lift Louisa out. What was it they had yelled? Regan wondered. Something like "The posse's here," and then "Clear the way, this lady needs some air." Well, that had to be the understatement of the evening, Regan thought. But they *were* helpful, and their cowboy boots were probably ruined.

The big surprise was Pammy. Before Regan could get out of the pool and do it herself, Pammy had flipped Louisa on her stomach, turned her head to the side, straddled her, and begun pumping her back. All her cutesyness evaporated as she'd taken charge, rhythmically pounding on Louisa's back until she'd begun to spit out water. Herbert had been beside himself with relief as everyone had cheered.

"I was a lifeguard when I was sixteen," Pammy had said crisply to Regan. "It's obvious she couldn't have been in long."

I was a lifeguard, too, Regan had wanted to say, but she didn't bother. She remembered with amusement the moment that Pammy had reverted to her usual persona. The reporters had been snapping pictures. Pammy had stood up, her halter dress damp and rumpled. "I must be just a mess," she'd said with a self-satisfied smile. Kieran had looked at her with an expression Regan still couldn't quite figure out. A combination of pride and wistfulness, she thought.

Of course, Regan had been standing there looking like a drowned rat.

There was something about the whole incident that didn't sit right with Regan. How could Louisa have just fallen in the pool? Did something else happen?

Stretching, she got out of bed. She pulled a bathing suit out of the suitcase on the floor. I'd like to go take a dip in the pool and wake up, she thought. The events of last night still seemed so unreal. She felt the need to go back out there.

It was nine-ten. She and Brigid and Kit were going over to her parents' house for brunch at eleven. Last night she had asked her mother if they could come by today. She knew then that she wanted to question Louisa.

Regan went downstairs, where the house was quiet. Everyone must still be asleep, she thought. Stopping at the refrigerator, she poured a glass of the orange juice Chappy had stocked and gratefully finished it off in about three gulps.

The day was bright and sunny. The ocean looked blue and sparkly, and boats dotted the horizon. At the pool area she found Duke in his bathing suit, using a skimmer to clean the pool.

"Hey, Regan," he called.

"Hi," she said, throwing her towel on a chair. The water in the pool looked calm and peaceful. It was incredible that this same place was the scene of such chaos less than twelve hours ago, she thought. "You're working early," she said to Duke.

"Oh yeah. It's my job to keep the pool clean. Chappy wants to make sure it's nice for you folks." He laughed. "Bettina got mad at me yesterday when we were cleaning up. I accidentally plunked the handle of the skimmer in a can of white paint."

Regan noticed the sign tacked to the door of the cabana: WET PAINT. She remembered Kit saying that they had been scurrying around getting ready for Brigid's arrival.

Regan smiled. "These things happen."

"Yeahhhh. They just happen to me a lot," he answered good-naturedly. "Say, you were a hero last night, Regan. Chappy was talking about how lucky Louisa was you went looking for her. He said you must have a lot of intuition."

"Well, thanks," Regan replied quietly. "Hey, did I hear you're an actor?" she asked.

"I've been working on it for fifteen years. I haven't had my big break yet but it's coming," he said, smiling broadly. He pulled the skimmer out of the water. "Done for now. Or until Chappy throws another lemon in the pool." He balanced the long pole on a table near the pool and looked at the slight coating of white paint on his hands. "The handle is still sticky, I guess," he said, half to himself. "I'd better go get some turpentine to wash this off. See you later."

" 'Bye," Regan said, and watched him walk away, shaking his head. She sat there quietly for a few moments, enjoying the peacefulness. The scene from last night was still so fresh in her mind. Someone had called 911. Within minutes the police had arrived with sirens blaring and lights flashing. By then Louisa had been sitting up and insistent that she not go to the hospital.

"Lambie will get too upset," she'd said, her speech slightly slurred.

So the maid had given Louisa a bathrobe to put on, and she'd worn that home, with Nora carrying her caftan in a plastic bag.

Regan walked over to the diving board and studied it. From the little she could get from Louisa last night, she'd come out for air and then been intrigued by the musical note painted on the bottom of the pool. She'd leaned over to have a look, lost her balance, and fallen, hitting her head on the side of the diving board.

The whole thing was strange. Even if she'd lost her balance, why would she hit the diving board like that?

Regan dove in and felt the cool water once again invigorate her. Two nights of weird sleep, she thought. I should always have an ocean or a pool at my disposal to jump into when I'm tired.

She swam several laps and got out. Time to grab a cup of coffee and go over to see how the world's most talkative patient was doing.

Regan, in the harsh unforgiving light of morning I feel mortified," Louisa called from the couch as Nora led Regan, Brigid, and Kit to the back of the house. Louisa was stretched out with a washcloth over her head. Her bad-luck red-and-white caftan had been replaced by a blue-and-green one.

Herbert was sitting at the other end of the couch silently massaging Louisa's feet.

"Don't be embarrassed," Regan said as she gently lifted the cloth. "You did get a good conk there. That diving board really jumped out at you."

"It sure did, Regan." Louisa started to get up.

"Don't get up," Regan cautioned as she accepted a cup of coffee from her mother. Luke was in the kitchen preparing brunch, the only meal he liked to cook. Blueberry pancakes were his specialty.

"I'm good as new. I guess I had more to drink than I realized last night. Regan, if it weren't for you . . ." Louisa grabbed Regan's hand. "Lambie and I thank you for saving my life. Isn't that right, Lambie?"

Herbert was in deep concentration, focusing on the little toe of Louisa's right foot. He looked up. "That's right. Thank you, Regan."

And this piggy toe goes wee wee wee, all the way home, Regan thought.

"He barely slept last night," Louisa said almost proudly, his insomnia making her feel well loved. *"Hnnnnn."*

She's definitely feeling better, Regan decided.

"Those waiters just kept pouring the wine. And I had a couple of those tropical drinks because it reminds me of when Lambie and I go to the islands. Lambie loves to snorkel." She looked fondly at her husband, who was now concentrating on the big toe of her left foot as if it held the same fascination as an exotic tropical fish. *"Hnnnnnn."*

If somebody did that to my feet, Regan thought, I'd make funny noises, too.

"Anyway," Louisa continued, "I was so busy talking to everyone there that I didn't notice how much I'd had to drink. When everyone was gathering in the drawing room, I knew I had to go out and get some fresh air." She turned to Brigid, who was sitting next to Kit on the other couch. "Brigid, I'm so disappointed I didn't get to hear you play that fiddle."

"That's okay, Louisa. I'll be playing it again this week," Brigid said as she sipped coffee. She had on a pair of khaki shorts and a blue short-sleeved shirt. Her long red hair spilled over her shoulders. "Although I'm not sure if I should," she added, laughing. "Something exciting always seems to happen, good or bad, every time I play it."

"The curse!" Louisa cried. "I know. Those young men from the radio station asked me to get material for them on superstitions and curses for your show tomorrow. Do you think they'd like to talk about my near drowning?" she asked hopefully.

"I couldn't say," Brigid replied.

"Something tells me they will," Regan said. "Especially since they're the ones who lifted you out of the water."

"Such strength." Louisa sighed. "And that girl who pounded on my back?"

"Pammy," Brigid said.

"I must write her a thank-you note. Her boyfriend is Kieran, isn't that right?"

"Yes," Brigid said quickly.

"He's so good-looking! And the other two boys are adorable. Where are they today?"

"Golfing," Brigid answered.

"Golf golf golf. All the men love golf. And I understand more women are out on the links these days. . . ."

"It's a great place to meet men," Kit said. "Although I'm afraid to get out there until I am sure I can swing without missing the ball."

Nora called from the kitchen, where she was cutting up fruit for the salad, "I keep telling Regan and Kit they should go to golf camp."

Regan laughed. "You see, Louisa, my mother keeps giving us suggestions on where to meet men."

"My mother wanted me to go on a field trip to Lourdes," Kit said. "It's pretty bad when your own mother thinks it's going to take a miracle for you to get into a relationship."

Louisa laughed. "Nora!" she cried, and then said, "Oh, my head." She readjusted the washcloth. "These girls will meet someone when they least expect it! Lambie and I met on a blind date set up by his aunt Phyllis and my aunt Gretchen. To think I didn't want to go! Kit, what about the men in your house? That Garrett seemed like he could be interesting. I was discussing the stock market with him."

"That's all he ever wants to discuss," Kit said. "What to do with your extra money, of which I have none."

"Pity. Oh well, I'm sure you'll meet all sorts this summer, Kit."

"I think we already have," Regan said. "Louisa," she began hesitantly, "now that you feel a little better, I just thought I'd ask. When you went out to the pool and leaned over, how is it that you hit the diving board?"

"I don't know. It's the oddest thing, Regan. I must admit I was experiencing the whirlies when I thought I saw something at the bottom of the pool. I went to the edge, leaned over, and then it was almost as if I felt jostled. But that's silly, isn't it?"

"Not necessarily," Regan replied. Not necessarily at all, she thought.

"I vaguely remember hitting the diving board, and that was that."

"Well," Regan said. "Just make sure to take it easy today."

"Oh, Regan, I couldn't possibly! After we partake of your father's wonderful brunch . . ." Louisa said, turning to look in the direction of the kitchen.

Luke, wearing a chef's apron Regan had given him, lifted his whisk and waved.

". . . I have research to do. I'll plug in my laptop and hook up to the Internet."

Regan set her cup down on the coffee table. "It might be interesting to see what you can find about Brigid on there."

Brigid waved her hand and laughed. "I hear they've reprinted a few newspaper articles about me. There are also some country music chat rooms where people talk about everything going on in the business."

"I'll drop in on them," Louisa declared. "I'll let you know what I find."

"Only if it's good." Brigid chuckled.

"I'm sure it's all good," Louisa pronounced. "You're a darling. Do you have a boyfriend?"

"No," Brigid said.

"You've got plenty of time, plenty of time," Louisa chirped. "Bettina invited me to the session with Peace Man this afternoon at the Chappy Compound. I wouldn't miss that for the world. Are you all going?"

"Yes," Regan said. "Bettina was dying to have Brigid attend."

"Wonderful. I'll be there taking notes on Peace Man's message for my article."

"Soup's on," Luke called as he carried a steaming tray of pancakes to the dining room.

"I'll be right back," Regan said. She hurried down the hall to the bathroom. Louisa's now-famous red-and-white caftan drooped from a hanger over the tub, looking as tired and forlorn as the last remaining item on a sale rack. It was in imminent peril of collapsing into a heap.

Regan stared at the outfit that could have been Louisa's last, then reached over to straighten it. After she evened the shoulders on the hanger, her fingers ran down the sides of the caftan, as she skimmed the pattern with her eyes. A shiny white mark caught her attention, a mark that was not in harmony with the white swirls in the fabric. It was circular. Regan touched it; it felt sticky. Turning over her hand, she saw that white paint was now visible on her fingers.

Her eyes flew back to the garment. It was stained on the back with white paint. She'd just been talking about white paint with Duke this morning. The stain was small, about the circumference of the end of the skimmer he'd used to clean the pool. Regan's heart beat a little faster. She knew the whole thing didn't sit right with her. Was it possible—no, probable—that someone had pushed Louisa with the sticky skimmer?

But why?

There was absolutely no way Louisa could have brushed into the skimmer so that the end of it would touch the small of her back. This is crazy, Regan thought. If the end of the skimmer left this paint stain, then someone deliberately held it against her.

"It was almost as if I felt jostled," Louisa had said not more than five minutes ago.

Regan could visualize a slightly tipsy Louisa bending over the pool to see the musical note . . . someone coming up behind her holding the skimmer . . . pushing her with it.

What should I do? Regan wondered. She had to get back to the table. I can't say anything to Louisa. Or to anybody, really.

She needed to think this through, to figure out who it could be. Who would want to kill Louisa? She hadn't known anyone at the party beforehand. All she had done was to go around telling everyone there she was writing an article on the Hamptons. Did someone at the party want to put a stop to that? Or could it have been someone coming up from the beach? Access was easy enough.

Or was that push meant for Brigid?

Oh brother, Regan thought. Could this in any way be tied to the letter Brigid had received? Or the fiddle?

There's not much I can do about the paint stain on the back of the caftan. I can't exactly question the people at the party.

But I will keep my eye out. For the safety of both Louisa and Brigid.

She hurried back to the table, not really feeling hungry anymore.

14

"At last!" Chappy cried as Duke, carrying a tray of coffee, juice, and donuts, entered Chappy's study. On Sunday mornings Duke would run out to Dunkin' Donuts and buy their favorites, and then they'd sit and discuss the projects at hand. It was a tradition they both enjoyed.

At this time Bettina was usually with her personal trainer in the exercise room, doing her ninety-ninth sit-up. She'd tried to get Chappy involved, but he had zero interest. "Generations of Tinkas lived to ripe old ages without ever having set foot in a gym," he always told her. "I'm not about to break a winning streak."

Right now he bit into a chocolate donut.

Duke picked up a cruller and began to munch. Usually they didn't talk until one full donut each was down their respective hatches.

"Thank God, our dinner guest didn't croak," Chappy finally said as he patted his mouth with a paper napkin.

"Oh man, that would have been bad," Duke agreed. He took a sip from his juice carton. "She really got bombed."

"Those drinks you made were too strong!" Chappy remarked as he turned and stared out the window at the sweeping view of the Atlantic. He always enjoyed going for a swim, his private beach making him feel as if he owned the ocean. A smile lit his face and his eyes shone as he voiced his inner thoughts. "The *Hamptons News* should print its story tomorrow. I'm sure it will be wonderful coverage of the party with Brigid O'Neill and Nora Regan Reilly enjoying a Saturday-night dinner at the Chappy Compound."

Duke, his lower lip protruding, looked at his boss with a puzzled expression. "But they were taking pictures of that lady spitting out water. What if they print those?"

"She lived, you idiot!" Chappy threw down his flimsy napkin. "All's well that ends well! That's all that counts. Yes, indeed. Tomorrow all of the Hamptons will be reading about the upcoming Chappy's Theatre by the Sea. It's good to start beating the drums, as they say, and let everyone know that, like it or not"—he rapped his knuckles on the desk as he pronounced each word—"Chaplain Wickham Tinka is a player in this town."

"Yeah."

Chappy sighed. "Did you skim the pool?"

Duke nodded. "Regan Reilly was out there this morning. I forgot to tell you," he said as he licked his finger. "Last night I heard she was a private detective."

"WHAT?" Chappy exploded. His voice became a harsh whisper. "A private detective?"

"Uh-huh," Duke said. "Angela told me."

"That one!" Chappy rolled his eyes.

"She's going to hear my lines for me. I told you I decided to memorize Shakespeare this summer."

God help us, Chappy thought. "This isn't the time to worry about your career. Our focus is the fiddle, and then you might have a chance at an acting career. How does Angela know that Regan Reilly is a private detective?"

"She said she read it in an article about Regan's mother, the writer."

"Just what I need!" Chappy cried. "I hope she doesn't get in the way when we switch the fiddles. It's not fair!"

Duke poured him another cup of coffee.

Chappy added two spoonfuls of sugar and stirred briskly. "My nerves! My nerves! Until we get that fiddle, I'm going to be a wreck. Let's see . . ." He paused, took a sip, and put down his coffee cup. "You know what today is, don't you?"

"Sunday."

"No, stupid. It's the first day we can go take a look at the fiddle by ourselves."

"Are we going in the tunnel?"

"Naturally. How else? We can't exactly barge in the front door. It'll also be a dry run for Plan A of swiping the fiddle."

"If Plan A is sneaking into the guest house through the basement, then what's Plan B?"

Chappy rubbed his hands together. "I've got this worked out. Brigid told me that the afternoon of the festival she wants to rest up and then get over there early. They're leaving for good in that bloody bus right after the concert, so we have to get it before she leaves. I'll ask her to come and play her fiddle one last time in the house here before the concert. That's if we haven't gotten it already. Then we drive her over there in style in the Rolls-Royce. We put the fiddle in the trunk, and while I talk to her in the car you switch them."

"That's a lot of pressure."

"Oh, be quiet. After our dry run this morning with the tunnel, we'll drop in on our friend the fiddle-maker."

"He doesn't want to be bothered."

"I don't care! We've got to prod him along."

"But he said he doesn't want—"

"TOO BAD ABOUT HIM!" Chappy paused and tried to calm himself. He pulled a Polaroid camera out of his desk drawer. "I thought we'd take a few pictures of the fiddle to give to our friend the fiddle-maker. It's a good excuse for stopping by. Now . . . you said they all went out?"

Duke swallowed the last of the carton of papaya juice and wiped his mouth with the back of his hand. "Yeah. The guys and Pammy went out of here this morning with their golf clubs. When I was coming back in just now, Brigid and Regan and Kit were pulling out. They were going to Regan's parents' house for brunch."

Chappy made a face. "We weren't invited?"

"Guess not."

"That's gratitude for you."

Duke crushed the carton in his hand. "Let's get our helmets."

Chappy turned around in his chair and rapped on the fake bookcase. It swiveled open, revealing a shelf holding two orange miner's helmets with special headlights attached. Chappy kicked his heels with glee and got up. Donning their special headgear they disappeared behind the bookcase and down the secret stairs into the bowels of Chappy Castle.

As the musty damp smell filled their nostrils, Chappy grew more and more excited. The sight of the gray walls with cobwebs in the corners and big dark pipes hanging from the ceiling contributed to the feeling of forbidden territory.

They went down a hall, past the wine cellar, past Chappy's baby buggy and all the other requisite junk kept in basements, and turned right. They stopped at a little dark corner that was now lit up by their helmets.

Chappy turned to Duke. "Do the honors."

Duke bent down and pulled away a stone near the ground, behind which was a door handle. Grabbing it, he pulled, and all the stones above moved forward in unison, revealing a secret room. The two of them hunched over and, once inside, shut the door behind them.

"Ah yes," Chappy said as he pulled the string to light the lone bulb hanging from the ceiling. "The Tinka Men's Lounge, a room created during the strain of Prohibition. Grandpa Tinka founded this little speakeasy so his buddies could come over for a few belts without the worry of being busted. Grandpa was a crafty bootlegger who would send his speedboat out to Rum Row, three miles offshore, just outside federal jurisdiction, where they'd stock up on supplies of booze from the boats that came up from the Islands. They'd rush their quarry back to shore, ever on the lookout for gangsters and the Coast Guard. But Grandpa had built his boat to be faster than the Coast Guard's. Oh yes," Chappy reminisced with a tear in his eye, "I'll never forget the first time my father brought me down here. I was thirteen . . ."

Behind him, Duke rolled his eyes. He'd heard this story every time they had come down here for the past ten years.

"Long after Prohibition," Chappy continued, "this was a special room for the men in the Tinka family. It was our escape. Grandpa and Papa and I would come down here and sit and talk, and they'd smoke their cigars. That's why, when I leveled the house, I made sure the foundation stayed the same. I wanted to keep this room!" He sat in a thronelike chair and looked around smiling. Boxes and boxes of junk were all over the floor. Girlie magazines dating back to Grandpa's days were stacked in the corner. The fiddle Duke had stolen from Malachy was propped up in the corner. "To think that this whole place survived the dreadful hurricane of 1938. I love it here!"

What a pit, Duke thought. But he knew to keep his mouth shut when it came to this historic room. He sat in the only other chair and crossed his legs. I should be doing summer stock right now, he thought.

Once seated, they usually didn't know what to do with themselves. They never even stayed very long. Just knowing it was there made Chappy happy. Today they had a mission, but Chappy always liked to sit for a few moments and pay homage to his rumrunning Grandpa.

They sat there listening to the faraway sounds of activity upstairs.

Finally Chappy stood. "Onward and upward."

"Okay, boss."

Through another secret door they went, this one opening onto the tunnel that led straight to the basement of the guest house. This tunnel was also where the booze was stored during the fourteen years of Prohibition, starting in 1920. Because Prohibition was so flagrantly violated, a popular song of the day had been "Everybody Wants a Key to My Cellar." That was certainly true in Grandpa Tinka's case. He'd had this long tunnel built to use not only for storing the bottles and bottles of contraband he always managed to procure, but also as a secret passageway for his drinking buddies to get to the speakeasy from the guest house. He never wanted them coming through the main house. Not only was he afraid of the main house being watched more carefully by the police, but he didn't want his wife, Agneta, having to cope with anyone stumbling out at the end of the night.

The tunnel was dark and damp. It smelled earthy and occasionally a bug or little animal would make Chappy scream. Now he and Duke moved, single file, through the subterranean passageway that opened onto the corner of the basement beneath Brigid's guest house. Another secret door had been built so as not to be noticed by the casual observer who happened to be in that basement.

No use letting people know about the tunnel and that Grandpa Tinka had been an outlaw, Chappy often thought. Chappy's mother had preferred that no mention of his colorful history be made in polite society.

The door upstairs in the guest house that led to the basement had no handle, per Chappy's design. It could be opened only from the other side by someone who was on the basement steps. Since no guest would have any reason to go to the basement, Chappy had in effect sealed it off.

"Well, we're here," Duke said, pushing his hair back as they opened the door and stepped out onto the cement floor.

"Shhhh," Chappy commanded.

"But nobody's home."

"You never know!" Chappy said sharply.

Silently they crept up the steps and stopped at the door to listen. They could hear nothing but the sounds of the surf outside and birds cawing as they flew overhead.

"You've got the camera?" Chappy asked.

Duke nodded solemnly.

His whole body trembling, Chappy slowly opened the door and looked around. No one was there. A breeze was blowing through the window. Papers were on the table. The sun was streaming in and the whole house was quiet. He turned to Duke. "Come on."

Leaving the door wide open behind them so as not to be locked in, they both ran through the downstairs room and bumbled up the staircase to Brigid's room. The door was closed. Chappy stopped and listened and then opened it. Brigid's brush and creams and perfume were arranged neatly on the dresser. Her suitcases were stacked in the corner. The bed was made.

"What a good guest," Chappy mumbled as he dove to the floor and checked under the bed. "Aha!" he cried. "Aha!"

He pulled out the fiddle case and lifted it onto the bed. "This case is a little better than the other," he said to the hovering Duke. When he opened it, his knees almost buckled.

The sight of the CT right there in front of him was almost too much to bear.

"Chappy Tinka!" he cried. "Chappy Tinka." His eyes grew moist as he lovingly lifted the fiddle and cradled it in his arms. The bow was in the case. "Too bad we can't take it now! Should I play, Duke? Should I play it?"

Duke shifted from one foot to the other. "I think we'd better just take the pictures. They might get back soon."

"You're right. Oh God, you're right." Chappy laid the fiddle on the white bedspread, and Duke started snapping away. They turned it over and snapped. They held it sideways and snapped. After Duke used up the whole package of film, Chappy lifted it again as if it were a newborn babe. "Mine, all mine," he said. "This will bring luck to our theatre, I just know it."

He laid it back in the case and had just slid it under the bed when through the open window in the hall they heard the sound of tires crunching up the drive.

A horrified noise emanated from Chappy's being. "Move!" he yelled to an equally horrified Duke, who was standing there frozen. "Move!"

Together they raced down the steps, the pictures in Duke's hand. They could hear the doors of the red station wagon Chappy had lent the band closing and the guys ribbing each other about golf balls that had ended up in the woods and ponds.

"Hurry!" Chappy whispered to Duke as they raced across the den. A gust of wind blew up and the door to the basement started to shut. Duke dove and caught it just in time.

Outside Kieran could be heard saying, "Teddy, when your ball hit the tree . . ." Then he stopped to demonstrate the swing, as the others laughed.

"Yeah, well," Teddy replied, "at least I didn't kill any fish with my shots."

Pammy could be heard giggling. "I was surprised to see you guys call it quits after nine holes."

Chappy raced through the basement door and down the steps. He turned to look up. "Shut the door!" he growled as Duke grabbed the handle, closed it behind him, and took the staircase in two leaps.

Upstairs, Kieran unlocked the back door to the guest house, and Pammy and the golfers stepped into what seemed like a perfectly undisturbed room. Chappy made a beeline for the entrance to the tunnel.

"Don't you want to stay and eavesdrop?" Duke whispered.

"NO! There's plenty of time for that later. We've got to get these pictures over to the fiddle-maker right now! LET'S MOVE!"

15

Malachy loved late summer afternoons. He loved the gentle light of the sun and the peaceful warm feeling in the air. Sundays were the quietest. He loved to sit outside his cottage and look out on the rolling hills.

But on this Sunday he was sitting out there feeling a little unsettled. It had been over a week since someone had come in and taken Brigid's fiddle right off his lap. Now all this talk about the curse and how the fiddle shouldn't have left Ireland. He was worried about Brigid.

She had called him so excited when she won the fiddling contest. Now she was out there in the Hamptons to play in a festival and then was going on tour. Everything should be all right, he told himself.

He walked into his cottage and looked around.

"A bit untidy," he said aloud. "I should really clean up." He started to straighten the piles of papers, then suddenly felt the need for human companionship. He didn't even have a fiddle around to cheer him up. I've got to get a new one, he thought.

I'll go into town for a bite and a pint, he decided.

He wheeled his bicycle out the door and rode on into town, passing numerous sheep and cows along the way. They all looked bored but strangely contented. Malachy loved to pedal and ride. The wind in his face and the feeling of the summer evening made him feel alive.

Parking outside the one and only pub, he went inside, thinking about Brigid's birthday party. Was that really only a few weeks ago?

The bar was humming. A television in the corner was tuned in to a sporting event.

"Malachy, what can I get for you?" Eamonn the bartender asked. "The usual?"

"The usual," Malachy affirmed.

"You're looking a little blue, my man," Eamonn said as he put the Guinness in front of him.

Malachy shrugged. "I guess I'm a little let-down after the excitement of the party and all." He sipped the frothy liquid. "Having Brigid's fiddle stolen didn't help, either."

The bar door swung open, and in walked Finbar, the journalist who had started the stink about Malachy giving away the fiddle in the first place.

Malachy looked at Eamonn. "More to add to my troubles."

Finbar sat at the end of the bar, three stools down from Malachy. He was a wiry, intense little man with flat brown hair plastered to his head. His plain face was ruddy. He was in his forties, and life had not provided too many thrills for him as yet. To many he seemed intent on getting back at people for injustices heaped on him as a child. Whatever the case, when he came a-calling, people looked the other way.

"Hey, Sheerin," he said loudly. "Are you going to get your fiddle back from Brigid O'Neill, now that the other one's been stolen?"

"None of your damn business," Malachy said.

"Well, you should. That fiddle belongs in Ireland. It belongs to all-Ireland fiddle champions. It belongs to the people in this country."

"Since when are you the self-appointed chairman of the preservation committee?" Malachy asked gruffly.

"Hey, bartender, I'd like a drink," Finbar announced. He pointed to Malachy's beer. "The same."

Eamonn nodded and filled a glass.

"It doesn't matter what I say," Finbar continued. "You should have remembered that that fiddle had a curse on it if it left Ireland. Do you want it on your conscience if Brigid O'Neill has an accident or faces death?"

Disgusted, Malachy stood up and paid for his drink. "Thank you, Eamonn. I think I'll be leaving now." He walked past Finbar without glancing in his direction, out the door, and hopped onto his bicycle.

The sweet summer evening no longer held any magic for him.

All he could do was worry about Brigid.

16

Things were hopping at the All Day All Night Diner in Southampton. It was Sunday noontime and the usual line ran out the door. Inside it was raucous, with music playing, plates clattering, the air-conditioning humming, and waitresses calling out orders to the cooks. Every few seconds plates were flung on the counter, piled high with an assortment of breakfast specials.

"I'll have some French toast, with sausage and coffee." Chuck snapped the menu shut and handed it with a smile to the waitress.

"And me," Brad added, "I'll take your western omelette with French fries, coffee, and a great big glass of apple juice."

"Coming up," said Lotty, a big fan of their country music station. She always greeted them with a "Howdy, fellas."

"Well, I guess we should be eating hero sandwiches, shouldn't we, partner?" Chuck said when Lotty walked off.

"You bet," replied Brad with a big smile. "Last night I went home and slept like a baby. Have your boots dried out yet?"

"No, sir. They're in sorry shape. But it was for a good cause."

A lone man slipped into a seat at the table next to them.

"A good cause it was. I wasn't even thinking of my boots when I jumped into that pool," Brad said proudly. "When Brigid O'Neill comes on our show tomorrow, we'll really have lots to talk about."

"We sure will, partner. We sure will."

Lotty came around and poured coffee in their cups. She handed a menu to the single diner, and when he nodded his assent, she poured him coffee, too. "Be right back to take your order," she said.

Brad and Chuck ate their meals in a hurry. They wanted to get over to the radio station and prepare for their big day on Monday. After they left, Lotty came out with the man's scrambled eggs.

"Here you go," she pronounced brightly.

"Miz," he said as he eyed his eggs, "I couldn't help overhearing those two talk." He pointed at the empty table. "They have some radio station or something?"

"It's new in town," Lotty responded as she gathered up their dirty dishes. "Country 113. They're really getting rolling. Tomorrow they're going to have that new singer Brigid O'Neill on the show. She's getting real hot." With that comment, Lotty disappeared around the corner and through the swinging door to the kitchen.

I know, he thought angrily. It bothered him to hear people talking about Brigid O'Neill. She was his, not theirs.

Those two cowboys were at the party last night, he thought. They were talking like they owned her. Somebody at that party was planning to hurt Brigid, I just know it. I have to get to her and show her that I'm the only one who can take care of her.

Whatever it takes, I've got to do it, he thought as his gaze returned to his meal and he dug in.

17

Bettina wiped the sweat from her brow with the white towel that hung around her neck.

"I'm pleased with your work today," her trainer, a thirtyish tanned hunk, said to her. "Your abs, quads, and glutes were really responding."

"I felt that, too," Bettina replied, patting her stomach. "This is the area where I need the most work, I think."

He nodded solemnly. "I used to have a gut, too."

Bettina blinked and looked down at her stomach. "Do you think I have a gut?" she asked with a nervous laugh.

Looking like a statue in tights, the trainer sighed. In a tone a reporter might use to announce the death of a world leader, he said, "Let's just say your fat percentage in that area is over the limit of acceptability."

Bettina took the news with the grace she had learned to call upon in charm school. Nonetheless the remark made her feel crabby. The endorphins that had been jumping around her body since the workout stopped dead in their tracks. "Okay. See you tomorrow," she said, closing the door behind him.

Scowling, she wandered into the kitchen, looking for someone to take it out on. The only thing that greeted her was the sight of an empty bag of Dunkin' Donuts. Oh yeah, Constance has off today, she thought. Not that it bothered her. Bettina never liked to have much staff around unless they were there to tend to her body, like her trainer or masseuse or hairdresser, or to take care of her soul, like Peace Man. A cleaning crew came in twice a week to dust and vacuum and mop the house. The minute their van pulled up, Bettina would take off to shop.

Where the hell is Chappy? she wondered.

"CHAAAAAAAPPPPPPPY," she called out.

Silence.

"CHHAAAAAAAAAAAAAPPPPPPPPPPPY," she shouted again.

Toenails clicked on the wooden floor down the hall, becoming louder and louder as Tootsie scurried into the room, a little ball of white fur jumping around in circles and wagging her tail. She looked very happy, as if experiencing her own endorphin rush from a workout session for canines.

Bettina leaned over to pick up her baby. She rubbed her neck. "I said Chappy, not Tootsie, baby. You're my Toot-sie. Tootsie Tootsie Tootsie." She buried her face in Tootsie's neck. "Does Tootsie think Mama has a gut?" Bettina asked.

Tootsie licked her face. "YIP. YIP. YIP YIP YIP," the little dog answered.

Bettina bent down and dropped her back on the floor. "CHAAAAAPPPPYYY."

She went down the long hall to his study. The double doors were closed. She knocked sharply. When there was no answer, she turned the knob and walked in.

A tray with coffee cups and donuts was abandoned on his desk.

Bettina charged over to the bookcase and rapped on it. It swerved open. The helmets on the little shelf behind it were gone.

"The men's lounge," she said under her breath. He must be down with Duke in that dusty old speakeasy, she thought. That place made her itch. Well, at least I don't have to sit here with his mother and grandmother like I used to in the old days when the three Tinka men would head down there. His grandmother did nothing but yak about the picnic club she'd formed in 1910 and all the fun they'd had. Talk about being bored out of your skull.

Bettina shrugged. She closed the bookcase, exited the room that her husband sat in to think up ways to waste their money, and bounded up the stairs to her second-floor room. Tootsie joyfully bounced after her. That lady who had nearly drowned was coming over for Peace Man's session this afternoon, Bettina thought. She wanted to interview her and Chappy sometime this week. Show what a lovely couple they were and all the culture they'd add to Southampton.

Wouldn't it make Chappy's mother spin in her grave? Bettina thought. Me and Chappy written up as the perfect Southampton couple! Bettina laughed out loud as she relished the thought. In her bathroom she turned on the shower that had nozzles firing water from six different directions.

I'll show you, Mother Tinka, she thought happily.

18

Claudia and Ned were lying side by side in the hammock behind their house in Southampton. The hammock wasn't facing in the direction Ned thought best for prosperity, but if it were the sun would have been in their eyes.

They were cuddled up, companionably reading the Sunday papers.

Clad in an old pair of swimming trunks, Ned was staring at a picture of a movie star's tastefully furnished living room. It was featured in the magazine section.

"He'll never be happy in that house," Ned grumbled. "How could he? Look at where he put that couch!"

Claudia, dressed in a pink bathing suit with green buttons, and a matching pink-and-green headband, glanced over. "Put him on the list to send a copy of your book to when it comes out."

"He'll have so much bad luck in that house, he'll have moved by then." Disgusted, Ned turned the page. "Until people around here understand how important feng shui is, I'll never be able to make a decent living at it."

Claudia took off her sunglasses and looked into her lover's eyes. "The movement is growing," she said. "It takes time."

"I guess, pumpkin," he replied as he took her hand. "It's just that the woman who fell in the pool tried to make me feel silly about feng shui."

"How so?" Claudia asked gently. She knew Ned's ego was very fragile. He hated being dependent on her to get him jobs. His last specialty had been the fine art of plant watering, and it just hadn't worked out.

"She said that sometimes there's only one good place to put a chair or a couch or a bed. And if that's the case, is the person doomed to a life of unhappiness?" Ned's eyes teared up. "I had to tell her yes. What did she do? She laughed."

Claudia rubbed his arm. "It takes courage to be a pioneer, honey. Are you sure she laughed at you?"

"It was a funny noise she made—sounded like a donkey. Like a *hnnnn*."

The phone in their kitchen rang.

"I'll get it," Claudia said. "I should have brought out the cellular phone."

Ned held on for balance as Claudia got out of the hammock. He watched as she disappeared into the house. Feeling miserable, he closed his eyes. Vaguely, he could hear her talking.

"Yes!" she finally yelled in a manner most unlike Claudia. She came running out the screen door. It shut with a bang. "It's always darkest before the dawn!" she cried.

"What do you mean?" Ned asked, his interest mildly stirred.

"That was one of the guys from the country radio station on the phone. They're having Brigid O'Neill on tomorrow, and they're going to be talking about superstitions and curses and New Age kind of stuff. They want you to come on and talk about feng shui!" With that pronouncement she jumped on top of him.

"Baby!" Ned yelled as he stretched his arms heavenward and then encircled them around Claudia's waist. When she raised her head to kiss him, he asked anxiously, "Do you know how good their ratings are?"

19

Tootling along in the dented Rolls-Royce, Chappy and Duke enjoyed the warm sunshine of a Hamptons afternoon as they cruised over to the home of the unsuspecting Ernie Enders.

They crossed busy Route 27 and took the back roads to Sag Harbor, about a twenty-minute drive away. As usual the traffic was considerable, but Chappy enjoyed being seen in his Rolls, even if it was only by the person in the car next to him caught in the same traffic jam.

They passed antique stores, restaurants, and an open field where a tractor was dragging a wagonload of watermelons. An old graveyard, a garden center, and little brick houses with flower boxes and hedges all contributed to the picturesque countryside.

They passed joggers and bicyclists out for a little exercise and fresh clear air.

And of course they passed multimillion-dollar estates.

"Ah yes," Chappy reminisced, the memory of holding the fiddle in his arms mingling with pleasant images from his early years. "Southampton is where I belong. Truly. I've been spending my summers here since I was a child . . . those days spent playing on the beach with my pail and shovel at the Tinka homestead. Mama and Papa and Grandma and Grandpa. Grandpa wearing his ever-present straw hat and monocle. It was glorious. That's why when Mother finally died a few years back, I had to knock down the house and build the castle. The memories in the house were too painful and I was all alone."

"I thought you said the house was too small."

"Well, that too," Chappy admitted irritably. "And I was anxious to try something different. I still don't know why the townspeople made such a fuss over the castle."

"Because it's so big," Duke commented as he turned his head to watch a water-skier skim across the surface of an inlet. "And the other house had been built by a famous architect. You even said it was the only house in the neighborhood that survived the hurricane of 1938."

"Oh, so what!" Chappy sniffed. "When that theatre is up and running and a big success, they'll forgive me. I'll be bringing culture here. They just don't know. Bettina will be so thrilled when we finally get on the A-list for parties."

"Where do they keep that list?" Duke asked practically.

"It's not a list that anybody keeps, stupid! It's just that people want you around. Everything has changed so much out here. It's hard to make a name for yourself with all the movie stars and celebrities"— Chappy punched his left palm with his right fist—"but having that fiddle with my initials planted under the stage is going to make a big difference in our lives." He paused. "I still can't understand why thumbtacks don't impress people."

"It's too bad Post-it Notes started cutting into the business."

"OH SHUT UP!"

No matter how much Chappy yelled at Duke, he remained unfazed. "Here we go," he said as they pulled down a winding street and stopped in front of a neat little house with a mailbox that read ENDERS.

Inside, Ernie was enjoying a little lunch with Pearl. She'd put out a nice plate of cold cuts and potato salad. They had a map spread out on the table and were in their umpteenth discussion about which route they should take on their cross-country trip. The only thing they knew for sure was that they'd be heading first to Gettysburg, Pennsylvania, for the big wedding this Saturday. After that, the sky's the limit.

Pearl had read a lot of articles about older couples discovering the country when they had the time to wander, but Ernie had drawn the line when she wanted to buy an RV.

"We won't use it enough, Pearl. I like to get back to my own house. This trip is a once-in-a-lifetime *ahhh* trip."

"I guess," Pearl had said.

When the doorbell rang, Ernie was helping himself to another serving of potato salad. "We expecting somebody?" he asked.

Pearl grimaced. "Nah." She got up from the chair. "I'll get it."

"Come in, come in . . . ." Pearl said a moment later. "We were just having a little bite to eat. Ernie needs to keep up his strength, you know. . . ."

Aggravated, Ernie pushed out his chair and got up. Here comes Mr. Big Shot and his Sidekick, he thought.

"Ernie," Chappy said with a forced geniality. "We just thought . . . ."

Not bothering to listen, Ernie shuffled out to the greenhouse, waving them along behind him.

"So," he inquired, "what's your excuse for being here now?"

The fiddle on the workbench was clearly still a work in progress.

"We have pictures!" Chappy said, proudly handing them to Ernie. He glanced at the fiddle, trying hard not to let his anxiety show.

Ernie squinted at the Polaroids. "Did you take these?"

"Yes," Chappy replied.

"So why didn't you bring me the fiddle? It would be better if I could see the fiddle, feel the fiddle, smell the fiddle. Then I can make this one more like it!"

"But but but," Chappy began, "it belongs to somebody else, somebody who needs it. This is a big surprise . . . ." His dismay was apparent when he glanced again at the fiddle on the workbench. It didn't look like the CT fiddle at all. Brigid would know the difference right away. "Besides, this still looks new, and the original one looks old."

"Give me time!" Ernie demanded. "You give me a rush job, and then you don't leave me alone! Here"—he picked it up—"take it and get out!"

"Please!" Chappy begged. "Please! I'll pay you double. I really need that fiddle!"

"Double?" Ernie asked, surprised.

"Double," Chappy agreed meekly.

"I'll call you when I'm done."

"Thank you, thank you," Chappy said as he pushed Duke, who'd been standing there silently, out the door.

They hurried past Pearl, who would soon find out that they could now plan two trips to Florida this winter.

Out at the car, Chappy and Duke both jumped in and shut the doors. Duke started the engine and pulled off down the block.

"That was an expensive little visit," Duke commented.

"Shut up and drive!" Chappy ordered.

20

In the turreted room of Chappy and Bettina's mansion, the group was gathering for Peace Man's enlightenment session. Bettina thought four o'clock in the afternoon was a perfect time for this particular kind of therapy. After a day of swimming, tennis, or golf, everyone could come and tend to the spiritual side of life before the evening's activities got under way. These activities could include anything from dining at a good table in a trendy restaurant, attending a worthwhile dinner party, or, lo and behold, simply taking in a movie. Spirits were ready for an awakening that would sustain the hard core through the important socializing hours in the Hamptons.

Louisa was there in a pastel jogging suit. Herbert had driven her over and gone for a walk on the beach, promising to be back in an hour.

Regan was sitting cross-legged on the floor between Brigid and Kit. They'd spent the last couple of hours on the beach. When it was time for the spiritual nourishment, they'd all three thrown shorts and T-shirts over their bathing suits and come hurrying over.

Angela was sitting behind them. She'd paraded around the beach in her bikini and then decided to come along to the session. I bet she's hoping to see Duke, Regan thought. She seemed to stick close to him at the party last night. But the only guy in the room besides Peace Man was Garrett.

Today Peace Man had on a pair of short shorts and a sleeveless shirt. With his wardrobe, Regan thought, his dry-cleaning bills must be pretty low. And with his shaved head, he doesn't have to worry about getting an expensive haircut. Talk about a low-maintenance lifestyle. Where will he go come September? Regan wondered. Will he get in his RV and head west? She couldn't picture him parking it outside of Chappy and Bettina's apartment on Park Avenue in New York City.

Garrett, whom Regan had at first judged to be your typical preppy Wall Street broker, was seated on the floor next to Bettina. Regan was surprised that he would be interested in a session like this. But he seemed to be trying to get into it. His eyes were closed and his hands were on his knees. Maybe it's an attempt to pick up stock-tip vibrations, Regan thought.

She looked up at Peace Man. He probably doesn't even know what a stock is, Regan thought. Garrett and Peace Man were two completely different types, yet there was something about both of them she couldn't quite put her finger on.

"Peace Man is ready for your souls," Peace Man announced. "First we must release all the tension from our bodies. We are constricted by negative tension caused by bad food, bad thoughts, stress . . ."

Cursed fiddles, Regan thought. People who push others into the pool when they're drunk. Threatening letters.

". . . So now we must get up and yell AAAAGH!"

The members of the group who had participated in these sessions previously jumped up with alacrity.

Regan, Kit, and Brigid eyed each other and stood cautiously.

"AAAAAAGH!" the group began.

"AAAAGHHHHHHHHH!" Peace Man yelled fiercely.

I thought he called himself *Peace* Man, Regan mused.

"AAAAAAAGGGGHHH!" went the crowd.

"HNNNNNN!" went Louisa.

Peace Man started to flap his arms and motioned them to follow him. Soon they were all going around in a circle looking like a bunch of chickens gone berserk.

"AAAGHHHHH! AAAAGGHHHHH! AAAGHHH!"

Why isn't this making me feel better? Regan wondered.

Fortunately the howling didn't last too long. Peace Man had them sit back down and do stretches while he talked to them about the universe and the importance of mind over matter.

"Matter doesn't matter," he said solemnly as he twisted himself up into a pretzel shape, with one foot dangling over his ear.

Is he auditioning for Gumby? Regan asked herself.

He then came around and made them stick out their tongues at him. "Peace Man judges personality by tongues and hands," he said. "There are many different kinds of tongues, many different kinds of hands. Next week Peace Man will discuss. Right now lie down."

They all lay silently on their mats, listening to the sounds of the surf outside. It reminded Regan of naptime in kindergarten. The same feeling of restlessness came over her now as it had way back when. Ten minutes later, Peace Man announced: "Peace Man will see you next week, but as of this moment Peace Man is going into a special seven-day period of fasting and silence. Peace Man will drink lots of fresh squeezed fruit juice."

Over the Fourth of July? Regan thought. No corn on the cob on the Fourth of July? This guy is not exactly a Yankee Doodle Dandy. So what is he?

Peace Man turned to unplug his lava lamp.

"But Peace Man," Louisa called to him, "I wanted to interview you for my article."

Peace Man shook his head and walked out of the room.

Louisa came over to Regan, an expression of frustration on her face. "Seven days of silence. I'd go mad. Maybe I can do a phone interview with him when he gets his vocal cords back."

Brigid and Kit got to their feet. Smoothing out her T-shirt, Brigid laughed and said, "I guess he won't need a ticket to the concert."

"That might be a good thing," Regan replied. "He might want to relieve tension in the middle of one of your songs."

"You know something?" Louisa said. "I'm even more fascinated by him now than I was before. What's his real name and where is he from?"

Bettina walked toward them. "I hope you enjoyed it," she offered anxiously.

"Oh yes," they all managed to mutter.

"Where did you ever find Peace Man?" Louisa asked.

Bettina smiled. "Chappy and I have a big Christmas party in New York. Last year I told Duke to invite his acting class. Peace Man had just signed up for it."

"Peace Man was in an acting class?" Regan asked with disbelief.

"He said he wanted to take it for a brief period so he could explore what it was like to be other characters. That way he could understand all of us better," Bettina said with another big smile. "Wasn't that a good idea?"

Now I've heard everything, Regan thought.

21

At 7:45 A.M., in Kit's car, which they'd borrowed, Regan and Brigid drove out of Chappy Compound onto the streets of Southampton. They were headed for the radio station. The air was fresh and clear with a lingering dewy feel, the birds were chirping, and not too many cars were on the road.

"What a day!" Brigid exclaimed. "I should get up early more often."

"Whenever I happen to find myself out and about in the early morning, and that's not often, I love it," Regan agreed.

Ten minutes later they pulled into the tiny dirt-and-gravel parking lot of the home of Country 113.

Inside the somewhat shabby entrance, a receptionist with an obvious fondness for large quantities of black eyeliner was busy removing her breakfast from a brown paper bag. "Can I help you?" she asked as she surveyed her blueberry muffin.

"Brigid O'Neill is here for her interview," Regan said crisply.

"Oh, that's right. I forgot. It's Monday, ya know." She looked at Brigid, who was holding her fiddle case. "I like your song."

"Thanks."

"Go through the door and make a left. They're at the end of the hall."

An ad for a local restaurant could be heard over the speakers in the station as Brigid and Regan were escorted into the studio by an employee who had encountered them in the hallway. Chuck and Brad were sitting in a room with microphones positioned around what looked like a command station with four seats. Both were wearing cowboy hats and seemed to be absorbed in reading material. A big picture window looked onto a control room, where the engineer was seated.

"Hey, guys," Brigid called out energetically.

They both looked up quickly. "Heyyyyyyy," they said in unison.

Enthusiastic greetings were exchanged, and Regan could tell that Brigid was getting in the "time to entertain" mode, something she knew from her mother can look easy but actually takes a lot of energy.

After Brigid was seated, Regan went in and sat on a couch in the control room. A burly, bearded engineer, preoccupied with his panel of knobs and buttons, nodded a quick hello as Regan settled herself in.

Suddenly the door opened and Louisa appeared. "I was just in the ladies' room," she whispered, her eyes twinkling. "I've been here for over an hour. I gave them all the research I had done, and I brought my laptop in case there was anything I should look up when they're on the show. There are some interesting curses to talk about. Have you seen the paper?"

"No," Regan said. "Why?"

"Hnnn." Louisa reached into her carryall and pulled out the Hamptons News. She placed it on the coffee table in front of Regan.

Regan looked down. The newspaper had blown up two pictures taken at the party Saturday night and printed them side by side on the front page. One was of Brigid playing her fiddle in Chappy's drawing room. Kieran was standing right behind her smiling, with his guitar in hand. Next to it was a snap of Louisa sprawled out next to the pool, with Pammy performing her lifesaving maneuvers. Above it was the caption "Is this fiddle really cursed?"

"Oh my God," Regan murmured. The article began, "As Brigid O'Neill played the legendary fiddle bequeathed to her by one of Ireland's most famous storyteller/fiddle-players, a fellow dinner guest nearly drowned in the swimming pool at the home of Chappy and Bettina Tinka in Southampton. . . ."

Louisa leaned over her shoulder. "I've never gotten my picture in the paper before," she said excitedly.

"Well, you did it with a bang, Louisa," Regan replied as she studied the pictures. "Two reporters were at the party. What about the other paper?"

Louisa plopped down next to Regan. "It's a weekly. It doesn't come out until Friday."

To Regan, Louisa looked as fit as a, well, fiddle. She was dressed in a pair of white pants with a coral-colored, short-sleeved shirt. She had on gold necklace, bracelet, and earrings and looked very much on the job. To think . . . "How did you get here today, Louisa?" Regan asked.

"I insisted on driving myself. I feel fine."

Regan smiled at her. "Good."

"Okay, we're back!" Chuck announced as the music from the last commercial faded out. "And we've got with us, Brigid O'Neill, who is sooooo hot on the country music scene these days. Her hit single, "If I'da Known You Were in Jail (I Wouldn'ta Felt So Bad about You Not

Callin'),'' has been in the top five of the country music charts these last couple of months, even reaching the number one spot. I love the title of that song.''

"Thanks," Brigid said.

"That's what I love about country music—the greatest lyrics. . . . Anyway, Brigid's debut album, entitled *Brigid,* which I have right here, is hitting the stores right now, available in CD and cassette. Brigid O'Neill is in the Hamptons to play at the Melting Pot Music Festival on Friday night. Are you excited, Brigid?''

"You bet," Brigid replied. "I'm looking forward to being in front of a New York audience."

"They're the best," Brad assured her.

"I should know, I'm from New York," Brigid said.

"Us too," Chuck said. "And we want more people in these parts to listen to country music. You like Country 113?''

Brigid laughed. "I love it."

"We do, too," Brad interjected. "Now, Brigid, did you see the *Hamptons News* today?''

"No. I just got up an hour ago.''

"Well, ladies and gentlemen out there," Brad began, "we were at a dinner party on Saturday night in the Hamptons, and Brigid played her famous fiddle, which you may have heard about. . . . By the way you can call our switchboard and give your guesses for what the initials CT carved into the side of the fiddle stand for. . . . We'll tell you more about that again later. . . .'' He handed Brigid the newspaper as he described how Brigid got the fiddle in the first place, the curse of the fairies for removing the fiddle from Ireland, and Louisa Washburn's tumble into the pool. "So what do you think about the fiddle's magic powers, Brigid?''

"I think the fiddle is blessed, not cursed. A good friend gave it to me, I won the Fan Fair fiddling contest with it, and I will always treasure it. I think our friend Louisa simply fell into the pool when she was leaning over to look at the musical note on the bottom. It has nothing to do with any silly superstition.''

"Okay, folks, we'll be back in a few minutes to talk about the fiddle, which Brigid has with her and promised she'd play for us. And we'll be taking your calls to see what you have to say about the fiddle. Don't go away.''

Next to Regan, Louisa seemed to be basking in the glow of her near disaster.

* * *

Across town, Chappy and Duke had gotten up early so they could listen. "Wouldn't you think they'd mention where the party was?" Chappy cried. "I fed them, for God's sake."

Duke shrugged.

"Go outside and start up the car. I want to buy that paper!"

In his little shack of a house, he sat in his bedroom listening, ready to pick up the phone and call the station. Sometimes he loved Brigid and sometimes he got so mad at her that it made his head ache and his stomach churn. He'd felt fine until they mentioned that song. Why was she letting them talk about it? It was his and Brigid's song!

At least she couldn't sing it on the air. It didn't sound like that guy who sings a little bit of it with her was there. That was good.

He lay back on his messy bed and waited for the commercials to end.

We're back, folks," Chuck announced. "Now Brigid, do you believe in curses and superstitions?"

"Well, they say we Irish are a superstitious lot. But I've never really taken it too seriously."

Brad picked up the pages of Louisa's research. "Those fairies from hundreds of years ago in Ireland were a tough bunch. We already know that they were mad as hell about the tree being cut down that was used to make your fiddle there, but did you know that these fairies used to carry off accomplished musicians to entertain at their feasts? If the human guest partook of any of their sumptuous food, then he wouldn't be able to return to his worldly existence. So you know what that means, don'tcha? You've got to eat before you leave home for a gig."

Brigid laughed.

"I've got a few more here," Brad said. "Horses sneezed to protect themselves from the fairies. . . . Hmmmm . . . Why do you sneeze, partner?"

Chuck scratched his nose. "Dust."

"Good answer. And Fridays are a day for storms, so people are loath to go to sea on that day. But get this, Brigid. If you encounter a red-haired woman before going to sea, that is definitely bad luck. Fishermen turn back if they see one on their way to the boat."

Brigid leaned into the microphone with a devilish grin. "Us redheads get blamed for everything. The one that I always thought was fun is that if you tie a little bag of clay around your neck when you're going to bed, then your future spouse will appear in a dream."

Chuck looked at Brad. "You'd better try that."

"I'm afraid I'd have a nightmare starring my ex-wife."

"I do think," Brigid continued with a chuckle, "that people invented these superstitions to deal with their fancies and their fears. Life is so unpredictable, and it was a way of trying to put a little order into it."

"Hey, I think we have some callers on the line here, Brigid," Chuck said. He pushed a button. "Hello."

"Brigid?" It sounded like the voice of a teenaged girl.

"Yes."

"Hi, Brigid. My name is Tiffany and I just want to tell you that I lovvvvve your voice . . ."

"Thanks, Tiffany," Brigid said softly.

". . . and you should keep that fiddle. Your friend gave it to you fair and square. Don't listen to anybody who tells you any different. It really bugs me when people try and, like, boss you around."

"Thank you," Brigid said. "I appreciate that."

"Thanks for calling, Tiffany," Chuck added as he pushed another button. "Hello. Hello." They could hear the echo of the seven-second delay on the caller's radio. "Turn off your radio, please," Chuck urged.

"Hello, I'm here," an older-sounding woman began. "My name is Marjie, and, Brigid, I just want to tell you that my parents came over from Ireland. My father used to play the fiddle, and that's why I love country music so much."

"Glad to hear it," Brigid said.

"I'm coming to the concert Friday. My husband and I want to get there early with our beach chairs and get a good spot."

"That's a good idea," Brigid said.

"The thing I like about country music is that it really gets down to the nitty-gritty of feelings, you know what I'm saying. It's not that noise you hear on other stations."

"You got that right," Brad said.

"Can you tell us a little about your album?" Marjie asked. "I'm going to buy it, but what about the other songs on it?"

"One of my other favorites on it is 'I've Got a Place to Live (But without You I Feel Homeless).' "

"Oh. Very good." The woman clucked approvingly. "Well, I'm trying to figure out what the CT on your fiddle could stand for. I've got the map of Ireland out and everything. When I come up with a good guess, I'll call it in. My husband and I would love to get to meet you personally."

"Thank you very much," Brigid said warmly.

"Okay," Brad interrupted. "We've got to take another break now. We'll be riiiight back." He raised his arm and wiggled his finger, a sign to the engineer to plug in the commercials.

The door of the control room opened and Regan turned. There with a big smile on his face was Ned Alingham. He was wearing a pair of plaid shorts, sneakers, and a short-sleeved button-down shirt with a pen clipped to the pocket. A folder was tucked under his arm. His big smile disappeared when he spotted Louisa.

"Hello," Regan said.

"How are ya, how are ya?" he responded.

"Here, sit down," Regan offered, pulling out a chair next to her.

"Hnnn," Louisa said, smiling. "Hello."

Ned looked at her suspiciously and sat. He held his folder close to him as though his life depended on it.

"Are you going to be on the show?" Regan asked.

"A little later," he said. "They want me to talk about feng shui and how it brings good luck to your life. It brought good luck to my grandmother. She practiced feng shui without knowing it and caught a thief."

"How did that happen?" Regan asked.

"She rented rooms in her house for extra money. One night she rearranged the furniture and put a little table with a lamp on the landing of the stairs. A boarder tried to sneak out in the middle of the night without paying. He had all her silver in his bag. Wouldn't you know he tripped over the cord of the lamp and went flying. Woke up my grandmother. She made him pay up and then called an ambulance. He broke his leg." Ned smiled. "Granny was a character."

"She caught him because she moved a table," Regan said.

Ned nodded. "As you can see, feng shui is in my blood. My grandmother was always rearranging people's furniture for them. When I first read about feng shui as a serious art form, I knew it was my calling."

Louisa gestured grandly with her arms. "I find the whole subject so fascinating."

His eyes narrowed. "You do?" he asked.

"Of course."

"I didn't think you felt that way the other night."

"Well, let's face it," Louisa said. "I still insist that there are some rooms where, feng shui or no feng shui, the dresser fits on only one wall. *Hnnn.*"

"A true feng shui expert would find a solution," he replied with a bit of impatience in his voice.

"Saw the dresser in half?" Louisa asked jokingly.

"If need be," Ned said definitively.

Regan crossed her legs, anxious to change the subject. "I understand you're working on the theatre at Chappy's," she prompted him.

Ned rolled his eyes. "It's taking forever. We were supposed to be done with that by now. I must say I was disappointed because it would have helped to drum up a little business over the summer."

He warmed up quickly and was talking in that hushed intimate manner that people seem to develop with each other in greenrooms before being interviewed on radio or TV. She'd seen it when she'd gone around with her mother. It's a kind of instant rapport, a shared kinship, resulting, Regan thought, from either nervous energy or boredom while you wait your turn.

"What's taking so long with the theatre?" Regan asked.

"It turned out Chappy's wife had rented out the servants' quarters to that guy Garrett for the summer. Chappy didn't know she'd done it. We wanted to get to work a couple of months ago and have the theatre ready this summer, but now we have to wait until after Labor Day."

Regan raised her eyebrows. "He didn't know she had rented it out?"

"Apparently not. She didn't think we'd be building the theatre until the fall."

"Had he ever rented it out before?"

Ned's eyes bulged behind his glasses. "No! He never did. They just got married again last September. Maybe she thought it was a good idea because of the money. Not that they really need it. In any case, it set us back a little bit."

"You said they got married *again?*" Regan asked.

Ned laughed with excitement. "Yeah. They were married more than twenty years ago, but it didn't last long. A couple of years ago, she called him up after she heard his mother had died. I guess they found what had been missing the first time around."

"Did either get married to anyone else in between?" Regan asked.

"Chappy, never. Bettina did once, I think."

Louisa, who'd been intently listening, her eyes going back and forth between them, shifted in her chair. "I'm going to interview them for the article I'm writing about the Hamptons. And I want to include a piece on you and Claudia."

Ned looked at her with a contented half-smile on his face. "I'm sure we can arrange that."

Suddenly a joyful strain of voices burst through the speakers singing "W-H-C-MMM. Hamptons Country Music."

"And we're back," Brad announced. "We have a lot going on this morning—this whole week, as a matter of fact. Brigid O'Neill is with us, and she told us during the break that she'd be happy to return on Thursday morning to announce the winner of the contest. Who can come up with the most original meaning for the initials CT carved into the side of her fiddle? She's going to play that fiddle for us in just a few minutes."

"I can't wait to hear people's guesses," Brigid said offhandedly.

"Me too. We have another caller here," Brad announced. "Hello, what's your name?"

"I don't give out that kind of information," a squeaky male voice said grumpily.

"Everybody has a right to their privacy," Brad replied good-naturedly as he rolled his eyes at the others. "What would you like to say to Brigid O'Neill today?"

"I want to tell Brigid that she should get rid of that fiddle."

"Get rid of it?" Brad asked, dubious.

"GET RID OF IT!"

"Why?"

"Because it is bringing her bad luck. I saw what happened at that party the other night. That lady was pushed into the pool!"

Next to Regan, Louisa inhaled sharply.

"Pushed?" Brigid asked.

"I was there. I saw it. Don't believe me if you don't want to, but SHE WAS PUSHED! And you know something? Maybe it was meant for you, Brigid. You have to be careful!!!"

Oh my God, Regan thought. He isn't a crank caller.

Brigid stayed calm. "So you saw what happened?"

"YES!" The squeaky voice was getting excitable. "And I'm coming to the concert. Then you and me can throw that fiddle into the ocean together."

Brigid sighed. "Well, I'd really like to keep the fiddle."

"I don't want you to! I have to protect you from the bad luck it will bring you. AND STOP SINGING THAT SONG ABOUT JAIL TO OTHER PEOPLE! THAT'S OUR SONG!" He slammed down the phone.

Oh brother, Regan thought. It sounds like our pen pal has blown into town.

22

"Brigid, you must be starved," Regan said when they walked out of the radio station.

Louisa had torn out of the parking lot a few moments before.

The interview had lasted a couple of hours. After numerous callers, Brigid had played the fiddle. Then someone had phoned in wanting to buy it for one hundred thousand dollars. When Brigid said no, the price kept going up. At half a million dollars, the caller, a very old woman who wanted to buy it for her husband, finally gave up.

"You'd better guard that fiddle with your life," Brad had urged upon her departure.

"I'm trying to think of where you should place it in the home," Ned had said, scratching his head.

"In a vault," Regan had answered.

Now, as Regan unlocked the car, Brigid looked over at her. "I am kind of hungry."

"What do you feel like having?" Regan asked.

"After an interview like that, something simple and hearty." Brigid laughed. "Like bacon and eggs at a greasy spoon."

"I've got just the place," Regan said as she turned on the ignition. "The All Day All Night Diner in Southampton. It's a classic."

"Two?" the waitress asked hurriedly, barely glancing in their direction as they entered.

"Yes," Regan answered.

The waitress's name tag read LOTTY. She grabbed two menus. "Smoking or non?"

"Nonsmoking," Brigid answered, and they followed her around the corner.

Suddenly Lotty turned, a look of recognition coming over her face. She glanced at the fiddle case and then stared at Brigid. "You're Brigid O'Neill, aren't you?"

"Yes," Brigid said, smiling.

"Oh, I was listening to you back in the kitchen this morning. Brad and Chuck come in here all the time. I love your music." She led them to a corner booth.

"Thank you." Brigid acknowledged the praise as she took a seat.

Regan slid in on the other side.

Lotty put her hand on her hip. "I love country music. The lyrics just kill me. *If I'da known you were in jail,*" Lotty began to sing softly, *"I wouldn'ta felt so baaaaad about you not callin'. . . ."* She laughed and let out a little snort. "Oh, excuse me. That song just cracks me up."

Sitting at one of the narrow tables no more than six feet away, he nearly choked on a piece of English muffin when he saw them. He'd just started to eat his soft-boiled egg when they walked in. It was perfectly cooked, and he had just put a little pat of butter on it and the right amount of salt and pepper.

One spoonful of egg followed by one bite of muffin, chew and swallow, was the special way he liked to ingest this particular meal. Now he was too nervous to take a sip of his nice hot coffee!

Brigid was right there! Just feet away. The rest of the tables in the section were empty. Within seconds he could be over there, touching her.

He started to sweat. His stomach hurt. He wanted to talk to her but he couldn't do it here. She might recognize his voice from this morning.

Who was that lady with her?

Why is the waitress singing their song? He could feel himself getting madder and madder.

I have to get out of here, he thought. They can't know it's me who called.

Look at how pretty she is!

Look at them laughing and talking! His eyes teared up and he felt like such a baby. He was so in love with her. He needed to be alone with her so she'd have the chance to fall in love with him. Just like in The Sheik.

He had to get to her. But how? He'd figure it out.

Since he'd gotten up this morning, it had been a bad day. Why was he feeling so confused again?

I can't wait for the concert Friday night," Lotty said as she came back with a steaming pot in her hand. "Coffee?"

Regan and Brigid both accepted.

"Be right back."

Regan watched as Lotty turned and walked over to a guy with a weird haircut dining alone.

"Everything okay?" she asked.

He nodded, picked up his napkin to wipe his mouth, and made the signal for the check with his right hand.

"You're leaving so soon?"

He nodded again.

Lotty whispered, but Regan could hear her. "You were asking about the country radio station yesterday. That's Brigid O'Neill over there. She was on this morning."

He glanced over at them, but when he saw Brigid and Regan looking, he turned away quickly.

"He's embarrassed," Regan said.

Brigid waved to him when he left. "Bless his heart."

In about as delicate a manner as possible for Lotty, she plunked their plates of eggs, crispy bacon, and whole-wheat toast down on the table.

"Two cholesterol specials," Brigid joked.

"You said it," Lotty replied cheerfully, then glanced around. All the tables in the area were now empty. She gestured with her thumb. "The guy who was sitting at that table over there before—he's come in three times in the past couple days. Doesn't matter if it's breakfast, lunch, or dinner, he always orders eggs." She laughed. "I don't know why he was in such a hurry to get out of here today. He didn't finish, and he usually licks his plate clean."

"Maybe he got sick of eggs," Brigid said.

"Or maybe someone rushed him over the results of his cholesterol test," Regan commented as she took a bite of the wonderful-smelling bacon.

"Well, he's a quiet type so at least I didn't have to listen to any complaints! Now enjoy!" Lotty said as she hurried off to clear a table of dirty dishes.

23

Arnold Baker had been the president of Welth College for ten years now. A graying man with a military carriage, he'd just turned fifty-seven and enjoyed his life in the Hamptons. His wife was involved with the various fund-raisers around town, his two children were grown and living in New York City, and he had a white clapboard house on a pond, which suited him just fine. It was filled with his books, pipes, and tweed jackets.

The only thorn in his side was Chappy Tinka. Here's a guy, Arnold often thought, who's a textbook case of being ruined by your inheritance. He would never have to lift a finger in life again. Never really had to lift a finger much before either. Arnold knew that since his twenties Chappy had worked, if you want to call it that, in the family business. When his mother died a few years ago, the entire Tinka fortune had plopped in his lap. He was an only child and so was his father, which of course meant Chappy got everything. Arnold knew that there were distant cousins who bore the Tinka name, but unfortunately for them they were not descendants of Alvin Conrad Tinka, the founder of Tinka Tacks.

What does Chappy Tinka do right away after he is freed from the iron hand of his mother and inherits all that money? He goes crazy! Builds a god-awful monstrosity of a house and ruins the look of the neighborhood for all those oceanfront houses on the block. Now he was planning on ripping down the servants' quarters and building a theatre on his property. How appalling! The worse part of it was that no one could stop him. The land had been in the family for so long that it was grandfathered and the zoning laws didn't apply to him.

Arnold knew the neighbors were worried that if his thespian efforts didn't work out, he might turn the whole place into a cineplex showing eight movies at once. The whole neighborhood would end up smelling of popcorn!

Not that Chappy wasn't generous, Arnold thought as he sat down at the antique desk in his office and looked out at the rolling hills of the lush green campus of Welth College. Tinka had made donations to the college even though he was not an alumnus, and he was one of the big sponsors of the Melting Pot Festival. It was just that ever since he had called and insisted that Brigid O'Neill participate in the festival, there'd been problems.

Brigid O'Neill was a fine singer and a great addition to the schedule, but Arnold had had to do some maneuvering of the lineup for the evening's entertainment and it had caused trouble.

Darla Wells was not happy. In fact, Arnold thought sadly, she was freaked out, as his students liked to say. Last week when Brigid O'Neill had agreed to come to the festival, it had been Arnold's unhappy task to inform Darla that the younger, hotter Brigid would be participating in the festival, and Darla would have to cut out a couple of her songs to make time for her. The other three bands, all male and known nationally, had agreed to the changes.

Darla was a different story. Talented though she may be, at age thirty-five she was still waiting for her big break in the music business. Up till now she'd been plucking her guitar at little out-of-the-way places in the Hamptons, hoping to be discovered. All to no avail. So her husband had cooked up the great idea to make a huge donation to Welth College—but only if Darla got to perform at the festival. Darla figured there'd be plenty of talent scouts in the audience and maybe she'd finally be discovered.

Well, Arnold thought, she certainly seems to possess the killer instinct you need to make it in the music business. It was definitely on display when I broke the sad news to her.

Darla knew that at the Melting Pot Music Festival the spotlight would inevitably shine, even when it literally wasn't on her, on the beautiful, charismatic Brigid O'Neill.

Darla would be the only local act at the festival, a festival that had started out small a couple of years ago and now was celebrated grandly, even receiving national coverage. Arnold had always secretly congratulated himself on that. It had been his idea to throw a fund-raising concert on the lawn of the college during the summer, when it seemed that the world was out in the Hamptons. Find a cause that the Hollywood types like to get into, like the wetlands or whatever, and make it a recipient of the evening's profits. Throw in a little publicity, stir, and what do you get?

One of the most exciting events of the summer.

Given the generosity of Darla's husband, why did he risk her wrath? Because Chappy Tinka donated *more* money to the college than did Mr. Wells.

Arnold Baker had to do some serious juggling. Trying to keep both families happy was an impossible task.

Now Brigid O'Neill was all over the paper and the radio. He'd caught part of her interview on the car radio this morning.

His secretary buzzed him.

"Yes, Dot," he said.

"I have a package here for Brigid O'Neill."

"Bring it in."

The gleaming wood door opened and Dot sauntered in. She'd been with Arnold since Day One at the college, and a more loyal secretary you couldn't find. Fifty years old, with a rounded girth and a practical air, the adjective that came to mind about her was sensible. Students waiting outside President Baker's office to speak with him were always comforted by her motherly presence; she'd raised four children of her own. Her husband was an electrician, and the two of them had known each other since her family had moved to Sag Harbor when she was in the sixth grade.

She was holding a small box wrapped in brown paper. Black lettering spelled out Brigid O'Neill's name and WEALTH COLLEGE.

Dot put it down on her boss's desk. The package sounded as if it had kernels of corn rattling around inside. "Whoever sent it can't spell, but they're not too far off the mark, are they?"

Arnold raised an eyebrow and looked up at her. "There's no address on this."

"It didn't come through the mail. Apparently it was left outside the door over the weekend. One of the security guys just brought it to me. He thinks it probably was left by that same crazy gardener who came to last year's concert. He left boxes of vegetable seeds for all the singers."

"Okay," Arnold said. "I think I'll take a ride over to Tinka's at lunchtime. I'd like to welcome Brigid O'Neill to town, seeing as I wasn't on the guest list for the other night."

"Did you get a look at the paper?" Dot asked as she pushed back her glasses on her nose.

Arnold nodded.

"I hope the festival is as exciting as Mr. Tinka's party," Dot deadpanned.

I don't, Arnold thought. I really don't.

24

Bettina sat on a lounge chair on the deck off the master bedroom, staring out at the ocean. Tootsie was cuddled up to her surgically enhanced right breast, busy licking her mama's neck and right ear. It was tough on Tootsie; she could never seem to get to the other ear. A cellular phone was always in the way.

The *Hamptons News* was on Bettina's lap.

Chappy had brought her a copy and then run back out into town to do God knows what. He was acting so neurotic lately. Even more than usual. Ever since we got back from Ireland, she thought.

Bettina scratched her leg and gave Tootsie a little kiss. As her eyes skimmed her toes, she made a mental note to summon the pedicurist. She then looked down at the picture of Louisa Washburn spitting up water and smiled. Hilda Tinka must be rolling in her grave, she thought.

She's got a lot to roll in her grave about these days, Bettina mused happily. Hilda had always thought of herself as so Gatsbyesque. When she wasn't playing canasta or going to a polo match, she'd been there to bug Chappy. And Bettina, for as long as Bettina had lasted during her first marriage to Chappy. Which hadn't been long. This time I'm staying till the fat lady sings, Bettina thought wickedly. She laughed aloud as she stared at the picture.

A picture like this taken at Hilda Tinka's estate just wouldn't do! Hilda had orchestrated so carefully all those prim-and-proper family pictures taken of everyone in their Sunday finest. She'd even once asked Bettina to step out of a shot.

"Mother, I'm married now!" Chappy had cried.

But Hilda had prevailed and gotten the picture of Chappy alone with his parents and grandparents.

Bettina sat there and wiggled her feet. She wished that Peace Man was giving sessions this week. It always relaxed her.

Why *was* Chappy acting so neurotic lately?

He couldn't possibly be unhappy with her. She'd been on her best behavior for nearly a year now.

I'll just have to keep closer tabs on him, she decided.

25

Everyone thinks you can have everything when you're rich, Darla Wells fumed. And it's just not true!

The brown-haired, doe-eyed singer with the cute little body was sitting in the primo chair of her hair colorist at his exclusive salon, Wendell's, in East Hampton, reading the *Hamptons News*. Actually she was staring at the picture of her arch enemy, Brigid O'Neill. The one who made it necessary for Darla to cut down the number of songs she would sing at the concert.

Wendell appeared from the back storeroom where countless bottles of dye and solutions and peroxide and conditioners were all lined up, just waiting to do their magic on the heads of anyone willing to pay through the nose.

Dressed in black pants and a black collarless shirt, his ever-mournful expression set firmly in place, Wendell solemnly approached the chair and planted his hands on the crown of Darla's head.

"What do we want to do today, darling?" he asked.

Darla looked at the reflection of his heavy-lidded, jowly, tanned face, surrounded by a cap of dark wavy hair. He was somewhere in his fifties, and everyone in town agreed that a more natural-looking dye job was hard to find on a man of that age.

"Highlights," Darla answered shortly. "The usual."

Wendell nodded ever so slightly, then looked down at the paper on Darla's lap.

"Ohhhhh. Brigid O'Neill is marrrvelous," he said. "She's got such a faaaaabulous head of hair. What I wouldn't give to get *her* in this chair." With that pronouncement he disappeared into the back room.

Inside her about-to-be-highlighted head, Darla seethed. I *hate* her, she thought. I just hate her.

Two hours later Darla exited the salon. She yanked open the door of her Mercedes-Benz sports car, reached in, and grabbed Brigid's CD off the passenger seat. Flinging it on the ground, she crushed it with her spiked heels.

"That's what I think of your singing," she muttered under her breath.

26

After breakfast, Regan and Brigid stopped in the village of Southampton to run a couple of errands. They got back to the Chappy Compound at eleven-thirty.

A battered gray sedan was waiting on the street outside Chappy's Castle and pulled into the driveway behind them.

When Regan and Brigid got out of their car, two boys who looked to be about seventeen or eighteen jumped out of the jalopy. Clad in sunglasses, baseball caps, college T-shirts, and baggy shorts, they smiled and waved.

"Brigid O'Neill," one of them called amiably as he hurried toward the women. He was tall and bony, and wore braces on his teeth. A tape recorder and a notebook were in his arms. A small backpack was flung over his shoulder. "I can't believe it's you."

The driver, stocky and tanned, shut his door and stood there shyly.

"Hello," Brigid said, smiling.

"Can I help you?" Regan asked immediately.

"I hope so," the tall one replied. "My name is Phil, and this is my buddy Nick. We're in high school out here and I work on the school paper. We heard Brigid on the radio this morning and thought we'd take a chance at coming over and seeing if you'd give us a quick interview." He grinned at them, his braces sparkling in the sun, his nose shiny. "It won't take long, I promise. It'll be awesome to have an interview with Brigid O'Neill all ready for the paper when school starts. All of my friends are coming to your concert."

Regan glanced over at Brigid.

"I don't mind," Brigid said.

Regan looked back at Phil. He seemed so young and eager. "Do you have an ID?" she asked.

"Huh?" he answered, looking embarrassed. "I don't have my license yet."

Brigid touched Regan's arm. "It's okay," she said. "It'll be fast." She motioned them to follow her. "Let's go inside."

The guest house felt cool, and there was a note on the table that said the others had gone golfing.

"We can do the interview right here," Brigid said. She sat on the couch, the fiddle case next to her.

Phil settled himself close to Brigid. Nick took a seat in a chair nearby.

"Regan," Brigid asked, "that bacon made me so thirsty. Would you mind getting me a glass of water?"

"Not at all." Regan turned her back and walked over to the refrigerator. I hope they make this fast, she thought as she reached in to pull out the bottle of ice water. Little did she know how fast they intended to make it.

"What are you doing with that rope?" Brigid asked suddenly. The fear in her voice was unmistakable.

"We have to tie you both up," Phil said quickly. "We're not going to hurt you. We just want the fiddle."

Oh God, Regan thought. She'd had a weird feeling about these two, an instinct she should have followed. Time to stop these boys. She reached down, pulled her pistol out of the sack tied at her waist, and spun around. While Phil was starting to tie up Brigid, Nick was heading toward Regan. "Hold it right there," she said.

The expression on Nick's face was priceless. "This was his idea!" he cried, pointing to Phil. "He thought we could look up the lady who called the radio station wanting to buy the fiddle. Or else we could find somebody else who would want it."

"Shut up, Nick," Phil squealed as he dropped the rope in his hands.

"I should have known something was up when you didn't take off your sunglasses when you came in here. Did you really think you could get away with this?" Regan asked.

"We weren't going to hurt you," Phil protested.

"Just tie us up," Regan said sarcastically. "And hopefully not give us rope burn. Brigid, why don't you get up and make room so these two buddies can sit together on the couch until the police arrive?" She gestured with her gun to the couch. "Nick, have a seat."

He almost tripped over his feet in his urgency to obey her.

"I'll call 911," Brigid said in a greatly relieved tone. She stood up. "You boys are off on the wrong track in life."

"We really like your music, Brigid," Phil said in what sounded like an effort to make amends.

"Then you shouldn't have tried to steal my fiddle. I like to make music with my fiddle."

Regan shook her head. "Boys, I suppose you're not on the school newspaper here in the Hamptons, are you?"

They both mumbled a negative response.

"Something tells me you don't even live out here at all. Who'd be stupid enough to try a stunt like this and live nearby? But I did notice that your car had New York plates."

"It's a Rent-a-Heap," Nick moaned. "We're here on vacation from Nebraska."

27

The wail of sirens pierced the ocean air as two police cars sped into the Chappy Compound for the second time in less than forty-eight hours.

Chappy and Duke were returning from a trip to Saks, where there'd been a sale on men's bathing suits. Since Chappy liked to take a two-minute dip in the ocean every morning and afternoon, his one concession to exercise, he collected bathing suits like Peace Man collected crystals.

Chappy also had begrudgingly agreed to go to the car wash with Duke.

"Oh all right," he'd said. "As long as we're out. But I don't know what I'm paying you for!"

Now, as they rounded the bend and caught sight of the commotion, Chappy screamed, "What's going on?"

Duke shrugged. "Don't know."

"Well, step on it."

Duke pressed down on the gas pedal and the Rolls-Royce sailed into the Compound. Duke kept going past the police cars parked at odd angles by the guest house—lights flashing, doors open, radios squawking—and drove around the circle in front of the castle.

"WHAT ARE YOU DOING?" Chappy screeched.

"After the car got dented, you told me to always pull it all the way around and out of the way."

"AGH! STOP!"

Duke slammed on the brakes, and the car lurched to a stop. Chappy unbuckled his seat belt just as Duke started to back up.

"STOP!" Chappy screamed as he was thrown forward. "LET ME OUT!"

Duke stepped on the brakes again.

Chappy fumbled with the door, jumped out, and went running to the guest house as Bettina, carrying Tootsie in her arms, scurried across the pool area in the same direction.

"I'm here!" he cried. "I'm here."

"Oh, Chappy," Bettina said breathlessly, grabbing his hand as they covered the rest of the ground to the door of the guest house together.

Inside two police officers were handcuffing the intruders. Another was questioning Regan and Brigid.

"What happened? What happened?" Chappy demanded. "Is everyone all right?"

Brigid answered. "We had a little excitement. It seems these two"—she pointed to the baby-faced criminals who were now being led out to the patrol car—"wanted to play cops and robbers with my fiddle."

Chappy's eyes almost popped out of his head. "What?"

"We feel terrible," Bettina declared, her hand still holding Chappy's with a firm grip.

Tootsie barked her agreement.

"I'm so lucky I had Regan here," Brigid said.

Regan shrugged. "I'm just glad everything's okay. I shouldn't have trusted those two. It's just that I've been around my mother so much when school kids want to interview her at book signings. We never think a thing of it. They usually act sweet and shy. Like those two."

"Who are they?" Chappy asked urgently.

The young sandy-haired patrolman sighed. "A couple of kids who aren't too bright. They heard someone offering big money for the fiddle on the radio this morning. They thought if they could get their hands on it, they'd be able to turn it over and make a quick buck. Miss O'Neill and her fiddle have been in the news a lot lately. Unfortunately the perceived value of that fiddle is all too inviting to the lowlifes of this world."

Chappy tsk-tsked and clucked his agreement. "How disgusting."

"Terrible," Bettina reiterated. "Terrible."

"Hey, what's going on?"

Regan turned. Kieran was standing in the doorway, his expression troubled as he looked straight at Brigid. Regan could see Hank and Teddy and Pammy following him.

The police officer quickly explained to him what had happened. "Crazy kids," he concluded.

Kieran hurried over to Brigid and put his arms around her. "When I saw the police cars I got so afraid. Are you okay?"

Brigid nodded and smiled and leaned her head against his chest. Regan could see a chemistry between them that she hadn't noticed before.

Kieran reached over and grabbed Regan's hand. "Thank you, Regan," he said simply.

"Hey, that's why I'm here."

"What's going on?" Pammy asked as she stepped into the room. Her expression was less than thrilled.

Kieran dropped his arms and turned to her. "It's okay now. The trouble is over."

No, it's not, Regan thought. It looks like it's just beginning.

Brigid quickly explained to Pammy what had happened.

"Well well," Chappy said. "Look who else is here."

Arnold Baker, the immaculately attired president of Welth College, appeared in the doorway. He was holding the small brown package addressed to Brigid O'Neill.

The patrolman tipped his hat. "Hello, sir."

Chappy made the introductions to the others.

"I just came to welcome you to town, Brigid," Arnold said, "and to deliver a package that was left for you at the college. I can see I picked the wrong time for that."

"Not at all," Brigid replied graciously. "It's great to meet you. I'm looking forward to the concert."

Arnold shook her hand and gave Brigid the box.

"Are you going to open it?" Bettina asked. "I can't wait to open the presents Chappy gives me."

"Hold on a minute," Regan said. "In view of what just happened, who knows what we might find in that box. It could be dangerous."

"My secretary thought it sounded like vegetable seeds," Arnold Baker offered. "That's what someone left for the performers at last year's concert."

"Let me take a look," the policeman said. He accepted the package from Brigid. It rattled in his hands. "Sounds like kernels of corn moving around." The tape over the flimsy brown paper came undone and the paper slid away, revealing a white box with a top. "It seems like it wants to unwrap itself," he observed.

"I'm dying to know what's inside," Bettina commented in her loud voice.

"Well, from the sound of it, it's definitely not a bomb," the policeman said. He turned away, lifted the top off the box, and pulled out a beanbag doll with long red hair and green eyes. The head was practically severed from the body. Scribbled in black letters across its white bib was the word BRIGID.

A collective gasp rippled through the room.

"Looks like there's a note here," the policeman said as he pulled a piece of paper out of the box.

"What does it say?" Brigid asked.

An uncomfortable look came over the face of the officer of the law. "It says, 'This could be you.' "

"Appalling!" Chappy cried. "I think this is appalling."

"Brigid, we're so happy you're our guest," Bettina declared. "We don't want you to think that this is typical of the way people act around here. It's true they can be pretty nasty in these parts but this is terrible. Terrible, terrible."

Two incidents within minutes of each other, Regan thought. Could a third be far behind?

Brigid smiled wanly. "I guess this means I've really arrived in show biz. Someone's sitting up and taking notice of me."

The police officer adjusted his cap. "Miss O'Neill, do you have any idea who could have sent this?"

Brigid looked perplexed. "No, not at all."

Regan turned to the officer. "On the radio show this morning, some strange guy called in. Someone also left a threatening letter for Brigid at Fan Fair in Nashville when she performed there. . . ." Briefly Regan explained what Fan Fair was. "Because the letter was just left there, it had no postmark. This box wasn't sent through the mail, either. . . ."

"Which means that the stalker or stalkers who wrote the note and dropped off the package have always been in Miss O'Neill's vicinity," the officer concluded. "Whoever called the radio station must be in the area."

"That's right," Regan said. "And you have the two who were here a few minutes ago . . . and the incident the other night with Louisa being pushed in the pool. . . ." She turned to Chappy and Bettina. "I think we should get some security guards to patrol the compound until Brigid leaves."

"Whhaaaat?" Bettina said.

"Oh my," Chappy uttered. "My my. I don't know whether that is, uhhh, really necessary, do you?"

Brigid straightened up. "Regan, no. I don't want to live like that, and this is supposed to be a vacation for everyone. You're here with me, this house is full of people, so is Kit's. Bettina and Chappy are right across the way."

"We'll all watch out for her," Kieran said firmly.

"That's right," Pammy declared.

Hank and Teddy nodded their agreement.

Brigid pointed to the box. "Whoever did this is not likely to come after me. And that letter from Fan Fair was left by someone in Nashville. That guy on the radio sounded like a loose cannon, talking about Louisa being pushed."

But I think she was pushed, Regan thought, envisioning the paint mark on the back of Louisa's caftan.

"What about the boys who barged in here today?" Pammy asked as she pushed her hair behind her ear. "That's really scary."

"They didn't want to get rid of me, they just wanted the fiddle. From now on, I've got to be more careful about who I grant interviews to. Right, Regan?" Brigid joked.

Regan nodded. "We can't let anyone who just shows up come in the door. Any interviews will be cleared in advance." And I'll bring the fiddle over to my parents for safekeeping, Regan thought.

"Besides a couple of phone interviews, the only other thing I have scheduled is going back to the radio station on Thursday. I have to call my manager, Roy . . ."

Arnold had been standing there quietly, taking it all in. He stepped forward. "Brigid, I'm so sorry."

"Hey, it's not your fault. I can't wait to play on Friday night."

"Good! Because as a representative of the college and the Melting Pot Festival, I find this whole business to be reprehensible. I can assure you that your presence at the festival is eagerly anticipated and will add to the evening's enjoyment immeasurably. Now, that said, I think I've done enough harm, and I'll get back to work."

Brigid shook his hand again. "Thanks for dropping by."

"Yes, oh yes," Chappy mumbled.

"Sir," Regan said as Arnold started to walk out, "I'd like to talk to you for a moment before you go." She followed him outside and made arrangements to stop by the college that afternoon. She wanted to talk with the security guard who'd found the package. Maybe he'd seen something.

"I'll be there all day," Arnold told her.

Regan watched as he backed out. The driveway was a sight: two police cars with flashing lights, the twenty-year-old station wagon Chappy had lent the band stopped behind them, Chappy's dented Rolls, and the tour bus and Peace Man's camper sticking out from the other side of the castle.

Where is Peace Man? Regan wondered. Did he meditate through all this commotion? Is he planning to spend the seven days of silence in his camper?

I have to watch out for him, she thought as her eyes swept the grounds of the Compound. The pool area where she was sure Louisa had been pushed the other night was calm and quiet.

Not only is that fiddle cursed, Regan thought, I think the Chappy Compound has a few ghosts haunting the place. She took a deep breath of the ocean air. An uncomfortable feeling was settling across her chest like a dead weight, a feeling that Regan was sure wouldn't go away until Brigid was safely out of the Hamptons.

Four more days until the concert, she thought. To think that this week was supposed to be a fun week for Brigid.

She walked back into the house and spoke again with the police. They agreed to let Regan keep the doll for her own investigation.

"Until Miss O'Neill files a complaint she can do what she wants with it," the officer said. "We'll keep the letter in case we want to check it for fingerprints."

"Thank you," Regan said, as the question kept running around in her head: Who would leave that doll? Let's hope my visit to Welth College this afternoon will shed a little light on that subject, Regan mused. Maybe I'll learn something that will be of help.

28

"Pearl, I can't believe I finished the damn thing." Ernie was sitting at the kitchen table having a cup of coffee. He'd just eaten breakfast, even though it was past noon. After Chappy Tinka had skedaddled out of his house yesterday, Ernie had worked nonstop, staying up until four o'clock in the morning putting the final scratches on the fiddle.

"It turned out so nice, Ernie," Pearl said as she cleaned out the refrigerator in preparation for their trip. She opened a jar of mayonnaise and sniffed. Deciding with a wrinkle of her nose that it wouldn't be any good by the time they got back, she chucked the jar in the garbage by her side. It landed with a thud.

"Nice, shmice. It'll have to do."

"Whatever you say, I'm proud of you." *Clunk* went an old hunk of cheese.

"Are you throwing everything out?" Ernie asked.

"Only what might stink or decide to grow mold before we get back."

Ernie stood up. Now that his task was completed, he felt satisfied but itchy. He'd been working on that fiddle day and night for a week. Instead of feeling worn-out, he was restless. Like he wanted to get away. Get out and see something new. Do things. He'd been cooped up for only a week, but dealing with Chappy Tinka made it feel like an eternity. "Are we all packed?" he asked Pearl.

"I've been packing and unpacking for days. There are a few more things to stick in the suitcases . . . and maybe a few others to take out."

Ernie stared out the window at the greenhouse. "Pearl, let's get out of here. Let's leave today," he blurted.

Pearl looked up from the produce drawer, where she had discovered a lime, now rotten, that she'd been searching for last week when her neighbor Bea had stopped by for a cocktail. Her mouth dropped open. "What?"

"You heard me."

"But . . ."

"No buts," he said, walking over to his wife. Tenderly he patted the soft skin on Pearl's face.

Pearl smiled. "Massaging my wrinkles?"

"I love your wrinkles. And I've been ignoring you all week. Why don't we throw our bags in the car and go into New York City?"

Pearl's eyes widened. "New York City?"

"Yeah, New York City. We'll get a room at the Plaza, buh buh buh, go out to dinner, buh buh buh, live it up for a couple of days, maybe go to a show, then we head to Pennsylvania."

"Are you feeling all right, Ernie?" Pearl asked suspiciously. Suddenly she got very frightened and her voice rose as she spoke. "Did the doctor tell you something was wrong at your checkup, and you've been keeping it from me? Did that cough you had turn out to be—"

"Oy! Pearl!" Ernie interrupted. "No! Can't I just do something nice?"

"It's a little unusual, that's all."

"Thank you very much."

Pearl laughed. "I'd love to go. But Ernie, New York City is so expensive! We made a budget for the trip."

"Forget the budget," Ernie said. "This is special. Tinka is paying me double, remember? We've got to live a little." He leaned down and gave her a kiss. "Why should I work like a dog if I can't enjoy the money?"

"Oh, Ernie! This is so exciting!" Pearl puckered up and kissed him back. "We haven't done anything this spur-of-the-moment since 1965!"

"What did we do in 1965?"

"We drove in to the World's Fair in Queens with no advance planning."

"Oh yeah."

Pearl looked around as if deciding what to do next. "I'll call Bea next door and tell her we're leaving today. . . ." All of a sudden a thought struck her. "Ernie, what about the fiddle? Isn't Tinka coming later this week to pick it up?"

"We'll surprise him and drop it off at his house on our way out."

"You know where he lives?"

"His address was on the check."

"He's getting it early and special-delivered!" Pearl said with glee. "Boy, will he be surprised!"

29

I can't believe I missed the excitement," Kit moaned as Brigid and Regan filled her in on all the details. They were sitting on the beach together in low lawn chairs, Brigid and Regan in their wet bathing suits. After everything that had happened, Brigid had wanted to go for a swim in the ocean.

"I want to let the water wash over me, Regan," she'd said. "I need to clear my head."

Pammy and the guys were up in the guest house making sandwiches for lunch.

Kit had been out with Angela, doing food shopping. When she got back and knocked on the guest-house door, Pammy had told her what happened and pointed to Brigid and Regan out in the water.

Kit had come running down and made them get out of the water and talk to her. "It figures that I'm in the grocery store when something like that happens. If I'd been here . . ."

"Kit!" Regan said. "We're just lucky the whole thing wasn't more serious."

"I suppose," Kit grumbled, her toes playing with the sand. "I can't believe it about the doll, too."

The three of them—one blond insurance saleswoman, one brunette private investigator, and one redheaded country singer—sat in silence for a few moments, staring out at the water, looking for all the world like any three friends in the Hamptons simply enjoying a sunny day at the beach. But in all likelihood very few conversations among the groups of women clustered in little groups up and down the miles and miles of shoreline vaguely resembled what these three were talking about.

"Brigid," Regan said, breaking the silence, "about the fiddle . . . I want to make sure nothing happens to it. What do you say I bring it over to my parents' house and leave it there for the next few days?"

For a moment, Brigid looked startled.

"Only if you want," Regan said, looking up at the guest house. "But there's no alarm system here for us to turn on when we go out. And we're all in and out to the beach, so the doors aren't always locked. Someone could easily slip into our place."

Brigid peered up at their living quarters. It looked peaceful and pretty and Currier and Ives-ish with its white exterior and black shutters, shining in the sunlight, sitting above the beach against the backdrop of a brilliant blue sky. A postcard-perfect image that only a couple of hours ago had been the scene of a foiled crime.

"What about asking Chappy to hold on to it?" Kit asked. "In all those rooms of his house, there must be a safe or someplace to hide it."

Regan shook her head. "There are so many people coming and going in that place. I'd rather get it away from here. You can be sure the word is going to spread around town about what happened. It might give somebody else ideas."

"Okay, Regan," Brigid said finally. "I guess it'll be a relief not to have to worry about it for a few days. Whoever said that possessions possess certainly had it right."

Regan nodded. "I think it will give us a little peace of mind. I'll go get it from my parents' place on Thursday or Friday before the concert. When you leave the Hamptons, maybe some of this hype will have died down."

"I hope you're right," Brigid said. "But you realize, don't you, that on the other side of this ocean, someone tried to steal what they thought was this same fiddle from Malachy?"

"Yes," Regan said.

"And they walked right into his house when he was sleeping and took it off his lap?"

"I know."

"You'd better bring it over to your parents' this minute!"

Kit stood up. "How about dinner at my place tonight? Angela and I bought the makings of pasta."

"I love pasta," Brigid said. "That sounds great!"

"You're cooking?" Regan asked Kit in mock disbelief.

"Well, Angela is in charge," Kit admitted. "I'm not a natural cook, but I can follow directions."

"Who's going to be there?" Regan asked.

"Angela and Garrett definitely. We'll see who else is around. Some of the others had to return to the City to work and are coming back out on Thursday for the weekend. Do you think the guys and Pammy would like to come?"

Brigid stood up. "We can ask them."

"Brigid," Regan said, "I want to run over to the college about the doll and then go bring the fiddle to my mother. But I want to make sure I'm not leaving you alone."

"Regan, I'll be fine," Brigid replied with conviction. "The others are here. I'd like to do some reading. I suppose I should call my mother. . . . I don't want her hearing about this from anybody else. She's in Ireland, but bad news always travels fast."

Regan thought again of Brigid's mother, Eileen. "Can you believe that's my kid?" she'd asked the group around her laughingly after Brigid had sung her hit song at the crowded party. Her face had been glowing with pride.

"I'm sure it will be easier for her to hear it from you," Regan said. "It's less upsetting. Just start the conversation with 'Mom, everything is fine but . . .' "

"But someone sent me a beheaded doll that looks like me. And another nut called me at a radio station. Other than that, things are just fine."

"I'm not going to leave you," Regan decided.

"Go! The guys are up at the house. Everybody's on their toes."

"Lock yourself in your room!" Regan said. "I'm not kidding!"

"Okay, okay!"

"Okay." Regan nodded. "Kit, can I borrow your car again?"

"Angela took it. She said something about going to visit a friend." Regan frowned.

"Regan," Brigid said, "take the station wagon. Chappy left it for all of us to use."

"Are you sure?"

"Take it."

"Okay. Kit, can I pick up anything for tonight?"

"There's a fruit and vegetable stand right around the corner. We were going to stop but it was really busy. If you can pick up some strawberries . . ."

Regan's eyes twinkled. "Kit, don't tell me you're going to make your famous strawberry shortcake."

"I just might," Kit said as she folded up her chair.

"Brigid, I've got to tell you," Regan commented with a smile, "tonight you're in for a real treat."

30

I can't believe she wanted a security guard around here," Bettina said for the twenty-fifth time since she and Chappy had walked back over to their house.

"I know, sweetheart, I know," Chappy said as they ate lunch together in the dining room. "As mother would say, it's so uncivilized."

Constance had served them a meal consisting of leftover chicken from the party on Saturday night, sliced and served on toast points. Chappy was drinking soda. Bettina was sipping a special herbal tea that Peace Man had suggested to soothe the spirits.

"Peace Man would see it as the presence of negative forces in our lives," Bettina declared.

"I think Regan Reilly was just erring on the side of caution," Chappy said as he sipped his soda, the bubbles tickling his nose.

The dining room door swung open. Clad in a pair of overalls with a bandanna tied around her neck, Constance appeared, with the same bored expression she'd worn since her first day of work at the Chappy Compound, when the castle had finally been ready for habitation.

"Ned Alingham, the feng shui specialist, is on the phone, Mr. Tinka," she said.

"Very well, very well!" Chappy cried in that resigned voice busy people use when they're being bothered. "Give me the cordless."

"Very well," Constance echoed, turning her back on them and whisking herself through the door as it swung back inward toward the kitchen. She returned a moment later and handed the phone to her employer.

"Chappy Tinka," Chappy declared as he held the phone up to his ear. "Huh . . . You heard about it already? . . . Where? . . . Oh my goodness . . . You want to what? I'm eating my lunch right now. I can't think about it at the moment. Good-bye!" Irritably, Chappy pressed the off button on the phone.

"He gets on my nerves," Bettina confided as she bit into a celery stalk. "What did he want?"

"He heard about the attempted robbery."

"Where?"

"That country music radio station. They must have a bug down at police headquarters."

"Oh my goodness." Bettina leaned down and fed Tootsie a piece of chicken. "So why did he call?"

"He said he'd never been over there in the guest house, and maybe the furniture arrangement was unlucky. He wanted to take a look."

Bettina groaned and sighed.

Chappy looked at her. "But I thought you believed in feng shui."

"I do. But that doesn't mean I have to like him."

The doorbell rang. "This place is a madhouse!" Chappy cried. "Will I ever get a minute's peace?"

Bettina shrugged.

Chappy threw down his napkin and yelled, "I'll get it!"

He sauntered through the living room with a purposeful stride and stopped at the front door, where he checked his reflection in the hall mirror before opening it. He was surprised to discover Regan Reilly standing there.

"Regan, hello hello," he said. "Yes, hello."

"I hope I'm not bothering you," she replied.

"Not at all! Come in. Come in."

"Just for a moment," Regan said as she stepped inside.

"Bettina," Chappy called. "Look who's here! Regan Reilly!" he announced, as though naming an old friend they hadn't seen for years.

"Yeah, hi," Bettina called.

Chappy led Regan into the dining room.

"I just want to make this quick," Regan said. Boy, is this a long table, she thought. Bettina at one end and Chappy at the other. It must be tough to pass the salt. "As you know by now, I'm a private detective."

"Yes . . . yes," Chappy mumbled. "I heard it mentioned when you were talking to the police."

Bettina nodded and lifted her dog onto her lap. "Uh-huh."

Suddenly the door from the kitchen swung open again, and this time Duke appeared. "Chappy," he said, and then he stopped in his tracks. "Hi, Regan."

"Hi, Duke."

"What do you want?" Chappy demanded.

Duke pulled some money and a receipt out of his pocket. "Chappy, I just wanted to give you the receipt for the car wash." He turned to Regan as he laid a green coupon down next to Chappy's plate. "If you save four coupons, you get the fifth wash for free."

"THANK YOU!" Chappy growled.

"You're welcome," Duke declared with a big smile. "A couple

weeks ago Chappy got mad at me because I lost the receipt," he said to Regan.

"GET OUT!" Chappy ordered.

Duke raised his hands. "No problem. Thank you. Nice seeing you, Regan." He turned and pushed open the swinging door into the kitchen, where a brief glimpse of Constance revealed her chasing down an airborne insect with a fly swatter.

"We're sorry about the interruption, Regan," Bettina said.

"Not at all. I just wanted to say that I got in the station wagon to do some errands and checked to make sure the registration and insurance cards were there, but the glove compartment door is locked. I asked the guys if they had the key, and they said they didn't. They admitted they hadn't thought about it when they drove the car. So . . . do you know where it is?"

"Oh dear, oh dear!" Chappy cried. "Of course. That glove compartment door is a funny thing. If you don't lock it, it flies open. All the time! Very distracting. No one around here drives that car very much. It's left over from the old days when Papa used to go off digging for clams and fishing and such and . . . oh dear. I'll be right back. The key must be in my study."

He disappeared down the hall in a frenzy.

"So, ya having a good time?" Bettina asked.

"Oh yes," Regan said, "although we could have done without the intruders."

"Yeah, I know what you mean." Bettina petted the dog, who was now licking from her plate. "Chappy and I always want our guests to be happy, and we get very upset when something bad happens."

"Uh-huh," Regan said. God, this woman is no rocket scientist, she thought. Something bad happens? That's putting it mildly.

"Here we go!" Chappy called ecstatically as he practically skipped down the hall. "Here is the key. Let me walk you outside and make sure it still fits."

Regan said her good-byes to Bettina and followed Chappy out the door. The red station wagon was parked right outside. She unlocked the door for Chappy.

"Locking the doors in front of our house?" Chappy joked.

In this place especially, Regan wanted to say. "Habit, I guess," she responded. She didn't want to tell him that the fiddle and the doll were under a blanket on the floor of the backseat.

Chappy quickly opened the passenger door, leaned over, and fit the key in the lock of the decrepit glove compartment. "Voilà!" he rejoiced as he pulled out the key and the unlocked door collapsed open with a thud. He rustled through some maps of Long Island and found the registration and insurance cards.

"Now you're safe to drive!" he declared proudly.

Regan briefly glanced in the car to make sure there was still a lump beneath the blanket on the floor behind the driver's seat. "Thank you, Chappy," she said. "I appreciate it."

"No problem." He got out, smiling, and handed the key to Regan.

Suddenly the noise of a car pulling into the driveway could be heard. They both turned to see a big, old-fashioned, four-door pale blue car slowly making its way through the Compound, as if the driver weren't sure of where to go.

"Who is that?" Chappy mumbled.

Regan went on the alert. After what had just happened, she wasn't taking anything for granted. Standing next to Chappy, she could almost feel the beads of sweat popping out on his forehead.

"Oh my God!" he said.

"What?" Regan asked quickly.

"Nothing," he said. "You'd better be on your way."

"Is everything all right?" Regan asked.

"Yes, of course." Chappy led her around to the driver's side door. "It's someone who used to work here," he whispered to Regan. "He drops by and never leaves. If I were you, I'd scram as fast as I could! I wish I could escape!"

Regan smiled and gave him the okay sign.

She put the key in the ignition. The car took a few starts to turn over. In the rearview mirror she could see an older man and woman getting out of the blue car. As she started to pull out, she could hear the man saying, "Mr. Tinka, it's ready! I finally finished it and it looks exactly the same . . ."

Regan shrugged and proceeded down the drive, anxious to get over to Welth College and talk to the security guard.

31

*S*omeone had tried to hurt Brigid! He knew it was going to happen!

In his little dark room with the flimsy bedspread, he sat at the tiny desk and stared at the sheet of paper in front of him.

"Dear Brigid," it began. "I love you."

He couldn't write anymore. He was so distracted and upset. After what had happened at breakfast, he'd come back here to calm down.

He stared at the unmade bed with the coarse white sheets all rumpled and messy-looking. He'd tried to lie down again but couldn't rest, even though he was so tired after staying up all night waiting for her to come on the radio.

He'd turned on the radio again and heard those two guys talking about the scary thing that had happened to her!

He had to save her now! He had to take her away. She would want him to. This morning she had smiled at him and waved. Maybe she loves me already, he thought. I wish I could have talked to her.

He banged the desk with his fist. When I called the radio station I should have disguised my voice, he thought angrily.

I'll come get you, Brigid. I'm not even mad at you for talking about our song with other people. As long as we can be together. The song is what made me notice you in the first place!

He rubbed his eyes. His head was pounding, as it always did when he started to get confused.

I'll be there soon, Brigid. I'll take you away and hold you in my arms and squeeze you to death.

I can't wait much longer.

32

Regan pulled up the long driveway of Welth College, past the rolling green lawn where the concert would take place on Friday night. She parked the car in the nearly empty lot behind the brick administration building. The campus had that quiet school's-out-for-the-summer look.

But Friday night this place will be hopping, Regan thought. Full of music and lawn chairs and cheering fans. *And who else?*

Regan made her way to Arnold Baker's office and was greeted by his assistant, an amiable woman who introduced herself as Dot. Through the partially opened door of Arnold's office she could hear his voice, which sounded upset and placating.

"Darla, I will try to give you more time at the concert. . . . I know it doesn't seem fair but we have to make time for Brigid O'Neill. . . . I think you're a wonderful singer. . . . Let me see what I can do. . . ."

"Can I get you a cup of coffee?" Dot asked Regan.

Regan got the feeling she was trying to distract her. She hesitated.

"I just put on a fresh pot," Dot informed her quickly.

"Actually, I would love a cup," Regan replied. She just didn't want Arnold Baker to think that she would be planting herself in his chair for a long visit.

Dot cocked her head. "I think he's off the phone now. Let me bring you in."

She led Regan into a stately office with oak paneling and shelves of books and floor-length, tie-back, red-and-blue curtains. Laminated diplomas hung on the wall, along with pictures of Arnold in his cap and gown posing next to various dignitaries.

He stood up and shook Regan's hand. In a somewhat embarrassed tone he said, "I'm getting so many calls. . . . There's so much to do about Friday night."

"I can imagine," Regan answered as she took a seat in one of his red leather chairs. She put the fiddle case and the doll box on the floor at her feet. There was no way she was going to leave the fiddle in the car in a parking lot.

"So you've had an exciting few days over at the Chappy Compound," Arnold remarked.

Regan nodded and picked up the box. "We have at that. It's all so unsettling." She shrugged. "I know it's a long shot, but I thought that if I talked to that security guard, I might find out something helpful about this." She held up the box.

Arnold nodded. "I called the security office and asked him to come over—Ah, it looks like he's here."

Regan turned to see an olive-skinned, dark-haired guy in his mid-twenties wearing a blue security uniform standing outside the office at Dot's desk.

"Come in, please," Arnold requested.

The guard turned and shyly walked into the office, introducing himself to Regan as Earl Barkley.

Arnold motioned for him to take the seat opposite Regan.

"As you know," Regan began, "the contents of that box you found were pretty disturbing."

Earl whistled softly. "Man, was I surprised to find out what it was. I never suspected a cut-up beanbag doll. The contents were rattling around. I actually thought it might be seeds." He shifted in his chair. "Like somebody left last year."

"I heard about that," Regan said. "So you found this box yesterday, which was Sunday?" she asked.

"That's right."

"Do you know what time it was?"

"Let's see." Earl squinted one eye and leaned back in the chair. "I'd say it was lunchtime. Yeah. Lunchtime."

"What do you consider lunchtime?" Regan asked.

"About twelve o'clock." He smiled. "I remember I was hungry when I drove around checking things out. After that I had lunch."

"And you found the box where?"

"The back door of this building. Just sitting there."

"The place was all locked up?" Regan asked.

"Uh-huh. There wasn't a car in the parking lot. It was Sunday morning. Things were quiet. School's not in session, so there's not much activity around here."

Regan sighed. "Had you driven by earlier that morning?"

Earl nodded. "I patrol the buildings around here several times a day."

"So you drove by in the morning?"

Earl nodded.

"How many times?"

"Once."

Do you know what time that was?" Regan probed.

Earl squinted again. "Nine o'clock."

"Are you sure?"

"Yes. It's my first loop of the day." With his index finger he made a circle. "It's always the same time, and I drive through here with a cup of coffee in my hand."

"And you didn't notice the box then?"

"It wasn't there," he said firmly. "I would have seen it."

Regan glanced at Arnold, who'd been intently listening. "So whoever left it here dropped it off between nine and twelve on Sunday morning," she continued.

Arnold's face looked grave. He shook his head back and forth slowly.

"Where do you go when you're not driving around?" Regan asked.

"Back to the security office to do paperwork. On days like that it's usually pretty slow. No parking tickets to give out . . ."

"So you didn't notice any cars around here?"

"No."

"No one else was on the campus yesterday morning, then?"

Earl sat and thought about that one. He gestured out the window. "A guy was using the tennis court down there in the morning."

Regan leaned forward. "Really?"

"He was by himself hitting the ball against the backboard."

"Do you know who he was?"

Earl shook his head. "No. I drove by the court and he waved."

"Don't you have to show a college ID to use the courts?"

Earl looked sheepish. He glanced quickly at Arnold. "Usually. But no one else was waiting for the court and he seemed like a nice guy, so I didn't bother to check."

Regan drew a quick breath. "Which time did you see him? At nine or twelve?"

"Twelve. Definitely twelve. I remember because it was getting hot out and he looked all sweaty."

"You can't identify him, then?"

"Well, I could if I saw him again, but I don't know who he was. He was about six feet tall with brown hair."

That really narrows it down, Regan thought.

"Did he look like he could have been a college student?"

"Yeah. He looked pretty smart."

Inwardly Regan groaned. "I mean his age," she said. "Did he look like he was in his late teens or early twenties?"

"I'd say he was early twenties. Like he might have graduated already."

Regan turned to Arnold. "I don't think the tennis player is the one likely to have left the box. One usually doesn't hang around after depositing a little present like that. But he might have seen something that could be helpful."

She turned back to Earl. "How well can you see the tennis courts from the back door here?"

"They're pretty far down. You don't really notice them. I didn't realize he was there at first because he was by himself in the court on the end. When I drove down by the courts I could see him."

"But he could see up here."

"Yeah. This building is on a hill, and from the courts you just look up."

"He didn't have a car here?"

Earl shook his head. "I didn't see one. A lot of times people jog over with their rackets in one hand, can of balls in the other, then they jog home."

Regan put the box with the doll on the corner of Arnold's desk. She wrote her number at the Chappy Compound and handed it to the guard. "If he comes back to play tennis, could you please call me right away? Don't let him leave without at least getting his name."

Earl nodded. "Of course," he said. He pulled out his wallet and placed the piece of paper inside. "I'll put up a notice in the security office for the others to be on the lookout for him, too."

"Thank you," Regan replied.

"Miss, if you don't mind. I'm just so curious. Could I see what the doll looks like?"

"Of course." Regan pulled the cover off the white box and gingerly lifted the nearly beheaded beanbag doll with the flowing red hair and the white bib that said BRIGID out of the box. Little white pebbles now lined the bottom of the box. The doll's head was bent to one side.

"That's nasty," Earl said. "Whoever did that is really nasty."

"I'm afraid they're worse than that," Regan said.

"Excuse meee," Dot murmured as she sauntered in with Regan's mug of coffee. "That coffeepot gets slower and slower . . . Oh dear!" she gasped as she took in the sight of the slashed doll.

"I know, Dot. It's disturbing," Arnold said quietly.

"No. You don't understand. That's my friend Cindy's doll!"

"What?" Regan asked quickly.

"She makes them."

"She makes them?" Regan repeated.

"Yes." Dot started breathing fast. "A few months ago just for fun she made one for her granddaughter. The child loved it and so did her friends because they like to play catch with it. . . ."

"Right," Regan said encouragingly, nodding her head as if that would make Dot continue.

"So Cindy made a whole bunch of them just the same." Dot stared at the doll. "Her granddaughter has red hair. . . . She'll be so upset that one of them was used for this."

"Where does she sell them?" Regan asked.

"She just started. Yesterday she had a table at the crafts fair in Water Mill. I spoke to her last night, and she'd sold all of them."

"How many did she sell?" Regan asked.

"A hundred."

Oh brother, Regan thought. "A hundred?" she repeated.

Dot shook her head. "She said it was a madhouse. One customer after another. I'm telling you, the kids love them. They're a perfect little present. Not too expensive. She made some nice spending money for her trip."

"Her trip?" Regan echoed. Don't tell me, she thought.

"She and her husband left on their sailboat today."

"Where were they going?"

"Points unknown," Dot replied with admiration. "They sailed out of Sag Harbor and were headed up the coast. Her husband has a serious case of wanderlust. He said he wanted to see which way the wind blew them."

Wonderful, Regan thought, just wonderful. "When will they be back?"

"In a month or so."

"Do you know if she had anybody helping her out at the fair yesterday?"

"Oh yes," Dot responded brightly. "She did."

"Who?" Regan asked eagerly.

"Her husband."

The words fell flat on Regan's ears. "Is there any way to get in touch with her?" she ventured.

"Not really. They were going to be out at sea for at least a couple of days and then check in with their daughter when they sailed into port. Whenever that is."

Knowing that it was a hopeless cause, Regan wrote down her number for Dot to give to Cindy's daughter. "Ask her, if she doesn't mind, to call me. Maybe she'll check in sooner than you anticipate."

When Regan drove away, all she could think about were the three people she'd love to talk to most at that moment. A couple out at sea and a certain six-foot, brown-haired male in his early twenties who plays tennis. She couldn't decide who'd be harder to track down.

33

Duke and Chappy scurried across the basement floor, fumbled with the door of their hideaway, and once inside shut it securely behind them.

"Duke! Duke! We got it! Will you look at this fiddle? Will you look at it?" Chappy demanded, his voice rising to a fever pitch, his heart beating wildly.

"Sit down, man," Duke urged his boss, whose chest was heaving up and down as they both breathed in the cool damp musty air of the Tinka Men's Lounge.

Chappy had snuck the copy of the CT fiddle into the house, been relieved to find that Bettina has disappeared, and then frantically located Duke. Now, tucked away in the depths of the Tinka homestead, they had a chance to examine their quarry.

With a case of the shakes, Chappy reached around with his free hand and sunk back into his chair. "Look at it!"

Duke leaned over, the light of his helmet shining on the initials CT. "Wow," he said. "It looks pretty good."

"PRETTY good?" Chappy countered. "PRETTY good? It looks great! It looks old! It looks like the real thing!" He caressed the wood, his fingers lingering over the carved initials. "Chappy Tinka," he said softly.

Duke sat on the other chair opposite Chappy. Spotting the fiddle he had lifted from Malachy in Ireland, he went over, picked it up, and brought it back to his chair. "Now we've got two extra fiddles," he said.

"But THIS"—Chappy indicated the one he was holding—"this is the important one. Brigid will never know the difference. Now we can switch them."

Duke adjusted the helmet on his head. "Now we don't have to drive over in that traffic and pick it up."

"UGHHHH! When Enders pulled in with his wife, I almost fell to the ground. Regan Reilly was standing right there!"

"She was?"

"Right there. Which reminds me: Keep the key to the glove compartment on the station wagon key chain, you moron. It was your fault she was hanging around."

"But I haven't driven that car in . . ."

"Never mind." Chappy waved his hand at Duke and hugged the fiddle closer. "I managed to get rid of Regan Reilly, and then Enders and his wife start hinting around to get invited inside! Can you imagine? If anyone had seen this fiddle . . ."

Duke nodded. "So do we go with Plan A or Plan B?"

Chappy's brow furrowed. He sat there thoughtfully in the gloomy dusk, his sneakered feet tapping up and down on the cement floor.

"Plan A!" he cried. "I think this should be done as soon as possible. After all, those thieves barged in there today, and if it weren't for Regan Reilly, they would have gotten away with my fiddle!"

"We oughta thank her."

"As long as she doesn't get in the way of us stealing it."

"True."

Chappy stood up. "I think the band is over at their house now, aren't they?"

Duke nodded. "I was out by the pool talking to Angela. They're all around."

"So we can't do it just yet." Suddenly Chappy felt a sense of urgency. "But it has to be done soon. Get out there and find out what their plans are for tonight. Hopefully they're going out, and we can make the switch then." Chappy took one last lingering look at the fiddle before they reentered the upstairs world. "Be good to Brigid," he said. "She will love you like you're the real thing." Laughing, he turned to Duke. "Now let's get out of here so you can get to work!"

Duke saluted.

"MOVE!"

34

Regan drove to her parents' house, her eye on the road but barely noticing her surroundings. Her mind kept going over the incidents of the last couple of days. She turned and glanced at the fiddle case on the seat next to her. "Maybe you are cursed," she mumbled.

I'm glad Brigid let me get this fiddle out of the way for a few days, she thought. Although that won't stop someone from trying to get it if they think it's still at the Chappy Compound. Regan squeezed the steering wheel. How long will Brigid have to put up with all this? Will things calm down when she goes on tour?

Who in the Hamptons would want to scare her with that doll? From what she'd overheard of Arnold Baker's conversation, there was at least one disgruntled singer who wasn't thrilled about Brigid being in the festival.

Regan turned onto her parents' street and navigated the big old station wagon down the block. I feel like I'm driving an enormous red boat, she thought. A boat with a funky glove compartment and a seat that's an ordeal to move forward. At least I won't have to parallel-park this bomb.

She pulled Chappy's clunker into her parents' driveway, turned off the engine, and sighed. Time to fill in the folks on what's been happening since this morning. If they haven't already heard. She picked up the fiddle case. "Let's go find a good hiding place for you."

With the case in one hand and the doll box in the other, Regan entered the front door.

"Well, look who's here," Louisa called from the den. "Hello, Regan! Long time, no see. What is it you've got there? A fiddle case? Don't tell me you've come over to play for us! *Hnnnnnn.*"

Regan smiled as she walked in. Louisa was sitting on the couch in a blue caftan with little orange open-mouthed goldfish swimming around the material, her feet propped on the coffee table, her computer on her lap. Regan could see through the window that Nora, Luke, and Herbert were just getting out of the pool.

"I think I'd need some lessons first." Regan put the fiddle case on the floor. "You look pretty busy."

Papers surrounded Louisa, and the plug to the phone was hitched up to the back of her computer. I hope no one is expecting any calls, Regan thought.

"I've been sitting here all afternoon with my laptop on my lap, which I naturally thought was the perfect place for it, and now my thighs are burning!" Louisa reached out her hand, but luckily Regan's elbow was too far away to clutch and shake.

"That must mean you're working too hard. Maybe you should put a pillow between your lap and the computer."

"Oh, Regan! You sound like my grandmother! When I was a teen-ager, she always said if you're going out in a group, bring a pillow in case you have to sit on a boy's lap in the car. *Hnnnnnnn.*"

Regan laughed. "She told you that?"

"Oh yes! It was much different in those days!"

"So I've heard."

"Regan, I've been doing research for my article on the Hamptons. A little while ago I called over and got that Chappy on the phone. I wanted to set up an interview with him and Bettina in the next couple of days, but now he wants to wait until after the concert, when Brigid is gone and the excitement has died down. The other night he said he'd do it anytime, and Bettina was most excited about it. But today he was a little short with me. He sounded distracted."

Regan thought about Chappy's reaction when that car with his for-mer employee had pulled up today. He seemed to be in a hurry to get me out of there, she thought. And he doesn't want to have a security guard on his property. Is he up to something? she wondered. Or is he just a wealthy eccentric who gets upset easily, like when the coupon from the car wash was lost?

"Well, Louisa, a few exciting things happened over there today, which I'll tell you about in a minute."

"As exciting as me falling into the pool?"

"I'd have to say yes to that, Louisa."

"Oh dear! I do want to hear all about it!"

Regan glanced outside. "I'd like to get everyone together. I'm sure they'll want to hear about it, too."

"Of course, Regan. It's nearly four-thirty. It's time for everyone to gather for libation."

"I can't stay long," Regan said as she walked over to the sliding doors.

"Oh, Regan, one thing! I looked up Brigid and her band on the Internet. There are pictures of them and articles and letters from fans."

Regan quickly turned back to Louisa. "Anything interesting?"

"Well, they all seem to love Brigid. . . ."

"That's good."

"I really just glanced at it. If anything juicy pops up, I'll let you know."

"Please do, and print it out."

A few minutes later, the whole group was sitting in the chairs by the pool with their drinks in hand. As the smell of the chlorine wafted into Regan's nostrils, she relayed the story of the would-be fiddle thieves.

"Oh my God, Regan," Nora said. She was wearing a white swimsuit cover-up, big round sunglasses, and a straw hat. "Of course you can leave the fiddle here. We'll keep it in our room in the safe."

"In our room?" Luke mumbled as he ran his hand over the top of his wet head. A towel was draped around his neck. "Maybe we should leave it by the front door."

Regan looked at her father. "Dad," she scolded.

He smiled at her. "I'll keep it in the bed right between your mother and me."

"Like my grandmother's pillow!" Louisa cried.

Lambie blushed and looked down into his drink.

Luke looked confused but didn't bother to ask.

Nora smiled understandingly. She turned to Regan. "Honey, we'll put it in the safe in our closet. It should fit in there. Lord knows we never use that space."

"Thanks, Mom," Regan said. "I'm glad the previous owner of this house had a lot of valuables to lock up. The other incident of the day," she continued, "was the delivery of this doll." She held it up for the group and explained its origins. "So as you can see, things have been a little tense. That's why I'd like to keep the fiddle here. At least it's one less thing to think about."

Nora put her drink down. "Whoever cut up that doll is really sick."

"I know," Regan replied quietly.

"Is there anything we can do?" Nora asked.

Regan looked at her mother's worried face. "Take care of the fiddle. That's it," she said. "Brigid wants to keep a low profile the next couple of days." She placed her soda glass on a poolside table. "I'd better be on my way."

Nora and Luke walked her to the car.

"Nice wheels," Luke said. "Where did you dig up this wreck?"

"It's Chappy's," Regan answered. "I didn't dare ask if I could borrow the Rolls."

Luke winked at her. "Who wants to drive a dented Rolls anyway?"

Regan smiled. "Not me."

As Nora kissed Regan good-bye, she urged her, "Regan, please be careful. I'm worried about you and Brigid."

"It's all right, Mom," Regan responded, trying to assure her. "We'll be fine."

As Regan motored down the dirt road, she tried to assure herself of the same thing. We'll be fine, she thought. We'll be just fine.

Won't we?

35

At the roadside vegetable stand on Route 27A, not far from Chappy's house, Regan took a basket and began to load it with several cartons of strawberries that were nestled among the raspberries, peaches, plums, blueberries, and watermelons. The brightly colored display of fruit was sweet smelling and appetizing. The scent of the strawberries was so pungent, Regan could almost taste them. So she did.

This place does makes you hungry, Regan thought, as her taste buds exulted with the flavor of the fresh fruit. And for the right kind of food. Heads of lettuce and plump tomatoes adorned the little stand. Peppers and carrots and celery were lined up and waiting to be bought.

"Is that all, miss?" asked a fiftyish man with leathery skin, a mustache, and tanned hands that looked as if they had personally picked all the fruits and vegetables, dumping the strawberries in a bag.

Regan nodded. As she pulled her wallet out of her purse, the sound of a horn honking blasted her ears. She turned to see Peace Man riding a bicycle on the other side of the road, swerving at the honk of the horn and losing his balance. He fell over into the bushes. What happened next Regan never would have imagined.

He jumped up and screamed at the passing car: "WATCH WHERE YOU'RE GOING, YOU BASTARD! I WASN'T IN YOUR WAY!"

Regan stood motionless. What happened to his seven days of silence? she wondered. I can see getting upset, but this is Peace Man!

"Miss?" The proprietor of the stand was anxious to get her attention back. And the money for the strawberries.

Regan blinked and turned back to him. "Sorry," she said. "That was just so surprising."

He shrugged and took her money. "I'd be mad, too. That car could have hurt him."

When Regan turned away once more, Peace Man was riding his bicycle down the road. He might have been provoked, she thought, but that's not a reaction I'd expect from a spiritual guru who claimed he was going to keep his mouth shut all week.

"Your change?"

Regan reached out her hand and then threw the money in her

purse. Climbing back into the station wagon, she decided that when she got back to the house, she would walk around the grounds. She wanted to stroll by his camper while he wasn't home.

Who is this guy? she wondered.

36

Back at the Compound, Regan found things calm and quiet. There was no one at the pool or out on the property. Everyone must be inside getting ready for dinner, she thought. I'll just take a quick look around while I have the chance.

She parked the car, locking her purse and the strawberries and the doll inside, and hurried across the driveway to the other side of the castle. The camper was parked next to the tour bus, but the tour bus was closer to the house. Regan walked between the two of them, glanced around, and then tried the handle of Peace Man's door.

It was locked.

Darn it, she thought.

Not wanting to be caught, she hurried down onto the beach. She kicked off her shoes and walked to the water's edge. It felt good to let the cool salt water wash between her toes. She turned and looked back up at Chappy Castle, looming large in the distance.

This place just doesn't feel safe, she thought. Not after everything that has happened. Anybody who wanted to get to Brigid could just walk up to the Compound's buildings from the beach.

But then what? Regan wondered. Where would they hide?

The deck where they'd had drinks and fixed their ice cream sundaes stared out at her. Regan found herself walking toward it, propelled by a desire to look underneath. It was supported by a row of thick logs, but there was enough distance between them that someone could slip through.

Regan crouched down and crawled under the deck.

This is roomy enough, she thought, as her eyes adjusted to the change in light. It was dark and cool and the sand felt damp. She looked around. Was that a bird chirping? she wondered. This was some listening post. You could hide under here and be sheltered and comfortable.

She gazed down at the sand. What in the world? she thought as she squinted her eyes. The damp sand held an indentation of a body, like the impression left by a head on a pillow.

Someone must have been here, she thought. But when? And who? The Phantom of the Chappy Compound?

She moved closer to the disturbed sand, started to examine it, and then something else caught her eye. Right past it was a little pile of

. . . what was it? Regan reached over and scooped the pieces up in her hand. She held them up to the light and recognized little bits of broken . . . eggshells.

How did *these* get here? she wondered. There were no eggs at the party the other night. Who would be peeling an egg under the deck?

Regan frowned. We were just talking about eggs today at the diner, she remembered . . . cholesterol specials . . . that strange guy who liked country music and was crazy for eggs. Suddenly Regan got a horrible feeling in the pit of her stomach.

Could he be . . . ?

Oh God, Regan thought as the pit in her stomach deepened. Was Brigid alone right now?

I have to get to her! she thought wildly.

Scurrying out from under the deck, Regan raced across the sand, past the pool area, and over to the guest house. Frantically she pushed open the door. The room was eerily empty. Where was everyone?

"BRIGID," she cried. "BRIGID!" Taking the steps two at a time, she ran to the second floor.

Brigid's door was closed. She knocked on it sharply. When Regan didn't get an immediate answer, she flung it open. Brigid was lying motionless on the bed, her back to the door.

"BRIGID!" Regan screamed.

Slowly Brigid rolled over, her eyes groggy from sleep. "Regan, what's wrong?"

With an overwhelming sense of relief, Regan leaned her head against the door frame. "You're all right, then?"

"Yes. I fell asleep. I didn't realize how tired I was."

Regan walked over to the foot of the bed and stood there panting. "What is it, Regan?"

Regan held out her hand. "These eggshells were under the deck at Chappy's house. It made me think of that weird guy in the diner. I'm sorry, I just thought . . ." Regan swallowed and struggled to catch her breath.

Brigid smiled. "Regan, I'm okay. I think we both have a right to be jumpy today."

Regan nodded. "I got this overwhelming sense that you were in danger again."

"I'm really fine."

"Where's everyone else?" Regan asked.

"Taking naps," Brigid said.

Brigid sat up and looked at the clock. "Oh, it's getting late. We'd better get ready for Kit's dinner, or we'll really be in danger!"

Regan laughed and shook her head as she slowly walked out of the room. "With Kit cooking, we're in danger either way."

Down the hall, crouched in the back of the dark closet, he was breathing heavily and sweating. He had come so close to being alone with Brigid! He had watched the house and seen Brigid on the beach this afternoon. Then he had watched her friend leave in the station wagon. And the others had come out at different times to walk out on the beach.

He'd slipped into the guest house to talk to Brigid because he had to. He couldn't control it anymore. He had to take the risk.

Then Brigid's friend had come running in and ruined it for him! He'd run to hide in the closet and heard her friend say he was weird! He'd like to get ahold of her and tell her a thing or two.

What do I do now? he wondered. In the darkness he smiled. Right now I'll just enjoy listening to Brigid, knowing she's right outside this door.

37

"I'll come down right away, love," Malachy said. He hung up the old-fashioned phone on the wall in his kitchen area and sat at the table. Suddenly his cottage did not feel as comforting as it usually did. Not with the news he'd just heard from Eileen O'Neill. The news that Brigid had had a close call today.

He looked down at the food on his plate, his hunger gone. The potatoes and vegetables that just a few moments ago had smelled so good didn't interest him anymore.

Maybe I shouldn't have given her the fiddle after all, he thought. She won the contest with it but now there's trouble. Nothing but trouble.

Why did that jerk Finbar have to make such a big deal out of it?

Malachy's eyes teared up. I had such a good time with that fiddle. It brought such happiness into my life. I wanted the same for Brigid.

He remembered the days when she was a teenager and would come up to the cottage to play.

"Let's practice," she'd say. "If we're going to perform together at all the parties around town, we have to be ready."

Oh, Brigid, he thought. I'm worried about you and I want to hear you play again.

Malachy stood up. He grabbed his jacket off the wall and headed out the door and down into the village to Brigid's aunt's house, where her mother, Eileen, stayed in the summer.

Life's too short, he thought. I'm going to ask them what they think about me flying over there and surprising her at her concert in the Hamptons.

Suddenly he found himself whistling as he rode his bicycle through the darkness.

38

I'm ready," Brigid announced as she came out of her room and across the hall into Regan's. "A nap, a shower, and a change of clothes can do wonders for the spirit."

"Oh, I know," Regan said. She had showered as well, putting on a pair of white jeans and a short-sleeved, black cotton sweater. Brigid had a pair of blue jeans with a rust-colored belt and a white blouse tucked in. Her red hair spilled over her shoulders.

Brigid sat down on the bed while Regan did a final check of herself in the mirror. She touched up her lipstick and ran a comb through her dark hair one last time.

"Ready," Regan said. "Are the others coming?"

Brigid shook her head as they walked out of the room and down the steps. "Hank and Teddy and Pammy came up from the beach when you were in the shower. Kieran had been asleep in his room. Anyway, Hank and Teddy went into town. They're meeting up with some old friends of Hank's. Kieran and Pammy went out to dinner and a movie." Brigid paused. "I think she let him know in no uncertain terms that she wanted some quality time alone with him."

"Ain't love grand?" Regan joked. They walked out the door and Regan locked it behind them. The early evening was upon them. The sky was streaked with purple and red, the water looked calm, and a soft breeze was blowing. Somebody must be playing taps somewhere, Regan thought. "How long have Pammy and Kieran been dating anyway?" she asked Brigid as they ambled over to Kit's cottage.

"About a year and a half."

"That long?" Regan said.

"Yes. Kieran just joined our band about a year ago and he was with her then."

"Oh. Where did they meet?"

"She's a nurse. Kieran was in a car accident near Nashville. He was banged up and hurt his hand pretty badly. She came upon the scene right after it happened and pulled over. She took care of him on the spot. Then she never stopped taking care of him."

"Really?" Regan said.

"Yes. Apparently he was pretty depressed. He didn't think he'd be able to play guitar again. She forced him to do occupational and physical therapy—she still makes him squeeze a rubber ball she always has with her. She encouraged him all the way. He credits her with bringing him back."

"She does seem like a take-charge kind of person."

"She is. She's even the one who found out we were looking for someone for the band. She scheduled his audition!"

"So they're pretty entrenched," Regan observed. "You know, I've saved a couple of guys' lives along the way but it never led to any romance."

"Maybe next time," Brigid said with a grin.

Regan laughed. "None of them looked like Kieran, I can tell you that."

They walked up the steps of the cottage, onto the wraparound porch, and opened the screen door.

"Hello!" Regan called.

"Come on in!" Kit yelled. She appeared from the kitchen wearing an apron over her jeans. "Welcome to Chappy's Outhouse."

"Oh, Kit," Brigid replied, laughing. "This place doesn't look bad."

"Not at all," Kit said. "The nice thing about it is it makes me appreciate my apartment when I get home. Now, how about a glass of wine?"

"After the day we've had, I think we both can use one. Right, Regan?"

"You said it."

They followed Kit into the kitchen. The aroma of marinara sauce and garlic filled the air. The stove looked as if it had served up a few meals during the War of 1812. The sink was huge and deep, with a divider running down the middle. "I think this sink used to be the bathtub," Kit said. "Red wine?"

They both nodded.

Kit filled the glasses, handed them over, and clinked hers against Brigid's and Regan's. "Cheers," she declared.

They all took a sip. "Where are the others?" Regan asked.

"Angela is getting ready. Garrett should be back any minute. I'm afraid we have a small group tonight. By Thursday this place will be crowded again, but . . ."

"That sounds fine," Brigid said. "It'll be nice to just hang out."

"Let's go out on the porch," Kit suggested. "We can watch the sunset."

"I *love* this," Brigid affirmed as they sat on the steps. "I'd like to make a toast to my two new friends."

"Hear! Hear!" Regan said, and they all clinked glasses again. "May we share many more adventures together, just none as exciting as this afternoon's."

"I'll drink to that," Brigid laughingly agreed.

"I'd like to make a toast, too," Kit said. "To the Melting Pot Festival. That's something we *want* to be exciting."

"It had better be," Brigid said, rolling her eyes. "Or else I'm in big trouble."

Big trouble is what I'm afraid of, Regan thought.

39

We've got to hurry!" Chappy cried. "We've got to get in there while it's still light out. It's too dangerous to use a flashlight."

Duke looked puzzled. "But we have the headlights on our helmets."

"What I mean is," Chappy growled, "if the house is dark and someone *outside* sees these flashes of light *inside,* they'll know something is up."

"Ahhhhh," Duke said, nodding his head in understanding.

"Ahhhhh, yourself."

They had rendezvoused in Chappy's study moments earlier after Duke had spied Regan and Brigid heading over to Kit's house. Chappy was sitting at his desk with a clipboard in front of him. The mission had to be completed soon, not only because of the impending darkness but also because he and Bettina were going to a dinner party at the home of one of the women who came to Peace Man's sessions. Chappy was dreading it. All he could think about was the original CT fiddle. If they pulled this off tonight, how could he go out and leave that fiddle at home while his fingers would be itching to play it without stopping?

Chappy picked up the Montblanc pen with his name engraved on it. On a sheet of paper before him he had a list of the names of everyone staying in the guest house.

"Brigid and the snoop Regan."

"Check," Duke said. "They've exited the premises."

"Kieran and his gal pal, Pammy."

"Check. They drove off in the station wagon to watch the sunset and then were heading out to dinner."

"Hank and Teddy."

"Check. I gave them a lift into town. They were meeting friends for a night of partying. They invited me to join them, but I said no."

Chappy looked up. "Well, bully for you."

"I also got invited to Angela's dinner party, but I told her I couldn't make it because I had to work."

"Well, aren't you the social butterfly?" Chappy asked with a little bit of envy. He put down his pen, first admiring the sight of his name in gold lettering, then dropped the clipboard into his desk drawer. "Our guests are all accounted for, and Bettina is upstairs with her masseuse." He checked his watch and then looked at Duke. "Are you ready to go into battle?"

"Aye aye, sir."

Chappy spun around and rapped the bookshelf. Within minutes they were downstairs, passing through Grandpa's speakeasy with nary a glance, just long enough for Duke to pick up the fiddle that was hot off Ernie's workbench.

Like two industrious miners, they traveled through the underground tunnel.

"It really gets damp down here," Duke commented.

"Shut up."

When they stepped into the basement of the guest house, Chappy nervously ran his fingers through his hair. "Not too much longer," he muttered.

"Not too much longer till we get the fiddle that will bring us good luck," Duke agreed, starting to get excited. "Maybe I'll finally be able to get an agent." His voice resounded in the empty chilly basement. "Maybe I won't have to wait until next summer to get a part in a play."

"sssssHHHHHHHH!" Chappy held a finger up to his lips. "We have to be careful."

With painstaking care, they opened the door at the top of the steps. As they expected, the coast was clear.

Upstairs in the closet, he was starting to feel restless. He had waited long enough. He was sure they were gone.

It had been so good to hear Brigid moving around, to hear her voice when she talked to that pain-in-the-neck friend of hers. Brigid sounded so nice. He could even smell the perfume that she sprayed on herself. It smelled so good.

I can't stay here. I'm hungry and I have to go to the bathroom. I'll have to try and see her another time, when she is alone.

Taking care to avoid bumping his head on the slanted ceiling, he untangled his feet and pulled himself up.

Chappy and Duke silently raced across the den floor. Through the open windows the waves could be heard breaking on the beach. Seagulls screeched overhead, oblivious to the intruders in the house below them.

They reached the staircase. Chappy almost let out a nervous giggle. Like a couple of cats, they crept up the stairs one by one, a big grin on Chappy's face.

They were almost at the top when they heard the creak of a door opening down the hall.

Adrenaline pumped through Chappy's body. He froze in place, terrified. Could it be the wind? he thought desperately.

Duke was hanging behind him, inches away.

Chappy waited.

Within seconds the door shut. Chappy started to feel relieved. It must be the wind! But then he heard the terrifying sound of a throat being cleared and footsteps in the hallway!

Chappy's body felt various biological urges. Valiantly he fought back the bile in his throat, turned around, and pushed at Duke's bulk. A tiny cry escaped from his lips. Sounding like a sick mouse, he squeaked, "Move!"

In record time they were back in the basement, running through the tunnel, pausing only a split second to tenderly place the fiddle on a chair in the men's lounge. They didn't stop again until they were in the sanctuary of Chappy's study, the bookshelf safely in place.

Panting, Chappy yanked his clipboard out of his desk drawer. "who was that?" he demanded of Duke. "I THOUGHT YOU SAID EVERYBODY WAS OUT!"

Duke, red-faced and sweating, collapsed into his chair. "I don't know, man. I swear, I saw them all leave."

Chappy put his head down on his desk and moaned. "I WANT MY FIDDLE!"

What was that? He stopped in place, ready to run back into the closet. He waited a few moments. Finally he relaxed. It must be nothing, he thought.

I'd better get out of here.

But first . . .

He opened the bedroom door that he was sure was Brigid's.

Oh! It had to be! A guitar was propped up in the corner. He went over to the dresser, where a picture of Brigid and a blond-haired woman with their arms around each other smiled out at him. I want to put my arms around you, Brigid, he thought.

He looked at her creams and comb and brush and perfume. He even sprayed a little of it on himself. On the bed was a little teddy bear. He grabbed it and sat down in the rocking chair by the win-

dow. *Squeezing the teddy bear as hard as he could, he rocked for a few minutes and looked out at the water.*

I love you, Brigid.

He wanted to lie on her bed, but he was afraid. I won't want to leave.

He put the teddy bear back.

I'll be back, he thought.

He went out into the hallway and found the bathroom.

After he used the facilities, he hurried down the steps, out the door, and raced along the beach, away from the Compound.

Time for a western omelette, he thought hungrily.

40

So how many does this house sleep?" Regan asked as Kit carried a steaming plate of pasta to the table.

"Eight upstairs," Kit said. "That's how many of us are scheduled each weekend. Down here we have the den, which closes off. There's a couch in there that's a Bernadette Castro special, so we can pull it out if we have extra bodies."

Garrett came in and sat across the table from Regan. His hair was gelled back and he smelled of cologne. With practiced affectation, he reached around and deposited his cellular phone on the sideboard. "I love staying in the den. It's so quiet and private," he said as he pulled his napkin off the table and positioned it on his lap. "Smells good."

"Expecting a phone call?" Regan asked.

"My office," he harrumphed. "The markets overseas are open now. . . ."

"Do we have everything?" Angela asked from the doorway, with wineglass in hand and the weary look of a chief cook who has tried to coordinate the presentation of all the food at the same time and is frankly sick of the effort.

"Angela, this looks great," Brigid said. "Sit down."

"Marinara sauce is my specialty," Angela replied with a smile, slightly placated. She had on a short skirt and a tank top that was stretched to its limit. Her blond hair was once again pulled up, and her tan looked as if it had deepened in the last couple of days.

Regan thought she looked like the Coppertone kid all grown up. The one who years ago had stared out from billboards, involuntarily mooning the country thanks to her frisky dog, who delighted in tugging on the back of her bathing suit.

Angela sank into the seat at the head of the table. "Kit helped some," she allowed.

"Kit loves to cook." Regan chuckled as she bit into a forkful of the green salad.

"Reilly the gourmet," Kit said sardonically. "What's your specialty? Washed chicken?"

"With a pat of butter and salt and pepper on each and every piece," Regan replied.

For a few moments, no one talked; they all ate hungrily. The pasta was delicious, the bread hot and garlicky, and the Chianti smooth. The candles on the table flickered, their soft light reflecting off the walls that boasted more old-fashioned wallpaper.

Regan was glad to see Brigid looking so relaxed. It had been quite a day for her.

As they were finishing, Brigid wiped her mouth with her napkin. "So, tell me how these group houses work," she said. "How do you find each other?"

Angela rolled her eyes. "It can be a big headache, believe me. I've been in charge for a while but Garrett took over this year. He worked it all out with Bettina. We've had pretty much the same group for three or four years now. Of course Kit is new."

"How did you get involved?" Brigid asked Kit, who was sitting back in her chair now.

Kit toyed with her wineglass. "A friend of mine from New York City was in the house. She had already paid for her share for this summer. But on her birthday in May her boyfriend popped the question. . . ."

Angela groaned and put her hand to her forehead. "They'd met only six weeks before. Can you believe it? That never happens to me."

Regan winked at Kit. How many times do you want to get engaged, Angela? she thought.

"So," Kit continued, "this friend, Sue, and her fiancé, Bruce, were making different plans for the summer. She asked if I'd like to buy her share. Because I live in Hartford, it's a bit of a schlepp, but I thought I'd give it a try. I met everyone when Angela had a party in her apartment before Memorial Day weekend."

Garrett cleared his throat. "You see, Brigid, everyone wants to get out of the City in the summer. Groups of friends get together to rent houses out here for the season. Around February you have to start coming out and looking at houses and see which ones will even rent to groups. Once you find a place, you divide it up into shares. Some people want to come every weekend, so they buy full shares. Others every other weekend, so they buy half shares, et cetera." He gestured with his hands. "On weekends like the Fourth of July, everyone wants to be here, so we're usually bursting at the seams. Like this weekend— it's not only the Fourth of July but everyone wants to come to your concert."

Brigid grinned. "Well, how did you find this house?" she asked.

"Ah!" Garrett pointed his finger. "Bettina found us because we're all country music fans."

Brigid's smile widened. "Glad to hear it."

"This past winter we got together at a country music bar in New

York to listen to a couple of new singers. Chappy and Bettina were at the next table. Bettina started talking to us—how did we know each other and so forth. She ended up suggesting that we rent her servants' quarters for the summer."

So that's how it happened, Regan thought.

"I hate the whole process of looking for a house. I drove out with Bettina the very next day to look at it."

Regan remembered what Ned had said: Chappy hadn't known until after the fact that she was renting it out. She cleared her throat. "Chappy didn't ride out with you to show it off himself?" she asked.

"No," Garrett said. "Apparently he was taking a workshop on how to audition for soap operas." He shrugged. "When I saw it, I thought it was a great deal. Right by the water . . ."

"The house could stand a few modern appliances," Angela commented.

"Well, the price was right. So I took it on the spot."

"Oh, I like it," Angela said, grunting. "But next year—that is, if I haven't gotten married by then—we're going to have to go looking again because they're tearing this place down to build a theatre."

"So next year at this very moment, someone might be in this exact spot emoting," Kit said.

"Yeah," Angela said as she picked at a crumb of bread on her plate. "Duke is memorizing his lines for *Romeo and Juliet*. He wants Chappy to put that on next year and let him play Romeo. I'm going to hear his lines for him."

That I'd pay anything to see, Regan thought.

Someone rapped at the screen door. Angela looked in that direction. "Who could that be?" She got up and adjusted the straps of her top, smoothed her hair, and walked to the door. She flicked on the porch light.

"Duke!" she cried. "I thought you had to work!"

It's Romeo, Regan thought. Wherefore art thou been?

Duke stepped in, dressed neatly in a pair of jeans and a black Lacoste shirt. "Chappy and Bettina went to a dinner party. I thought I might stop by and say hello."

"Come on in, Duke," Kit called. "You're just in time for dessert."

Over Kit's strawberry shortcake, which consisted of store-bought individual shortcake patties generously laden with whipped cream from a can and sliced strawberries, they talked about Brigid's upcoming concert and tour.

Duke scarfed down the contents of his plate. "So where are the others tonight?" he asked Brigid.

"They're all out," she said. "Didn't you drive Hank and Teddy into town?"

"Yeah, I did." Duke put down his fork. "So Pammy and Kieran went out, too, huh?" he continued.

"Yes," Brigid answered.

"Do you have anybody else coming to visit this week?" he asked awkwardly.

Brigid frowned, puzzled by the question. "No. Do you, Regan?" she inquired.

"Not me," Regan answered. "We're Chappy's guests, so I wasn't going to go inviting more people." Why is he so interested? she wondered.

"Duke, would you like some more dessert?" Angela asked. Her whole demeanor had changed with Duke in the room. There was a lot of lifting up of her arms to play with her hair—and, not so coincidentally, to show off her assets. But at the moment her Romeo doesn't seem to notice, Regan Thought. *Why is he here?*

"No, thanks," he said.

A few minutes later they cleared the plates and took their glasses outside to sit on the porch. The night air was cool and the crickets were chirping.

Angela seated herself in the glider next to Duke. By now she was smiling and giggling and refilling everyone's glass.

Nothing like getting a boost from the presence of someone you've got the hots for, Regan thought. But Duke seems so distracted. Oh well, maybe that's the way he always is.

By the time they finished the wine and Brigid and Regan got up to leave, it was nearly eleven o'clock. Much to Angela's disappointment, Duke insisted on walking them over to the guest house.

"You can't be too careful," he said.

"Well, let me know when you want me to hear your lines," Angela called as they stepped off the porch.

"Okay, Angela," he said. "Maybe sometime in the next couple of days."

Regan and Brigid and Duke wandered over to the guest house. It was completely dark.

"I guess no one is back yet," Duke said.

"Guess not," Regan answered.

Regan and Brigid said their good nights to him and, agreeing they were both tired from the long day, went directly upstairs, turning on lights along the way.

Brigid went into her room and collapsed on her bed. "Oh!" she called out to Regan. "I'm glad we don't have to get up so early tomorrow morning."

"Me too," Regan said as her fingers fumbled to turn on the bathroom light. She shut the door and stopped dead in her tracks.

The toilet seat was up.

The guys left before us, she thought nervously. And I was the last one to use the bathroom before we walked out the door to go to dinner. What's going on?

Duke had been asking all those questions about who was home tonight. Had he slipped in here? But why?

A sense of dread swept through Regan. Don't jump to any conclusions, she told herself. Maybe one of the guys stopped back at the house for some reason.

But why would they use *this* bathroom?

Regan leaned against the pedestal sink and slapped the seat down into a female-ready position. It landed with a bang.

After Chappy builds the theatre, he can turn the guest quarters into a haunted house, she thought. Complete with a handle-free door downstairs.

Regan stared at the commode. There might be a good explanation for this, she thought. But what can I do? I can't go asking the guys tomorrow if they left the toilet seat up. I won't sound like an investigator, I'll come off like a nag.

And if the only lead I have to go on is a guy who leaves the toilet seat up, most of the male population would end up on the list of suspects.

She sighed. I'd better go downstairs and make double-sure the doors are locked. She knew the others had keys.

Regan hurried down the steps and checked the back door that faced the beach. She and Brigid had come in this way, and, as she had expected, it was securely locked. She went around the ground floor making sure that all the windows were closed and locked as well. She pulled on the front door, which no one really used, to open it. She wanted to slam it shut and make sure the lock was in place. The door was the kind that stuck. It required a couple of pulls for Regan to get it open. When she did, the sight of a smashed cassette propped up against the screen door made her gasp. She leaned down to pick it up.

A cassette of Brigid's hit single, all crushed and bent, looking as if someone had pounded it with a hammer. Someone in a rage, Regan thought. She shut the door, locked it, and hurried upstairs with the cassette. Brigid is not going to see this, she thought. I'm not going to let whoever is doing this ruin everything for Brigid.

She sat on her bed and stared at the cassette. A smiling Brigid staring out through the crushed, fragmented plastic holder. It eerily reminded Regan of the nearly beheaded doll.

Oh, Brigid, she thought, who wants to hurt you?

41

Regan slept fitfully. All night she kept awakening, staring at the clock, thinking about everything that had happened. Finally, before dawn, she fell into a deep sleep.

When her eyes started to flutter, she looked at the clock for what felt like the twentieth time since she'd gone to bed. It was 8:37 A.M.

The room feels too dark for 8:37, Regan thought. Even with a shade. And it's chilly. She threw back the covers and hoisted her body out of bed. Walking over to the window, she yanked on the shade. Obediently it flew all the way up to the roller, disappearing out of sight except for its cord, which slapped the ceiling several times before calming down.

Outside the day was gray and overcast. It was still dry but it didn't look as though it intended to remain that way for long. The smell of rain was in the air.

Oh great, Regan thought. There's nothing like a rainy day at the beach to drive everyone bonkers.

Yawning, she threw on a pair of jeans and a sweatshirt and went out into the hallway. Brigid's door was closed.

Regan hurried into the bathroom. The tile floor felt cold and damp against her bare feet. Rainy days at the beach, she mused as she applied toothpaste to her curved toothbrush, whose makers promised it removed more plaque than you could ever imagine in your wildest dreams. Rainy days can seem endless, making you feel like a kid again, all cooped up and restless. Severe cabin fever can set in before the ground is completely wet.

Regan turned on the tap and ran water over her brush. You don't have your bills with you to pay, you don't have your closets to clean out, you don't have your laundry to do. You just don't have your stuff around to keep you busy, she thought.

Regan stared in the mirror and began to brush.

You have too much time to think and worry.

Down in the kitchen she found Brigid and Pammy sitting at the table drinking coffee. Brigid was in her robe but Pammy was dressed. Bagels and donuts were set out on plates and several newspapers were stacked up on the table.

"Good morning," Regan said.

Brigid smiled. " 'Morning, Regan."

"Regan, I made a pot of coffee," Pammy announced cheerfully. She gestured to the table. "And there are donuts and bagels here. Help yourself."

"Thanks," Regan said. She reached for a mug and poured herself a cup. "Did you go to the store already?"

"Yes. I was up early. The guys aren't going golfing until this afternoon, so I thought I'd pick up some breakfast and the newspapers."

Little Suzy Homemaker, Regan thought. There's always one in every crowd. She sat down at the table. I shouldn't be like that, she thought. Especially because those donuts do look good. She chose a glazed one and took a bite.

Pammy put down her cup and hesitated. She crinkled up her little nose and pushed back her long, golden brown hair.

"Brigid had a rough night," Pammy finally said.

So did I, Regan thought. She turned to Brigid. "What happened?"

Brigid looked up from the newspaper and waved her hand as if to dismiss the whole issue. "I had a few bad dreams. No big deal."

"About what happened yesterday?"

"Yes," Brigid replied. "Someone was chasing me with a gun."

Pammy got up from her chair and walked behind Brigid. She put her arms on Brigid's shoulders and began to massage them. "Ever since his accident, Kieran sometimes gets a stiff neck. He loves it when I do this to him." She started working her way up Brigid's neck to her scalp. "How does it feel, Brigid?"

"Good," Brigid said quickly.

Regan thought she seemed uncomfortable but was too polite to say anything.

"You're very tense," Pammy declared. "But it's a natural reaction," she said with an air of authority. "Post-traumatic stress syndrome can manifest itself in many ways. I've seen it with patients." She paused. "I've seen it with myself."

Regan looked at her. "You have? What happened?"

Pammy's voice dropped to a near whisper. "When I was a kid my cousin drowned. Right in front of me. She was my best friend."

"Pammy, I'm so sorry," Brigid replied.

"It's okay," Pammy said. "After that, I learned CPR. I said if that ever happens again and I can get to whoever is in trouble, I want to know what I'm doing. That's why I jumped in the pool so fast the other night to help Louisa. I couldn't help my cousin, so I feel as if I'm making it up to her by helping other people. I guess it's one of the reasons I became a nurse. I like to help people. Nothing gave me greater satisfaction than nursing Kieran back to health . . ."

I'll bet, Regan thought.

". . . and encouraging him to play again."

"I'm so sorry about your cousin," Brigid murmured.

Pammy nodded. "I took it real hard. I kept dreaming about her calling out to me. That was over ten years ago and I still dream about it sometimes."

They all remained silent for a moment.

What a revelation, Regan thought. Especially at this hour of the morning.

". . . So I know how upsetting it can be to have those kinds of dreams," Pammy continued. "When I came down this morning, Regan, I could tell Brigid was a little out of sorts."

"Well, thank God it turned out all right for me yesterday. Thanks to Regan. Hey, I'll write a song about it. In the meantime . . ." Brigid sat up straight as Pammy stopped the massage and sat down at the table. "Thanks, Pammy," Brigid said, handing Regan a couple of the newspapers. "Everyone can read all about the cause of my nightmares."

Regan looked at the snippet in USA Today. It talked about Brigid O'Neill and her cursed fiddle, which a couple of teenagers had tried to steal only to be thwarted by the quick action of her bodyguard. The Hamptons News had a bigger piece that asked again if the fiddle was really cursed.

"I'm surprised the reporters didn't call about this yesterday," Regan said.

Brigid slathered a hunk of cream cheese on a sesame bagel. "They might have tried. We were out at the beach, and then I was on the phone with my mother and Roy yesterday afternoon. There's no call-waiting here, so they would have gotten a busy signal. Last night everyone was out. Like I said yesterday, it was a good idea to call my mother to let her know what happened."

With that pronouncement, the phone rang.

Brigid started to get up.

"You want me to get it?" Regan asked.

"Nah," Brigid responded. "I may as well bite the bullet." She started to laugh. "Bad pun, I guess."

Out in the pantry she picked up the cordless.

Regan looked out at the ocean. Whitecaps were doing their dance on the churning surf as the waves angrily thrashed the shoreline. "I don't know whether the guys will be doing any golfing this afternoon," she said to Pammy.

"Oh, I know," Pammy answered as she turned to look out at the water, "they'll be disappointed."

"Do you golf, too?"

Pammy laughed and rolled her eyes. "Not at all."

"You don't?" Regan continued. "What do you do? Ride along with them in a cart?"

"Sometimes," Pammy admitted. "Or sometimes I'll sit in the clubhouse and read."

Talk about keeping a watchful eye, Regan thought. "Are you going on the tour with them?" she asked.

Pammy's expression became dejected. "I can't. I have to get back to work. When we leave here Friday night, they'll drop me at a hotel near Kennedy Airport and I'll fly home in the morning."

"Oh," Regan said. "Where do you work?"

"I'm a private nurse in Nashville."

"Will you meet up with them at all during the tour?"

"I'm planning on it."

Regan turned to see Brigid walking over to them, the cordless up against her ear. She was laughing. "Hold on a second, Roy. Regan, Pammy, guess what? My album's gotten some great reviews!" Brigid turned back to the phone. "What's that, Roy?" She looked at Regan. "They said my voice is 'rich and pure and' . . . what? . . . 'and has a wide range. Brigid's songs will make you laugh and cry. She's someone to watch.' " Brigid stomped her foot. "All right!"

Regan raised her hands over her head and clapped them. "Brigid, that's great."

"Wonderful," Pammy murmured.

"Who else has called?" Brigid asked into the phone. She was laughing and giddy, the demons of the night seemingly banished from her thoughts. "Hey guys, Garth and Clint and Dolly have already called Roy this morning to make sure I'm okay. They saw the papers. Hey Roy, anybody else? No!" Brigid guffawed. "Well, it's still early. Hey, maybe that fiddle is bringing me good luck after all!"

Regan sat back in her chair. It was great to see Brigid looking so elated. Elated because she's getting great reviews for the album somebody took the trouble to smash. Inwardly, Regan shuddered.

Pammy was across the table, bent over the newspaper.

"Yes!" Brigid yelped as she turned off the cordless phone and plopped it on the table. "Things are looking good!"

"That is fantastic!" Regan said.

Pammy looked up. "Congratulations, Brigid."

"Thank you both!" Brigid sank into her chair. "Suddenly the day doesn't look so gloomy. I just wish that festival wasn't three whole days away! I want to get out there and make some music!"

"Once you start on Friday, you'll be doing it practically every night all summer!" Regan said.

"I can't wait!"

Pammy got up with her cup of coffee. "I'm going to see if Kieran is awake yet. I'm sure he'll want to hear the good news."

Brigid's smile faded ever so slightly. "Please tell him."

"Oh, I will. Now let's hope nothing happens to ruin this fun for you, Brigid. We wouldn't want you to have another day like yesterday that you dream about tonight."

"Oh, I bet my dreams tonight will be good ones," Brigid assured her with a smile. "Because having my first album well received is a dream come true. A dream I've had all my life."

Pammy smiled at her and nodded as she walked out of the room.

Regan turned to Brigid. "We're in for some lousy weather. How about a walk on the beach before it starts?"

"I'll be walking on air," Brigid said. She jumped up. "Let's go!"

42

Ned and Claudia were at their office bright and early on Tuesday morning. Ned had insisted on it. Thanks to his appearance on the radio, their office had been deluged with calls for consultations about feng shui, and Ned was practically out of his mind with joy. Claudia had to drag him out of there on Monday night to go home.

"I don't want to miss a call," he'd complained.

"That's why we have voice mail," Claudia had said. She'd been firm with him. Loving but firm. "You need your rest."

From one day to the next, Ned's self-esteem had quadrupled.

Claudia was now at the table in her office poring over plans for a house that the owner kept changing his mind about. Ned had tried to tell him he should by no means have a bathroom by the front door. It was bad luck. But the owner had wanted one for guests, and that was that. After catching the show on the radio the home owner had made an emergency call to Claudia. Scrap the bathroom by the front door, find a new place for it.

How about in the backyard? Claudia had thought. She'd spent hours on the plans, and now he was rushing her to change everything before the builders started their work. But she was happy that he was finally listening to her beloved.

Ned poked his head in the door. He was wearing a blazer, shirt and tie, and a pair of blue jeans. He'd decided that this would give him the air of being conservative yet a little hip. The shoes were a bit off, but it was a vast improvement.

"I'm going to Darla Wells's house, honey," he called.

Claudia looked up. Today her headband color combo matched a blue-and-green cardigan.

"Good luck!" She flashed him the victory signal.

Ned gave her a thumbs-up and turned on his heel. He was off to give feng shui advice to someone who could send a lot of business his way in the Hamptons. She had called yesterday afternoon and wanted him to come over first thing this morning. If she talks it up to her friends, who knows what could happen?

All of this because of the dinner party at Chappy Tinka's house! What a night that turned out to be! Ned climbed into the Range Rover and steered into the traffic of Main Street in Southampton. Darla lived in East Hampton, which could take more than a half hour to get to. But he'd left plenty of time.

He glanced at the cloudy sky as he headed toward Route 27. We're in for some bad weather, he thought. At least it's good for the shopkeepers and theatre and restaurant owners. Everybody will be looking for something to do.

Humming to the music on the radio, he drove along, thinking about how busy he was, about how important this meeting could be for his future. Exactly fifty-seven minutes later, when he turned down Darla Wells's block, he groaned audibly.

A cul-de-sac! She lives on a cul-de-sac! That was very very bad for feng shui. He shook his head back and forth. I guess we'll just have to make do.

He inched his vehicle down the long white graveled driveway. He was happy to see that the property was level and no trees were blocking the front door. No bad luck to worry about there. And thank God she didn't have a number four in her address.

The house was impressive-looking. It was large and white and exuded the traditional Hamptons look. A wraparound porch and columns and a vast lush lawn with trees and flowers completed the picture of old money.

Ned walked up the porch steps, rang the bell, then stood there, nervously tapping his folder with his fingers.

He waited.

He looked at his watch. It read 9:30 A.M.; he was prompt, as always. He had even parked his car in town for a few minutes and grabbed a cup of coffee so he wouldn't be early, which was as bad as being late, if harmony and balance were your goals in life.

With a sinking feeling, he rang the bell again. He could feel his body starting to cave in.

Suddenly the door burst open. Darla Wells, wearing pink stretch pants and a black top, started to apologize. Ned hadn't met her but had seen her picture in the society pages of *Hamptons* magazine and *Dan's Papers*. Her highlighted hair was shoulder length. Her doelike brown eyes and olive skin made him think she looked exotic. A completely different type from his Claudia.

"I'm sorry," she said, running a hand laden with a big diamond ring through her hair. "I just got off the phone with my agent. We're deciding which songs I should sing on Friday night at the concert."

"Oh, how wonderful," Ned replied as he followed her inside and into the living room.

"Well, I don't know how wonderful," she said. "It's hard to choose. I've got so many good ones I want to sing and not enough time."

Ned's eyes were roaming the room wildly. Although it was furnished tastefully, it could use a lot of work.

"I heard about you when I was having my hair done yesterday," Darla commented. She indicated for him to sit down on the couch.

"Oh, I thought you heard the radio show," he said, easing himself into a pristine white couch that he was relieved to see was properly placed.

"I shut it off after Brigid O'Neill's interview." Darla sat down at the opposite end.

Terrific, Ned thought.

Darla continued, "Someone at the salon was talking about your interview and said it was very interesting."

"Good," Ned said. "Good."

"So what's Brigid O'Neill like?"

"Very nice. She likes feng shui."

"Feng what?"

"Feng shui."

"What's that?"

"That's what you called me here for, isn't it?" Ned laughed politely.

"Oh, of course! Of course! You rearrange furniture."

Ned clenched his jaw. "It's a little bit more involved than that. It's about living harmoniously using the energy of your surrounding environment to create wealth, happiness, and fame."

"That's right!" Darla crossed her leg and started swinging it. "I don't have to worry about wealth. It's the fame I'm interested in."

Ned scratched his chin and looked around. Before he could answer, Darla asked another question.

"Have you done this for Brigid O'Neill?"

Ned looked at her. "No. How could I? She lives in Nashville. But she told me yesterday she wants me to fly down there after her tour and take a look at her house."

"So she's gotten famous without feng shui."

"Yes. But she'll get more famous after she puts it into practice. guaranteed!" Ned said forcefully.

"She's staying over in Southampton," Darla observed.

"Yes," Ned said. "At the Chappy Compound."

"I hear you were there at that dinner party they wrote about in the paper yesterday."

"Yes. And they wrote about Brigid O'Neill again today. In the national newspapers, no less."

Darla's stomach turned. "Why?"

"A couple of kids came right up to the Compound yesterday, pretending to want to interview her for the school paper. She let them in and they tried to rob her of her fiddle. But she has a bodyguard who took care of things."

"She has a bodyguard?"

"Yes. Do you want to talk about feng shui?"

"Of course."

Ned stood up. "I'd like to walk with you through your house and show you little things you could do."

Darla nodded. "I'll follow you."

"First of all," Ned said, "you should have a crystal in the far left, which is the wealth-and-power corner of a room . . . put mirrors behind the kitchen stove to create more wealth . . . face your bed toward the door. If you were single, I'd tell you not to put it up against the wall because you might not open up to a relationship. . . ."

Darla tailed him, eagerly taking notes. Anything to make me famous, she thought.

An hour later, he drove home happy that she had signed up for an in-depth analysis of her Four Pillars of Destiny and seemed anxious to tell her friends about him.

He had agreed to come backstage with Claudia and say hello to Darla at the concert Friday night. I'll have to bring flowers, he thought. Butter up the client.

He couldn't wait to tell Claudia about the meeting. I know what else I want to do, he thought. This afternoon I'll drive over to the Chappy Compound and take a look at the guest house. A free feng shui consultation. I won't even tell Chappy. Let it be a surprise for him. After all, it's thanks to him that things have really started rolling along.

Ned smiled, pleased with himself. There was only one thing bothering him. Why did Darla Wells keep questioning him about Brigid O'Neill?

43

Regan and Brigid walked barefoot down the beach quite a way before turning around and heading back. The sky looked as if it could open up at any time, and they didn't want to be caught in a downpour. It felt good to be out in the air meandering along the cool sand.

Brigid picked up a couple of rocks and threw them in the churning water. "I'm so excited, Regan," she said. "Those reviews are so important. Roy says it means the difference in getting booked on important shows, too."

"You should let Austin know the good news," Regan said. "And you should let him know about yesterday's adventures before he reads about them in the paper. He was really worried about you."

"I know," Brigid said. "He's such a good cousin. We're more like brother and sister. I'll call him when we get back to the house."

They came upon Chappy Compound and the area where the tour bus and Peace Man's camper were parked.

"So that's where you'll be spending the summer?" Regan smiled as she pointed at the bus.

"Sleeping with feet facing front in case we stop short."

"Really?" Regan said. "I guess it makes sense."

All of a sudden the sound of Bettina's mutt barking her head off assaulted their ears. Tootsie came bounding around from the front of the house and started barking at Peace Man's RV.

Bettina's voice could be heard following behind. "No, Tootsie. No. Mama says no bark. No."

Apparently Tootsie didn't agree. She stood there between the tour bus and the RV barking her head off.

Bettina and Garrett appeared from around the front of the house. Regan waved at them as she and Brigid passed. "Hi!" she called.

"Oh yeah, hi!" Bettina said.

Is he selling her stocks or are they discussing the lease on the summer house? Regan wondered. Or is something else going on between them?

Peace Man came out of his trailer and gave the peace sign to Bettina and Garrett.

"Forgive us, Peace Man," Bettina said. "Tootsie is a little wound up today."

Peace Man nodded, locked the door of his camper, jumped on his bicycle, and drove off.

What a weirdo, Regan thought.

Back in the kitchen, Teddy, Hank, and Kieran were sitting at the table having breakfast and reading the papers. Pammy was busy refilling their coffee cups.

"Congratulations," Kieran said to Brigid. "Great reviews!"

"We're proud of you," Teddy added sweetly.

"That's right," Hank agreed.

"Proud of *us!*" Brigid corrected. "You guys are a part of it, too."

With that pronouncement, a clap of thunder boomed and rumbled across the sky.

"Drumroll, please," Brigid said as she looked up at the ceiling.

Another booming noise filled the room.

Everyone laughed as the rain started to thrash down.

Pammy handed Kieran the rubber ball he used for therapy. "Why don't you squeeze this while you read the papers, honey?" she suggested.

"Later," he said.

The rain bounced off the roof as thunder and lightning cracked the air. And they all spent most of the next forty-eight hours in the guest house as it rained and rained and rained.

Later that afternoon, after everyone had nibbled and read and watched TV, Brigid went upstairs and Kieran and Pammy and Hank and Teddy went into town to buy food for dinner. Regan was on the couch reading when there was a knock at the door. She looked up and saw Ned Alingham standing there holding an umbrella over his head.

She got up and let him in.

"Hello, Regan," he said.

"Ned, what's going on?"

"I don't want to disturb you. I thought I'd take a quick look at the living area here to see what I can do to make it better. I want to surprise Chappy. After all of you have gone, I'll take a look at the bedrooms and rearrange the whole house. For free, I might add."

Regan raised her eyebrows. "Great," she said, silently wondering how it was possible to meet so many strange people in such a short period of time.

Ned put down his umbrella and glanced around the room. "Aha!" he exclaimed. "Will you please tell me what that couch is doing in front of the window when it should be against the wall facing the window and that beautiful ocean?"

"I haven't a clue," Regan said.

"Care to help me move it?" he asked.

"Of course," Regan said.

The couch felt like a ton of bricks. Grunting, the two of them pushed it against the wall in front of the door with no handle.

"I've never seen a door with no knob like that," Ned declared. "I'll have to look up what that means in feng shui. Because it has no handle, I see no reason to not have the couch right in front of it."

Regan sat on the newly placed couch. "This is much better," she said. She also didn't mind having the door blocked. What could Chappy be hiding down in that basement? From the windows outside it looked dingy and empty. She wished they weren't too small to squeeze through.

"It opens up the room to peace and harmony," Ned announced proudly. "I promise you, you will feel the difference."

He looked around the rest of the downstairs. "Not too bad," he said. "I don't want to disturb your quarters at this time. As I said, I'll be back when you're gone. Don't mention anything to Chappy that I was here. I want to surprise him when the whole house is done."

"My lips are sealed," Regan assured him.

"See you at the concert."

"Right." Regan walked him to the door and watched as he stepped outside and opened his umbrella with a flourish. Energetically he bounced down the walkway to his car.

There goes someone who enjoys his work, Regan thought. She turned and looked at the newly placed couch. He's right, though. It does look a lot better. The question is, what will Chappy think?

44

*H*e looked out the window of his shack and sighed. Look at that rain! It was coming down in cats and dogs, like his mother used to say.

Now what? He couldn't exactly go walking on the beach near Brigid's house. Not in this weather. They'd lock him up for being a nut.

And I'm not a nut! he thought.

He turned on the television set. So many of his favorite game shows had been canceled over the years. Why did they have to take "Supermarket Sweep" off the air? And "Hollywood Squares"? And "I've Got a Secret"?

He laughed out loud. "I've Got a Secret." That was a good one. I've got a secret, too, he thought.

How about "The Newlywed Game"? He'd have loved being on that show with Brigid as his bride. He sat down on the bed, black depression suddenly overwhelming him.

I want to see her! But I can't until it stops raining! It had better stop soon or I'll go crazy, he thought.

Brigid is waiting for me. I just know she is.

Today is Tuesday, and she'll be leaving on Friday. I have to get to her before then, and this weather is not cooperating!

He pulled the covers over him, curled up in a ball, and started to cry.

45

Rain rain go away, come back on saturday!" Chappy wailed at the window of his study. "if you must come back at all!"

It was teatime. Duke sat in his chair in front of Chappy's desk, sipping from his mug and shaking his head. "It's wet out there," he said.

"Of course it's wet out there! It's been raining nonstop for a day and a half!" Chappy moaned. "How am I going to get my fiddle?"

"I don't know. They don't seem to want to leave the house. And there's no way of keeping track of everybody," Duke said. "When I called to see if they needed anything, Regan said they were all reading and watching TV and lounging and napping and playing board games."

Chappy's eyes bore into Duke's. "Board games?"

"Yeah. Parcheesi, Monopoly, Chutes and Ladders . . ."

"Where did they come from?"

"You had me buy them last year when your cousins visited and you didn't want to spend time with them."

Chappy slapped the desk. "That's right." He put his hands up to his head. "I've got a headache that's not going to go away until I get that fiddle."

Duke looked at him. "Would it make you feel better if we went over and eavesdropped?"

Chappy's face softened. "Maybe," he said in a way that meant "Yes, but force me."

Duke stood up. "Let's go."

Within minutes they were in the basement of the guest house. Music resounded from above them.

Duke cocked his ear. "It sounds like they're practicing."

"Ohhhhh," Chappy moaned.

They stood on the steps and listened as guitars played and Brigid sang.

Tears filled Chappy's eyes. I want to be able to sing like that, he thought. And have my theatre and act and perform.

The music stopped and several people applauded.

"Who's that?" Chappy whispered to Duke.

"I think Angela and Garrett and Kit are in there," Duke answered with a sigh.

A female voice asked, "Should we go out to dinner tonight?"

Chappy grabbed Duke's arm, waiting.

"Nah," the others chorused.

"Too crowded."

"Can't get a parking space."

"My hair will frizz."

"We'll get all wet."

"Let's order out and rent a couple of movies."

"Good idea!" they agreed.

Chappy shook his head woefully as each answer bore into his soul. Duke patted his back. Silently they went back through the tunnel and returned to Chappy's study.

"I don't get it, Duke," Chappy said painfully as he stifled a sob. "Why do things have to be so difficult?"

Duke cleared his throat and began to sing the title song from the Broadway play *Annie*. "The sun will come out, tomorrow, bet your bottom dollar that tomorrow, there'll be sunnnnnn."

Chappy looked at him with an expression of horror that Duke had never seen before. "GET OUT OF HERE!"

"Okay, man, sorry." Duke got up and hurried out the door. Shutting it behind him, he stood and waited to hear the thud of Chappy's airborne shoe making contact with the other side of the wood.

Chappy did not disappoint.

He'll get over it, Duke thought. But I do wish it would stop raining. He looked at his watch: 5:15 P.M. Time to get something to eat, he thought, and study my lines. With a spring in his step, he headed to the kitchen.

46

Arnold Baker sat at his desk listening to the rain pelt his windows. With each noisy raindrop he shuddered. The concert was two days away, and the weather showed no signs of clearing up. If the concert had to be canceled, it would cost the college a fortune. Too many tickets had been sold to hold it inside.

No rain date was possible.

The bands all had other commitments after Friday. Everyone except Darla Wells. He laughed miserably. She could do the concert herself on Saturday and sing her heart out, he thought. Every song she'd ever heard of in her life. She's probably out in East Hampton doing a rain dance right now, he thought.

Dot poked her head in the door. "I'm going home. Don't look so depressed. They said good weather is heading our way."

"Where is it now?" Arnold asked. "In the South Pacific?"

"No." Dot laughed. "It's coming from Pluto."

Arnold shook his head.

"Oh, before I forget," Dot said. "If you talk to Regan Reilly, tell her that my friend Cindy, the one who made the dolls, left a message on her daughter's answering machine. They're sitting out the storm in a boat dock somewhere." Dot waved. "Good niiiighhht."

Arnold managed a little wave. " 'Night." I won't have a *good* night until this bloody rain stops, he thought. And the field dries and is squishproof.

Is that too much to ask? he wondered. Is it?

Getting up from his desk, he turned out the lights and headed home.

Pulling out of the long driveway of Welth College, Arnold was dismayed to see that the field looked like it would be squishy for days to come.

47

Malachy was busy tidying up his cottage. If I'm going abroad, he thought, I'd better leave my place clean. If I die, I don't want them to think I was a slob.

Singing to himself, he sat and started going through a month-old pile of newspapers next to the fireplace. Brigid's going to be so excited, he thought. At least I hope she will be!

He had it all planned. He'd fly to Kennedy Airport on Thursday, stay overnight, and then take a bus to the Hamptons on Friday. He'd surprise Brigid at the concert. It was going to be so grand.

The more he had thought about going to see her in concert, the more it made sense. And the more it made him think he should have planned it a long time ago. I'm getting on in years, and how many times do you get a chance like this? he thought. A chance to see someone you love doing so well. He'd been everywhere in Ireland but had never traveled outside the country. It was high time, it was. The ticket was expensive but what was he saving his money for anyway? Not that he had much.

Brigid's mother and aunt had thought it was a wonderful idea. They couldn't wait for him to get back in a week and tell them all about it. A week was all the time he wanted to be away. Stay in the Hamptons a few days and then head into New York City and look up some old mates who'd moved there. That would be enough.

A green slip of paper that was hanging out the side of one of the newspapers fluttered to the floor. "What's this here?" he said to himself. Picking it up, he held it up and examined it. " 'Hamptons Car Wash. Good toward one free wash,' " he read. The date stamped on it was June 15. How did this get here? he thought. I don't even own a car. The Hamptons is where I'm headed now.

None of my pals have been up here lately. Malachy leaned back in his chair. He looked down at the pile of newspapers the coupon had been hidden in. They were all from the month of June.

Could this have been dropped by the person who stole the fiddle? Where else would it have come from?

The thought made him nervous. Was that person in the Hamptons right now? Near Brigid?

I'll bring this with me to New York and show it to that Regan Reilly, Malachy thought. See what she thinks. She's already done a good job of taking care of our Brigid.

He put the piece of paper in his wallet.

Just two more days, he thought, and I'll finally be with Brigid. I can't wait.

48

Regan stood at the door of Brigid's room. They both had come upstairs to go to bed. Kit and Angela had just run to their house after staying for dinner and a movie.

"Back to the radio station in the morning," Regan said. "Are you up for it?"

"I should be," Brigid replied. "I've had two days of rest."

"They'll announce the winner of that initial contest. What do you think the initials CT stand for?"

Brigid paused for a moment. "How about Chappy Tinka?" she blurted, cracking up.

Regan burst out laughing. "I never thought of that," she said, shaking her head. "You should win the prize, Brigid!"

"Tickets to my own concert! If it ever stops raining!"

"It will," Regan assured her. "Good night, Brigid."

"Good night, Regan."

Regan walked across the hall, smiling to herself, and closed her door.

Later, as she lay awake in the dark, listening to the rain and waiting for that magic moment when she'd fall asleep, she didn't think it seemed so funny. It was just another weird element about this place that made her uncomfortable.

Regan pulled the covers around her. Only two more days. I'll miss Brigid, but I'll be glad when she's safely away from here.

I'm probably crazy, but I can't get the initials CT out of my mind. Chappy Tinka! That's some coincidence.

Regan rolled over and finally fell asleep. She dreamt of doors that had no handles.

49

When Regan woke, she could tell it was still raining. But the sound of raindrops hitting the leaves of the trees was somehow softer, more muted, as if slowing down.

She got out of bed, pulled up the shade, and looked out. Is that a break in the clouds? she wondered. We can only hope, she thought, as she started to get ready.

Down at the radio station, things were in full swing. Brad and Chuck were jazzed. It had been a good week. Ever since Brigid had been on their show Monday, people had been tuning in and calling the station. The excitement in her life following the show hadn't hurt the momentum, either. People were starting to take notice of their station!

Brigid was sitting in the studio with the two of them now, her headphones on, during a set of commercials. Louisa and Regan were in the control room with the engineer.

"I was going through Brigid's Web site last night," Louisa whispered.

"Was there anything unusual?" Regan asked

"No. But she's getting so many letters now!"

"Let me know if anything strange shows up on it."

"Okay." Louisa pulled some papers out of a folder. "I thought Brigid might like to see these pictures I printed out. They were new on the Web last night."

Regan glanced at them. There were shots of Brigid signing autographs and playing the fiddle. A group shot of the band had Pammy in it with her arm wrapped around Kieran. How did Pammy manage to get in a band shot? Regan wondered. She certainly insinuates herself into the middle of things. I can't imagine that Brigid will be too thrilled about this. "I'll give these to Brigid later, Louisa. Thanks." Regan dropped them in her bag.

"We're back!" Chuck declared. "And have we got great news for you people who are inside like we are and not near a window. The rain has stopped! The sun is out! That is the official word!"

"You said it, partner," Brad exulted. "The land is drying, and that concert is going to happen tomorrow night. The forecast is for smooth sailing and sunny skies. What do you think of that, Brigid?"

"I'm absolutely thrilled! One more day and we'll be out there playing our music!"

"Which leads us," Chuck said, "to declaring the winner of our contest. The winner, of course, will receive a free pair of tickets to the concert, a personally autographed copy of the hot—and I do mean hot—new CD, *Brigid,* and a chance to meet Brigid O'Neill in person."

"I think," Brad said, "before we announce the winner we should give a sampling of the entries."

"Shoot," Chuck ordered.

"For those of you who are just tuning in," Brad continued, "we had a contest to see who could come up with the best meaning for the initials CT carved into Brigid's very famous fiddle."

Brigid leaned into the microphone. "I can't wait to hear these."

"Well, here goes. The responses included the following: County Tipperary; Connecticut, because CT are the initials for that state; Cursed Trinket; Can't Travel; Colleen's Tool; Connor's Thunder; Catherine's Tiger; Charley's Toy . . . and the list goes on."

"Those are good ones," Brigid said.

"Well, Brigid"—Chuck looked at her with a hint of mischief in his eye—"the one we picked was simple, but we think it fit the best . . ."

Brigid laughed. "How long are you going to keep me in suspense?"

"Not much longer," Brad assured her. "He just likes to drag this stuff out."

Chuck ignored him. "The one that had the most meaning for us and for you, we think, is . . . drumroll, please . . . COUNTRY TUNES!!!"

"How perfect!" Brigid said. "That is just perfect. I can't wait to meet whoever thought of that."

That does work, Regan thought.

Twenty minutes later, after Louisa had hopped in her car, Regan turned to Brigid. "How do you feel? Do you want to get something to eat?"

"Not with that blue sky up there! This is my last full day to sit on the beach and swim. Tomorrow we'll be rehearsing. Let's go back and grab something at the house."

"Sounds good to me," Regan said. They got in and pulled away, not noticing the nondescript little two-door car that came out behind them.

When they turned right instead of left, its driver groaned and pouted.

They're not going to the diner again! he thought angrily. I wanted to go in after them and sit where I could watch her. I wanted to try and be with her. I have only one day left, and then she leaves. I've got to do something.

Well, at least he'd definitely get to talk to her tomorrow. They were meant to be together. She even said she couldn't wait to meet him. After all, he had won the contest.

50

Now I can't decide which is worse, THE RAIN OR THE SUN! Either way our guests are always around. Sitting in the house or plopped on the beach right outside. And we can't risk going in the house when they're so close by!" Chappy griped.

Duke nodded. "I wish I'd thought of Country Tunes as the answer. I never win anything."

"Oh, shut up! Those initials don't stand for Country Tunes. They stand for Chappy Tinka!"

As usual they were sitting in Chappy's study. Duke had gone on a special trip this morning to buy Dunkin' Donuts without being asked. He thought Chappy needed the lift. Together they had listened to Brigid on the radio.

"Maybe they'll go out tonight," Duke said.

"Well, we still haven't figured out who was in there the other night when we thought they were all out," Chappy growled. "I still wake up with the sweats about that one."

"Hmmm," Duke said. "I haven't had any problem sleeping."

"You never do! To be quite frank, sometimes that worries me."

Duke shrugged.

"Bettina woke me up last night, said I was talking in my sleep. She's concerned about me and wants to spend more time together. 'After Friday!' I wanted to say, but I could hardly do that."

Duke tried to look understanding.

"Now she's insisting on going to the concert together. She wants to ride over in her car because she'd be embarrassed to be seen in mine with the big dent in it. UGGHHHH."

"So what does that do to our plans?"

"I will still ask Brigid to come over here and play one last time in the house. We'll walk her to the car. . . . I'm sure that thumbtack Regan will be attached to her side, so it will be my job to distract them and get them in the car. You'll put the fiddle in the trunk, where the other fiddle will be waiting. You have to quickly open the case and make the switch, then put the good fiddle in the golf bag. . . . Are you listening?"

Duke blinked. "Yes."

"Did you prepare the golf bag so the fiddle will fit inside it?"

"I cut out the separators. The fiddle will slide right in."

"Hallelujah! Now what are you supposed to say when you take the golf bag out of the trunk?"

"Oh, I forgot to remove these," Duke said, sounding as if he was auditioning.

"Work on your delivery," Chappy ordered. "I'll take the bag from you and insist on carrying it inside while you drive them off to the concert. I'll drive over later with Bettina."

"What if they don't want to put the fiddle in the trunk?"

"The trick is to not give them a choice. Get it out of Brigid's hands and put it in the trunk before she has a chance to say no. Can you handle that?"

"Of course, I'm an actor."

"Me, too, you know," Chappy said indignantly.

"You've never been in a play."

"You call those plays you were in?" Chappy screeched. "Those ramshackle productions I sat through! I should have gotten a rabies shot before I went into that last rodent-infested basement."

"It was performance art."

"Oh, shut up!" Chappy picked up his coffee cup and took a sip. "Getting back to the fiddle, we don't want to have to resort to that plan of action. I'd rather get my hands on the magic fiddle *today*. Keep an eye out for what they're doing over there." He pointed in the direction of the pool and the guest house.

"Yes, sir!"

"I have to find Bettina. I promised I'd go for a swim with her this morning. She's probably off reading the business section of the paper again. Checking out the stock prices." Chappy shook his head. "She really surprises me sometimes. And this time around she seems to be so much more loving and affectionate."

"Probably because your mother's not here to bug her all the time," Duke replied.

"Don't talk about Mother like that!" Chappy snapped.

"But you do."

"It's different when I say it. She could be difficult at times, but she's now resting in peace, and let's leave it at that."

"Aye aye, sir."

Chappy stood up and wordlessly walked out the door. Under his breath he mumbled, "Country Tunes. How ridiculous."

51

The day passed quickly. Everyone took advantage of the much-welcomed good weather and spent most of their time on the beach.

The other members of Kit's house had started arriving in the morning, ready to celebrate the long Fourth of July weekend. They came out on the sand and pretty soon several blankets were spread in the same area.

"This is heaven," Brigid said.

They went into the water, chilly thanks to the rain and the relatively early point in the season, but the waves were big enough to keep everyone bouncing around and warmed up.

When Brigid and Kit and Regan came out of the water and headed to the blankets, Regan told Brigid that she'd go pick up the fiddle from her parents' house.

Brigid lowered her sunglasses. "I hate to make you get in the car again. . . ."

"That's okay. I'd rather get it now. Tomorrow will be hectic, and I know you want to practice. But I don't want to leave you alone."

"Regan," Brigid said, motioning to the group around her, "I'll be fine."

"I promise I won't leave her side," Kit said in an uncharacteristically serious tone. "My keys are under the seat."

"Thanks, Kit," Regan replied. Kit's reassurance made her feel better. She had to get the fiddle and knew Brigid didn't want to be dragged along. Not on her last day of vacation.

Regan ran up to the guest house, quickly changed, and on her way out walked around to look once again in the basement windows. She leaned down and pushed her face against the dirty glass. Yup, she thought. It looks like a basement.

She hurried to Kit's car and drove over to her parents'. It felt so good that the sun was out again.

At the house she found the foursome out by the pool.

Louisa was sunning herself. "I decided to enjoy the sunshine, since Lambie and I will be leaving on Saturday. How we hate to go!"

I'll bet, Regan thought.

"Brigid sounded good on the radio this morning," Luke said. "How is she doing?"

"Her reviews have put her in great spirits. She's excited to start the tour."

"Did you show her the pictures, Regan?" Louisa asked.

Regan squinted. "Not yet. To tell you the truth, I don't think she'd love seeing Pammy in the middle of a band photo that's going out over the Internet."

"Oh my," Louisa said. "And I bet Pammy wouldn't like to see some of the letters that fans have posted on the Internet. So many of them ask why Brigid and Kieran aren't together. I quote, 'When you sing together, it looks like you're really a couple.' "

"No kidding?" Regan asked.

"No kidding."

"I've really got to get back now. Mom, could you get that famous cursed fiddle out for me?"

"Of course, dear."

Regan and Nora went inside. In her room Nora unlocked the safe and handed her daughter the object of so much speculation. "It's been some week."

"I know," Regan said. "Thankfully, it's almost over. By the way, I've decided to stay through next week with you."

"Wonderful."

When Regan pulled back into the Chappy Compound, Duke was coming out of Kit's house. Angela was standing at the screen door. Regan waved to them and parked Kit's car.

"Regan," he said as he walked over, *The Complete Works of William Shakespeare* under his arm. He pulled a letter out of his pocket. "Someone left this letter in the mailbox for Brigid. Would you mind giving it to her?"

"Not at all." Regan took it and looked at the writing on the envelope. Oh God, she thought. It was the same big black angry lettering. There was no address on it. No return address on it either. Just Brigid's name.

Duke started to walk off.

"Duke?" Regan called.

He turned and looked at her. "Yo," he answered.

"When did you find this letter?"

"This afternoon when I went out to get the rest of the mail."

"Was anyone else around?"

"I didn't see anybody. Why?"

"Just curious," Regan said. She didn't need to tell him her concerns. When he walked off again, she ripped the envelope open. She read it quickly and gasped. Except for the last sentence, it had exactly the same sentiments as the message in the letter left in Nashville.

DEAR BRIGID,
YOU'VE TAKEN SOMETHING THAT DOESN'T BELONG TO YOU. I DON'T WANT TO HEAR YOU SINGING THAT SONG ABOUT JAIL ANYMORE. YOU'VE BEEN WARNED. WHAT IS IT GOING TO TAKE TO MAKE YOU FINALLY LISTEN?

No. Regan decided. I don't think I'll pass this on to Brigid. After the concert I'll turn the doll, the smashed cassette, and the letter over to the police. There's nothing they can do about them now, and I don't want to upset Brigid. When she's left the Hamptons, I'll call her manager and have a long talk about measures they should take to ensure Brigid's security in the future.

The thought made Regan shiver.

They're having a BARBECUE!" Chappy cried. "Doesn't any one of them ever plan to spend a dime on a restaurant in this town? Won't they ever go out?"

Duke shook his head back and forth. "They're going to set up a grill on the beach."

"Were you invited?" Chappy asked suspiciously.

"Yes. So were you and Bettina."

"My nerves can't take it."

That night, Angela sat in the sand, holding a script. "Romeo, Romeo, wherefore art thou, Romeo?" she asked Duke as she bit into a hamburger.

Well, this is it, Brigid," Regan said as they talked in the hallway before calling it a night. "Tomorrow is the big day."

"And what a day it will be," Brigid answered cheerily. "It's going to be so exciting."

"No doubt," Regan agreed.

* * *

*H*e lay in bed, staring at the ceiling. He'd had the country music radio station on, and they'd done nothing but talk about Brigid and play the song. He was about to go crazy.

He'd made his plans. He couldn't bring Brigid back here right away. He'd packed the car with his camping equipment. He'd take her to the woods, like he'd planned to do in Branson, and she would fall in love with him.

Then he could bring her back here and they'd live together happily ever after.

All night he stared at the ceiling.

52

On Friday, the Fourth of July, there was a sense of excitement and anticipation in the air. It felt like the day of a prom or graduation or wedding.

The morning dawned brilliantly, and as the sun ascended into the sky, it shone down with a vengeance on the field at Welth College, doing its best to continue desquishing it.

Arnold Baker was a happy man. Casually dressed, he was outside his office, checking the progress of workers as they set up the stage on the field. Thanks to the rain, the grass looked greener and more lush than ever.

Tonight this field will be filled with music lovers having a good time, he thought. The day was saved. He looked up at the sky, smiled, and uttered three words: "Thank you, God."

Over at the Compound, the day was just beginning in the guest house.

When Regan came down to the kitchen at nine o'clock, Teddy and Hank were walking in the door with bags of bagels and the newspapers. Brigid was at the table by herself.

"Hey, Brigid," Hank said. "Your face was staring out at me from this paper this morning, so I thought I'd better buy it."

Brigid laughed heartily. "Throw it over."

Regan leaned over Brigid's shoulder to get a glance at the *Southampton Sun*. A publicity photo of a smiling Brigid looked back at them.

"Great shot, Brigid," Regan said.

"Thanks."

"What does that say?" Regan asked and began to read aloud. " 'Country music singer Brigid O'Neill will be appearing at the Melting Pot Music Festival on Friday, the Fourth of July. As with most country music singers, her songs will be about love and heartbreak, but Brigid herself has yet to find the man of her dreams. However, with her looks, talent, and charm, it shouldn't be long before she steals someone's heart and is singing from her own experience of being in love. . . .' "

Brigid looked up at Regan and rolled her eyes. "How embarrassing."

The phone rang. Teddy and Hank were both in the kitchen getting out the cream cheese and jelly and butter. Hank walked into the pantry and grabbed the phone. "Hello . . . yeah. Hey, Roy! . . . What? . . . Oh, that's great! . . . Here's Brigid." He walked over and handed the cordless to Brigid. "You're booked on Imus's radio program next Tuesday morning, and that night we'll be playing on Conan O'Brien's show."

That ought to sell a few albums, Regan thought. Millions of people listen to "Imus in the Morning." If he likes an album, he'll play it on the air and talk about it. Regan knew that he particularly liked country music. And Conan O'Brien's late-night television talk show was known for being a great jumping-off point for young new bands.

"Yes!" Brigid said, giving Hank the thumbs-up as she grabbed the phone and started walking around. "Roy, that's great news!" she exulted.

Regan whispered to Hank, "Does that interfere with your tour?"

"No, they scheduled the shows for when we'd be swinging back past New York anyway."

Kieran came into the room and sat down at the table. "What's going on?" he asked.

As Hank told him, he caught sight of Brigid's picture. He pulled the paper over to him and began to read the article. Regan thought his expression looked troubled. Before he could finish the article, Pammy came bounding down the stairs and into the room with Kieran's rubber ball in her hand.

"What's all the excitement?" she asked. "I heard Hank and Brigid and . . ." She looked at Kieran, whose nose was buried in the newspaper. "Kieran, what are you reading that's so important?" She leaned over his shoulder.

Regan poured herself a cup of coffee and watched the animation on Brigid's face as she talked to her manager. The image of the mutilated doll bearing Brigid's name raced across her mind. Only a psychotic would have done that. If that person wanted to harm Brigid, the concert would be a logical place to try. I'll stick to her like glue today, Regan vowed silently.

* * *

Chappy woke up and was shocked to see that it was after nine o'clock. Actually, I shouldn't be too surprised, he thought to himself. I was tossing and turning so much, I didn't fall asleep until dawn.

He turned on his side, disturbing Tootsie, whose snout was resting on the edge of Chappy's pillow. A low growl emanated from the dog's throat.

Bettina, sprawled out on the other side of Tootsie, slowly opened her eyes. "What'sa matter, baby?" she asked lovingly.

"Ohhhh, nothing, I guess," Chappy replied.

"I was talking to my other baby." Bettina reached out her manicured hand and stroked Tootsie's back. The dog rolled over and stuck her four legs straight up in the air, quickly taking on the look of deep rigor mortis. It was her favorite position for a doggie chest rub. "Did Daddy wake you up? Daddy didn't mean to wake you, did you, Daddy?"

"I'd have to say that wasn't my intention," Chappy answered wryly. God, how I hate that mutt, he thought.

"Daddy, say Happy Fourth of July to Tootsie."

Give me a break, Chappy thought. "Happy Fourth of July, Tootsie," he said quickly, throwing back the covers. "I'm getting up."

Bettina grabbed Tootsie's paw. "Wave good-bye to Daddy. . . . That's right, honey. . . . 'Bye, Daddy . . . 'byyye."

Chappy turned away from the sight of Bettina aiming Tootsie's paw in his direction and moving it up and down. The best piece of luck that could come from that fiddle, he decided as he headed into the bathroom, is if that four-legged bark factory decided to run away. Even Lassie had managed to get herself lost. Chappy shut the door behind him and gazed in the mirror. Look at the bags under my eyes, he thought. Stress is doing me in.

Oh well. It will all be over with today. Either I get that fiddle before Brigid O'Neill departs the Chappy Compound, or I'm doomed to a life of the humdrum.

He reached for his swimming trunks hanging by their white netting from one of the many shower heads. A quick dip is in order, he thought. Hopefully it will make me feel better and help me cope with what will be a most dramatic day in the life of Chaplain Wickham Tinka.

I can't wait for the concert tonight!" Louisa cried at the breakfast table. "It will be such fun."

"Regan said we should get there by five to set up our chairs. It starts at six. I'm putting together a picnic basket for us," Nora commented as she spooned a piece of juicy cantaloupe from its rind.

"I've got my cowboy hat ready," Luke drawled.

Lambie looked up from the bran muffin he had just sliced into four perfect bite-sized sections. "I left mine at home, darn it."

Louisa smiled at him. *"Hnnnnnn."* She turned to Nora and Luke. "Lambie bought a cowboy hat years ago when we decided to take horseback riding lessons in Central Park. I had one, too, but it flew off when we went into a quick trot, and was trampled by the six horses behind me."

"That's too bad," Nora said.

"Actually, I was glad to lose it. It gave me hat hair." Louisa drained her cup of coffee. "Do you have any phone calls you'd like to get out of the way? Because I'd like to plug in my computer to the telephone line again and get some work done."

Luke and Nora shook their heads.

"Good. I'd like to take a look at Brigid's Web site for anything interesting she might like to know about. Besides Pammy's picture. If there is, I'll print it out so she can see it when she's on that bus roaming around the country. Those tour buses must get awfully cramped and cozy after weeks on the road." Louisa stood up. "World Wide Web, here I come!"

A taxi bearing Rudy, the rested, relaxed tour bus driver, pulled into the Chappy Compound at ten-fifteen and stopped near the guest house.

Rudy paid the fare and got out, hurrying to ring the bell in the hopes that he could avoid contact with Chappy Tinka. The image of the dented Rolls-Royce was still fresh in his mind.

"Hi, Rudy," Brigid called as she ran down the stairs to let him in.

Dragging his duffel bag, Rudy stepped inside as she opened the door. "Brigid, good to see you. Are you ready for life on the road again?"

"Ready as I'll ever be," Brigid said with enthusiasm. "We're all about packed."

"Great. I'll get the equipment over to the college right now. Your rehearsal's at noon?"

"Yes."

"Okay. After everyone's back from that, we'll load up the suitcases and be all ready to roll out right after the concert. We should make it up to Boston before the sun comes up. I hear your concert tomorrow night is sold out."

Brigid laughed. "I know. Roy called before."

Rudy reached over and squeezed her arm. "You deserve it."

"Thanks, Rudy," Brigid said quietly.

He sat in the diner, eating his scrambled eggs. He'd gone to a barber yesterday and had him cut his hair short. He also was wearing a blue baseball cap. The last thing he needed was Brigid's friend who'd called him weird recognizing him. He felt himself getting nervous. Today was his last chance to get Brigid to come away with him. He put down his fork and stared at his plate. His appetite was gone. It's not going to work, he thought. Brigid's going to leave me and I'm going to be all by myself.

Tears welled up in his eyes. I've got to get out of here, he thought. Or that waitress will think I'm a big baby.

The rehearsal went well. Everything at the college was all set up and ready to go.

At four o'clock the groaning tour bus, packed with the band's and Pammy's personal gear, pulled out of the Chappy Compound in the afternoon light.

"Welth College or bust," Rudy called. He made a point of announcing the next destination, no matter how close by, at the start of every run.

Kieran and Pammy were the only ones on board.

Teddy and Hank had driven over earlier in the station wagon, which Kit would drive back after the concert. She and a couple of the others from her house were already on the college grounds, staking out a plot for the ever-expanding number of friends who would be joining them. Angela, in charge of the food detail, had organized a smorgasbord of delights that would be spread out on a blanket.

Now, with everyone else gone, Regan and Brigid looked around the house one last time to make sure that nothing was forgotten. Brigid's fiddle was in its case by the door.

"I think we've got everything," Regan said. "Time to say good-bye to this place."

"Even though we had a few problems at the beginning of the week," Brigid added, "this has been fun."

"It has," Regan agreed, thinking of both the smashed cassette and the letter she didn't dare mention. She looked over at the couch. "I hope Chappy likes the new position of his couch."

Brigid shrugged. "It looks a lot better where it is now. Heck, he probably won't even notice."

Regan laughed. "You know, Brigid, I'm glad we won't have to say good-bye to each other today. I'm looking forward to seeing you next week in New York."

"Doesn't that work out great?" Brigid commented. "You and Kit can come to watch the show, and then we'll all go out to dinner. Where should we eat?"

"Elaine's. It's been around for years on the Upper East Side. It's very hot. It started out as a hangout for writers, but now she gets a lot of different celebrities in there." Regan laughed again. "Now that you're a celebrity, it's high time you showed your face."

It was Brigid's turn to chuckle. "I don't feel any different. But I don't want anything to burst this bubble."

Regan looked at Brigid's face. She was so young and hopeful and excited. But Regan also could see a vulnerability under the surface. "Nothing will," Regan said firmly. She only wished she could be so sure.

Together they walked out, shut the door, and ambled over to Chappy's house. Chappy, Bettina, and Duke were there to greet them.

"We feel so privileged," Chappy cried, "that you are giving us this private recital before you go onstage!"

"It's my pleasure," Brigid said as she pulled the original CT fiddle out of the case. "It'll get me warmed up."

Chappy had led them into the drawing room. Brigid stood in the same spot where she had played last Saturday night. It seems like ages ago, Regan thought. And in the middle of it, I found Louisa in the pool. Regan inhaled sharply and leaned on the arm of her chair.

"Before I start," Brigid commented, holding the fiddle in her arms, "I want to thank you for having us here this week."

"We loved it," Bettina declared.

"It's a memory we'll always cherish," Chappy insisted.

Brigid smiled, placed the fiddle against her shoulder, paused for a moment, and then hit it with the bow. The fiddle jumped to life. Joyous, stimulating music filled the room.

Chappy looked around, smiling, tapping his foot on the floor. Bettina, clad in black stretch pants, a white oversized T-shirt, and low sandals, her arms folded in her lap, seemed to be enjoying it as well. Duke was keeping time by rapping his thighs with his cupped palms.

When Brigid finished the second song, she took a quick bow.

Chappy stood up. "Bravo!" he cried. "Bravo."

Bettina, Duke, and Regan joined in the applause. Finally Regan stood. "Brigid, we'd better get going. Duke, you're driving us over there, aren't you?"

"Yes," he said as he got to his feet.

Brigid leaned down, placed her fabled fiddle back in its case, and snapped it shut.

Chappy hurried over to her and grabbed both of her hands, shaking them with enthusiasm as she started to straighten up.

"Marvelous. That was just marvelous."

Duke picked up the fiddle and started to walk. "I'll carry this."

"Will we be seeing you at the concert?" Brigid asked.

"Of course. Of course," Chappy said. "They have a special place for us to sit. Bettina and I will be driving over a little later, in time for the show!"

"I'd better start to get ready," Bettina said. "See you later." She turned and headed upstairs.

The others walked out to Chappy's Rolls. Duke hurried around to the back and quickly opened the trunk. With a flourish Chappy opened the front and back doors of the car for Regan and Brigid. "I'm going to miss you two. This place won't be the same. I just know I'm going to wake up tomorrow morning and feel as sad as can be."

Brigid laughed. "I guess that means you'll have to invite us back."

"Anytime! Please come anytime!"

"Hey, boss," Duke called as he shut the trunk, "here's your golf bag. I forgot to take it out of here."

Regan turned to see Duke holding a green-and-white golf bag very high in the air. That's pretty cheap-looking for someone like Chappy to be toting around the golf courses in the Hamptons, Regan thought. It also didn't seem to have any golf clubs bobbing around in it.

"Oh, that!" Chappy cried. "I'll take it inside. Good-bye, ladies." His hands fluttering, he ushered them into the car, shut the doors, and walked around to the back, where Duke handed him the golf bag.

Brigid turned around from the front seat. "Here we go, Regan."

"That's right."

Duke jumped in and they sped out of the Compound.

* * *

Louisa, all dressed and ready to go to the concert, was sitting with her laptop, waiting for the others. A pile of pages from Brigid's Web site was on the couch next to her. She was just about to turn off her computer when she decided to read a couple more letters. May as well keep going until the others are ready, she thought. She pulled up another fan letter on the screen and began to read it.

"Oh my God," Louisa murmured. Quickly she pressed the print button on her machine. I'll have to show this to Regan as soon as we get to the concert.

Chappy was delirious. He stepped back from the car and waved as it pulled out of the driveway. He turned around and headed into the house, quickly shutting the door behind him.

Bettina's upstairs, he thought. She said she wanted to take a Jacuzzi and be ready to leave in an hour. I told her I wanted to have a quick swim. That's good. I have at least forty whole minutes before I'll have to run down and get wet, then come back and get changed. Holding the golf bag with both hands, he ran to his study, closed the door, and within seconds had changed into his yellow-and-black bathing suit and disappeared behind the bookshelf. Awkwardly, he scurried down the steps with the golf bag, ran across the basement floor, and opened the door to the men's lounge. Once inside, he shut it and stood there panting.

"Thank you, Grandpa, for building this private room!" he said.

He pulled on the string of the lightbulb, and with tender loving care he lifted the fiddle and bow out of the bag. His whole body quivered with delight. We did it! he thought. We did it! Tears filled his eyes. I can't believe that I'm holding in my arms the legendary fiddle that will bring me good luck. The fiddle that moments ago had filled his house with such beautiful music!

Chappy looked up impatiently at the lightbulb. It's so dingy in here; I want to get a good look at this and play for a few moments in the light of day.

Aha! he thought, almost jumping up in delight. The guest house is free! Everyone is gone! I can go there and play to my heart's content. Or at least until it's time to go to the concert.

He hurried through the tunnel, cradling the fiddle in his arms. "If I were a rich man, diedle diedle diedle diedle diedle diedle diedle dummmmm, all day long I'd diddy diddy dum, diedle deedle diedle

diedle dummmmm," he sang. "I'll be playing that part with this fiddle, I just know it," he said, his voice echoing in the tunnel as he scampered through, his feet moving as fast as possible, trying to keep up with the commands from his brain.

He opened the door to the guest house basement and silently gave thanks that he didn't have to tiptoe around anymore. He ran across the floor, humming, and up the steps he went. He turned the door handle and pushed. It wouldn't budge. What? he thought. What's going on? He pushed again, and the door opened a crack. Huh? Is that the back of the couch? Good God. Who told them they could move the couch? Was there another feng shui specialist in their midst? He threw his weight as hard as he could against the door, but the couch only moved another inch or two.

"PLEASE!" he groaned. Sighing, he decided to give up. There's no use throwing out my back. I have the magic fiddle, and that's all that counts. I'll have plenty of time to play it later in the light of the guest house. For now I'll do it in the men's lounge.

He turned around and ran back down the steps, across the floor, and through the door to the tunnel. He resumed his singing as he ran toward Grandpa's speakeasy. "Diedle diedle diedle diedle diedle diedle diedle dummmm."

Back in the lounge where he had spent many a happy moment, Chappy sat down in his favorite chair, lovingly inspected the initials CT on the fiddle, drew it close to him, and began to play.

He had no idea that two people were on the other side of the door listening.

Darla was in her assigned classroom, preparing for her big moment. Each performer had been given a "dressing room" equipped with a couple of comfortable chairs and refreshments. Darla's husband wasn't there yet. He'd be coming over soon.

There was a knock at the door. She opened it to find Ned, the feng shui master, with a blond-haired woman next to him. He was holding a large bouquet of flowers.

"We wanted to wish you the best of luck!" he cried, peering into the classroom. "Would you like me to rearrange those chairs they set up for you?"

As Duke pulled into the winding road at Welth College, which had been closed off except for special vehicles, a broad smile came across Brigid's face. The lawn was crowded with concertgoers who were busy with their picnics and socializing.

"Where do you want me to let you off?" Duke asked.

"Up on the left near the radio station booth," Regan said. "Brigid's supposed to meet whoever won the contest. What are you going to do, Duke?"

"I thought I'd go have a beer and then come back when it's time for the concert."

He let them off at the top of the hill, near the stage and in front of the administration buildings, where the Country 113 booth was set up. Brad and Chuck were there, clad in their C&W regalia. People were wandering around all over, and music was playing over the sound system.

A birdlike woman who must have been in her eighties stopped them, putting surprisingly firm hands on both their arms.

"Well, this is my lucky day—to come face-to-face with country music's current star. I always wanted to be a singer and you're just wonderful."

"Thank you." Brigid smiled.

"And aren't you Regan Reilly, whose mother writes those books?"

"Yes," Regan said.

"Could I get autographs? My grandson collects autographs." She fished in her bag for blank three-by-five-inch cards, presenting the first one to Brigid.

Quickly Brigid signed it.

"And Miss Regan, would you ask your mother to please—oh dear!" She dropped her pocketbook. Glass cases, a wallet, loose change, handkerchiefs, cough drops, family snapshots, medicine vials, more three-by-five-inch cards, key rings, and a compact were among the many items to scatter on the ground.

As Regan and Brigid bent to assist with the picking up, Brad from the radio station tapped Brigid's arm and pulled her back a few feet. "Brigid," he said. "The contest winner is here, but he's all upset. He won't tell us why. We've got to calm him down enough to accept the award on the air. We made such a big deal out of it, we'll look like dopes if we can't get him to take it. He said he might just go home."

"The poor guy," Brigid said. "Why is he upset?"

Brad shrugged. "Oh God, look. There he goes." He pointed to the administration building. A man with a blue baseball cap was coming out and heading for the parking lot. "I'll go get him."

Brigid put a restraining hand on his arm. "Let me try."

* * *

Look, the lens came out of my reading glasses!" the old lady cried. Her voice was trembling. "Regan, don't let anyone step on it."

Regan could hear Brad and Brigid talking as she felt in the grass for the lens. "We'll find it," she said hurriedly. "It can't be far."

I feel like such a baby, he thought as he came out of the building where he'd gone to the bathroom. He wiped his nose and sniffled. There are too many people here. He headed to his car. I'll put in Brigid's cassette and blast it. How did I ever imagine I'd be able to get her away from here, too?

Just then he heard her voice. He turned his head. She was running toward him! Oh my God! She wants me!

"Hello," Brigid said breathlessly as she approached him. She was holding a fiddle case. "I hear you're our contest winner."

"Yes," he replied.

"Will you come with me and accept the award?" Brigid asked.

I want you to come with me, he thought.

"Yes, but could I take a picture of you first? My mother won't believe that I really met you if I don't get a picture with my camera."

"Sure," Brigid agreed. "Where's your camera?"

"In my car. Right here." He walked the ten feet over to the special space that had been reserved for him, opened the passenger door, and reached in for his camera. He picked it up and turned to Brigid. "Would you mind sitting right in the passenger seat here? Everybody will laugh, thinking that I got Brigid O'Neill to ride in my old car."

"Okay," Brigid answered. She sat down in the car, keeping her feet on the ground and the door open. "Cheese," she joked.

"I need a close-up," he said, leaning toward her. With all his strength, he pushed her back. She dropped the fiddle case as her head smacked against the steering wheel. He forced her feet inside, slammed the door, and ran around to the other side.

I'm finally taking her away with me, he thought.

Regan's hand closed over the eyeglass lens. She handed it to the old lady and looked around. Brigid was gone!

"Brad, where's Brigid?" she yelled.

He turned to her and pointed. "She's with the guy who won the contest."

Regan squinted and saw Brigid getting in the car of a man who had a camera in his hands. As he shut the door and started hurrying around the car, Regan took off like a thunderbolt, sprinting across the lawn.

"Stop him!" she screamed.

He was turning on the ignition when Regan reached the car. She yanked open the door and grabbed the keys as people came running.

"You're not going anywhere," she said breathlessly.

"Go away! I want to be alone with Brigid!" he started to cry.

It was the guy from the diner! The one who liked eggs. I guess my theory about the eggshells was correct, Regan thought.

Brigid sat up in the car, rubbing the side of her head.

"Are you okay, Brigid?" Regan asked.

"I think so," Brigid said as she turned and opened her door.

Ned, Claudia, and Darla had come running out of their classroom when they heard Regan screaming. "He had a special parking space that would have enabled a quick getaway," Ned declared. "The car was positioned perfectly, facing the exit."

"Are you all right?" Darla asked Brigid tentatively.

"Yes," Brigid said. "I'll be fine."

"I suppose you're the one who wrote Brigid those letters and bought her that lovely doll," Regan hissed at the would-be kidnapper.

"No, I didn't," he sobbed.

"Sure, and you didn't try to kidnap her either, you creep. Get out of the car."

When he got out, Regan spotted Brigid's cassette on the front seat of the car.

"I see you like cassettes. You also like to leave mangled cassettes lying around for people to find?"

"NO!" he cried. "I just want to be with Brigid!" His whole body convulsed with sobs as two security officers handcuffed him and led him away. "I love you, Brigid," he called out to her. "I heard your song when I was in jail. You were singing it to me, weren't you? I would never hurt you!"

A crowd had gathered. Regan took a look at Brigid's head. "That guy gave you a good wallop. You've got a little bump there, just like Louisa had." I can't wait to find out if he has an alibi for the night Louisa was pushed, Regan thought. Pushing seems to be his MO. "Let's get you inside." She picked up the fiddle case from the floor of the car and put her arm around Brigid for support. They walked the short distance to the steps of the building.

A distressed Arnold Baker came out the door. "I'll show you to my office upstairs. There's a couch in there where Brigid can lie down."

A familiar voice called from behind them: "Brigid!"

Regan and Brigid turned to see Malachy standing there with Pammy.

"Malachy," Brigid cried as he reached out and hugged her. "What are you doing here?"

"I couldn't miss your first big concert. Not for the world. Are you getting yourself into more trouble?"

"Word travels fast. I can't believe you're here."

"He was looking for you backstage. I told him you were probably in your dressing room and I'd bring him over," Pammy said cheerfully.

"Why don't we walk Brigid inside?" Regan suggested, explaining what had just happened.

In Arnold Baker's office, they helped Brigid onto the couch. Pammy put a pillow behind her head. "She needs rest," she said firmly.

Regan put the fiddle case down on the floor next to the couch.

"Hey, Malachy," Brigid joked. "Maybe that fiddle you gave me really is cursed."

"Oh, love!" he replied. "Bite your tongue!"

Arnold Baker stood there awkwardly. "I'll leave you here in some peace and quiet. I'll be out by the stage if I can be of any help. . . ."

After he departed, Malachy knelt on the floor next to Brigid. He opened the fiddle case and pulled out the instrument. "Let me get a look at my old friend here," he said. When he picked it up, he looked distressed. He ran his fingers over it. He squinted and held it closer. "This isn't our fiddle," he finally pronounced.

Brigid's half-closed eyes opened. "Oh, Malachy, don't even joke like that."

"I'm not joking, pet. This is a spitting image, but before I gave mine to you, I carved BON in the tiniest of lettering on the side. You'd barely see it if you didn't know it was there."

"Malachy, I just played it forty-five minutes ago," Brigid protested.

"And I played it for more than forty-five years. This feels a little different. If it had your initials on it as well as CT, I might not have noticed. But where are those initials? Could someone have stolen the magic fiddle the way they stole the other fiddle from my house?"

Regan's mind was replaying the events from the time Brigid played at the house up to this moment.

"I believe that whoever tried to steal the fiddle from Ireland was from the Hamptons." Malachy pulled out his wallet. "Look at what I found in my house. I think it was dropped when the fiddle was stolen." He handed Regan the slip of paper.

A green coupon for the Hamptons car wash. The same type of coupon that Chappy collected. The same kind of coupon that Duke said he'd lost a couple of weeks ago. A couple of weeks ago was when Malachy's fiddle was stolen.

It slowly started to make sense. That golf bag in the trunk had no clubs in it. Had Duke put the original fiddle in it and substituted this copy in the case Brigid was carrying? What about that older man who had pulled into the driveway and said, "It looks exactly the same"? What was *he* talking about? Out of the blue, Chappy had invited Brigid to stay at his home. And the initials CT stood for Chappy Tinka!

"I've got an idea where it is," Regan said grimly.

Brigid, Malachy, and Pammy all looked at her.

"Where?" Brigid asked.

"With Chappy. I think Duke switched them when we were in the car."

"No!" Brigid cried. "We have to get it back! Regan, do you think you could get it from him?"

"Brigid, I don't want to leave you again."

Brigid started to cry. "I'll never see it again. Malachy gave it to me and now it's gone."

Malachy turned to Regan. "Do you think you could go and try to get it back? I'll stay right here with Brigid, I promise."

"So will I," Pammy declared.

Regan hesitated. Brigid was so upset about losing the fiddle. The person who had been threatening her was now in police custody. Malachy and Pammy promised to stay right here with her.

"I'll go," Regan said. "But I don't want Brigid to set foot outside this room until I get back. I mean it."

"She won't. I guarantee it," Pammy said. "We'll stay with her and lock the door."

Brigid smiled. "Thank you, Regan. Why don't you take the police with you?"

"No," Regan said. "We have no proof that he did it. Besides, I want to catch him by surprise." She turned to go.

"Regan, please be careful!" Brigid called after her as she hurried out of the room.

Feeling wildly uneasy, Regan ran the length of the hallway, down the stairs, and out the door to the end of the parking lot, where she knew the red station wagon was parked. She hopped in and reached for the keys under the seat. She knew the guys had left them there so Kit could drive it home later. She backed out of her space and was ready to throw the car into drive when she heard someone calling her name. Up from the tennis courts came Earl, the security guard, with a man dressed in tennis whites. She rolled down the window.

"This is the guy," Earl said proudly. "The guy who was playing tennis last Sunday when the doll was left here. I recognized him."

"Oh yes," Regan said quickly. "I don't have much time and I think we have our man anyway, but I was wondering if you saw anything last Sunday when you were playing tennis. Did you notice any cars driving around?"

He looked at her quizzically. "Yes, I did."

"What did you see?"

"A car pulled up in the parking lot and stopped."

"What kind of car?"

He laughed. "You're sitting in it."

"What?" Regan said. "This kind of car?"

"I believe it was this car. How many big old red station wagons do you see being driven around out here? I remember because it's so distinctive."

"Last Sunday?" Regan said almost to herself. It didn't make sense.

You've got quite a bump there," Pammy said to Brigid. She turned to Malachy. "I noticed a soda machine downstairs. Do you think you could see if it has any ice, or even a cold can, to hold up against Brigid's head?"

"Yes, indeed," Malachy said, anxious to help. He got up from his chair and hurried out the door.

With a decisive motion, Pammy locked it behind him. She turned menacingly to Brigid, whose eyes were closed.

Well, thank you," Regan said. "I've got to run, but I might be calling you to discuss this later."

"Okay," the tennis player replied. He and the security guard started to walk off.

Regan was about to accelerate when she heard her name being yelled yet again. The passenger door opened, and a panting Louisa plopped down next to her.

"Louisa, I can't talk right now," Regan said abruptly.

"This might be important," Louisa insisted. She thrust a letter in Regan's hands.

"What's this?" Regan asked.

"A fan letter for Brigid I printed off the Internet."

Quickly, Regan began to read.

Dear Brigid O'Neill,

I love your songs, and so I decided to look you up on the Web. I saw that picture of your band. Was that Pammy Wagner with you? She is a murderer!

There was never any proof that she was guilty, but a little more than ten years ago something happened in our town, the town Pammy grew up in. Pammy's cousin drowned. Everybody knew Pammy got her drunk on purpose and then decided to take her swimming in a lake by themselves late at night. Her cousin was not a drinker or a good swimmer, and she drowned. Why did Pammy do this? Because her cousin was going out with a boy Pammy liked.

She's a PSYCHO. *Big time. Or what you call a bunny boiler. Remember that scene from* Fatal Attraction? *I really liked that movie.*

How come that guy in your band likes her?

Yours truly,
Your #1 Fan

Inside Arnold Baker's office, Pammy came around behind Brigid.

"Let me give your neck a gentle massage," she offered. "It'll make you feel better."

"Okay," Brigid agreed.

"Do you know what just happened to me, Brigid?"

"No."

"Kieran just broke up with me. He told me it's over. He said that he was grateful for all the help I'd given him, but it wasn't working for him anymore. That it hadn't for a while."

"I'm sorry about that, Pammy," Brigid said softly.

"No, you're not. You'll be glad to get rid of me. I see the way you two look at each other."

"No . . ." Brigid began to protest.

"Yes. Oh yes. But if I can't have him, then you won't, either," she declared as she slipped a plastic bag over Brigid's head.

* * *

What do you think?" Louisa asked.

"This is unbelievable," Regan said, thinking out loud. "The tennis player said he saw *this* car driving around the day the package with the doll was dropped off. It was Sunday morning. The guys were golfing and Pammy was with them. She doesn't golf. She said she read in the clubhouse. She must have taken the car while they were playing and dropped the doll off."

"Where is she now?"

"In the President's office with Brigid and Malachy. Louisa, hold on tight!"

Regan floored the gas pedal and sped down to the entrance of the administration building. She threw the car into park and went racing out the door, Louisa at her heels. She yanked open the door of the building and ran into Malachy in the first-floor hallway. He was carrying a container of ice.

"Brigid's alone with Pammy!" Regan shrieked. Without waiting for a reply she raced up the stairs, two at a time. She reached the door of Arnold's office, but it was locked. She twisted it frantically and banged on it. "Pammy, I have to get in!" she yelled.

From inside the door she could hear Pammy shouting.

"I DON'T WANT TO HEAR YOU SINGING THAT SONG ABOUT JAIL ANYMORE. I DON'T LIKE THE WAY YOU SING IT WITH KIERAN!"

"Regan, look out," Malachy said from behind her. She stepped aside as he threw his weight against the door. It went flying open, and Malachy fell to the floor.

Brigid's right hand was limp, her left hand fluttering in a feeble attempt to claw at the plastic bag Pammy was pressing against her face.

Regan lunged across the room and threw herself at Pammy as Louisa's nails dug into the bag and ripped it open. She pressed her mouth against Brigid's and began to perform CPR.

Regan wrestled Pammy to the floor and twisted her arms behind her.

An instant later the room was filled with people as Louisa's final "HNNNNNNN" down Brigid's throat brought her back to life.

Regan could see that Brigid would be all right. "You take over," she said to Malachy and the security guards who'd come running when they saw her speeding car. "There's something I've got to do for her."

* * *

Chappy was in heaven. He recognized that the fiddle was not giving out the same sounds as when Brigid played it, but that did not deter him. Practice, practice, practice, he thought.

Outside the door of Grandpa's speakeasy, two listeners looked at each other and winced at the screech of the high notes.

"ARF! ARF!" Tootsie came bounding down the basement steps.

"I told you to lock that fleabag in the bedroom," one of them said.

Tootsie was upon them, her tail wagging joyously.

Bettina turned to scoop her up but Tootsie wriggled away and bounded back across the basement floor. "I thought I had closed the door. Mama's baby is so smart."

"Well, go lock her up. I don't want her barking when we put this loser to sleep."

Bettina made a face. "She looks as though she wants to play tag. I can never catch her, so I'm always 'It.' "

If I run into a cop, I'll get the escort I didn't want, Regan thought as she sped to the Chappy Compound. She pulled onto the property and didn't stop the car until she was in front of the castle. She jumped out and rang the bell. There was no answer.

She tried the door. As expected, it was locked. She ran around to Peace Man's trailer and knocked on the door. No answer. It was locked as well.

She ran around the back of the house, onto the deck, and peered through the sliding glass doors.

No signs of life.

Chappy, much as he hated to, decided he had better call it quits. It was time to fetch Bettina and go to the concert. Reverently he laid the fiddle on the chair, opened the door to head upstairs, and was shocked by who was standing in front of him.

"Peace Man! Bettina! What are you doing here?"

"Peace Man invented some special vitamins we want to try out on you," Bettina said.

"But we have to go to the concert now," Chappy replied nervously.

"We're not going to the concert," Bettina answered him. Unnoticed, Tootsie slipped by her, ran through the speakeasy, and discovered the long tunnel on the other side.

"You've heard your last song," Bettina said.

Peace Man raised a gun to Chappy's head. "Get back inside there."
"Surely we can discuss this!" Chappy cried.

Regan stood quietly on the deck of Chappy's house. The waves of the ocean were breaking behind her. What else had she heard? It sounded like a faint barking. Bettina's dog? It was coming from the direction of the guest house.

I may as well try it, she thought.

As she drew closer, the barking grew louder, coming through the open windows of the main room. Regan, glad they hadn't locked the door upon their departure, opened it and went inside the house where she'd stayed all week.

Tootsie scampered over to her.

"Hello, Tootsie," Regan said. "Where is everybody?"

Tootsie ran over to the couch. When Regan followed, she realized that the door with no handle was . . . open a crack! The couch was at a slight angle, as though someone had tried to push it out of the way with the door. Tootsie continued barking, trying to squeeze behind the couch to no avail.

"Did you come in this way?" Regan asked. With effort she pulled out the couch enough to make room for herself and Tootsie, then followed the dog down the steps into the musty, dimly lit basement.

Tootsie ran to the other end of the room, where a door stood open. Regan felt for her gun. Who knows what I'm going to find? she thought. Over at the door she was astonished to find that there wasn't a room behind it, there was a tunnel!

Tootsie raced ahead, her barking echoing through the tunnel. Cautiously Regan made her way through the damp, dark passageway. She saw a light at the end.

Is this what it's like when you die? she wondered. The old light at the end of the tunnel. But this light did not give her the warm, welcoming feeling you were supposed to experience. As she approached it, she slowed. What was it she heard?

Bettina's voice!

"Take Peace Man's pills!"

"I don't want to. You know I have terrible trouble swallowing pills. I'll give you any amount of money that you want."

"I'm going to get it anyway. Your mother will really roll in her grave about that." Bettina cackled. "She never liked me, did she?"

"No, she didn't. Now I can see why. Now I know why you've been studying the stock prices. Figuring out what to do with my money!"

"Yeah, Garrett's been teaching me all about investments. I told him I had a little nest egg that I wanted to see grow. Why do you think I rented out the servants' quarters this summer? I didn't want to see more money go down the drain with that theatre. I knew we were going to kill you this summer. What better time to stage your suicide than when you've got a stolen fiddle in your posession? Everyone will think you went bonkers, you'll be completely disgraced, and the world will feel sorry for me!"

"Peace Man!" Chappy said. "I'm shocked by you! Well, Duke said you were a good actor."

"Gee, thanks," Peace Man said. "I took that class so I'd get invited to your party."

"You did?"

"Yeah," Bettina said with a big smile. "We wanted to make it look as if I just met him at the Christmas party."

"Where did you meet him before?" Chappy asked.

Bettina stretched out her arm. "Say hello to my second husband."

"WHAT? You're Arthur? This is really galling, Bettina."

"Yeah. We were afraid somebody would find out. That's why he pushed that nosy Louisa into the pool. It looked like she was going to be a relentless busybody. He went into his seven days of silence so she couldn't interview him."

"I see he's broken it now," Chappy observed.

"Just for you. Arthur and I loved each other but we were poor; we divorced so I could remarry you. He's not really a guru, you know."

"Duh," Chappy said flatly.

"Duh, yourself. I told him I'd get back together with you only after I heard that that old bat of a mother of yours was out of the way. No amount of money would make me marry you again with her still around!"

"Don't talk about Mother like that!"

"Well, you'll be seeing her in a little while. Say hello for me. If you don't take Arthur's pills, which will put you to sleep for good, we're going to have to shoot you. Take your pick."

They have a gun, Regan thought. She pulled hers out.

"Give me the pills," Chappy said. Maybe Duke will find me, he thought, before it's too late. They can pump my stomach. Mother said I drank turpentine when I was a toddler, and the doctors were amazed at my resilience.

"We even brought a whole bottle of water for you to wash them down," Bettina said.

Peace Man handed Chappy a fistfull of pills. "Take them!" he ordered.

I've got to move now, Regan thought. She burst into the room. "HOLD IT RIGHT THERE!" she demanded.

Peace Man and Bettina both jumped. Chappy spit out a mouthful of pills. "Regan! How good to see you!" he practically sobbed.

"Drop the gun, Peace Man!" Regan shouted.

He looked at her with hate as he threw his weapon on the floor.

"I want you and Bettina against the wall with your arms up. And I don't mean for exercise."

The two of them slowly complied.

Chappy burst into tears of relief.

Tootsie, who'd disappeared through the door, came bouncing back.

"That dog saved your life," Regan observed.

Chappy leaned down, and the dog jumped into his arms. Brigid's fiddle was on the chair.

"I see the stolen fiddle is here, too," Regan said.

"I had nothing to do with that!" Bettina insisted.

"Quiet!" Regan commanded.

"I stole it," Chappy admitted as Tootsie licked his tears. "I am terribly sorry. And I'll tell you now: I had Duke steal the one over in the corner there from that guy's house in Ireland. Now that I have my life back, I want to come clean!"

Regan shook her head in disgust, which only made Chappy start crying again.

"I'll do anything for penance," he cried. "Anything! But before you send me to jail, would you mind if Tootsie and I came to the concert with you?"

"I'll think about it," Regan said. "Now go call the cops."

After the police came and handcuffed Bettina and Peace Man, Regan turned to Chappy. "Because you were almost murdered, I'll let you come to the concert. I can't say how Brigid's going to feel or if she's going to press charges. That's up to her. Right now I just want to get this cursed—and I do mean *cursed*—fiddle back in her hands."

Chappy's eyes flooded with tears. "You're a wonderful woman, Regan Reilly."

"Yeah, I know. Now get in the car."

Accompanied by a police escort they raced back to the college.

Brad and Chuck were onstage introducing Brigid and her band to the audience when the cars came roaring up.

Luke and Nora, Louisa and Herbert, Ned and Claudia, and Kit's group were all sitting in a special section in front. Even Darla and her husband had come down to join them after Darla's performance as the opening act. It had gone great, and after seeing what Brigid had gone through, Darla had decided that being famous wasn't worth it. Unless of course someone offered her a really good record deal . . .

"Hey, partner," Chuck said into the microphone. "It looks like we have more excitement."

Regan and Chappy ran over to the side of the stage. Malachy was standing in the wings.

Regan tapped him on the back. "Malachy," she whispered. "I've got something I'd like you to give Brigid." She handed him the magic fiddle.

Malachy winked at her. "Ah, Regan," he replied. "You're grand." He walked out and handed it to Brigid.

Brigid jumped for joy when the fiddle was back in her arms. She embraced Malachy and then held up the fiddle for the crowd.

"It looks like Brigid has her fiddle back," Brad said as the crowd went wild.

"The magic fiddle you've heard so much about was a lost fiddle for a while today," she said. "But thanks to my friend Regan Reilly, it's back."

The crowd cheered again.

"I'd love to have my friend Malachy here play a duet with me, but his other fiddle was stolen in Ireland, and we haven't gotten that one back yet."

"Yes, you have," Chappy cried, running onstage with Tootsie under one arm, the fiddle under the other. "It's right here." He handed it to Malachy.

"Well, thank you," Brigid said.

No thanks to him! Regan thought with a smile.

"Well, folks, we have a real treat for you tonight," Brad announced as Regan and Chappy walked around to join the group seated in front of the stage. "We have Malachy Sheerin, the former all-Ireland fiddle champion, who will play a song with Brigid O'Neill, the little girl he taught to play when she was thirteen years old."

The crowd roared its approval.

Nora looked at Regan with a puzzled expression as she sat down with Chappy. "Don't ask," Regan urged as she turned to watch Malachy and Brigid standing side by side, playing together, just as they'd done so many times over the years, across the sea in that little town in Ireland.

And when Kieran and Brigid started singing "If I'da Known You Were in Jail," she saw another kind of magic. A magic between the two of them that cast a spell. A spell that despite the efforts of two crazy people, just couldn't be broken.

I have the feeling they'll be making music together for a long time, Regan thought.

53

Regan sat at the large table at Elaine's and looked around at the whole group. There was certainly lots to celebrate.

Brigid and Kieran were sitting together, Kieran's arm firmly around her chair. Everyone could tell they were in love. "I felt such an obligation to Pammy," he'd said. "But finally I realized I couldn't do it anymore. I had to be with Brigid."

It must have eased his guilt considerably to find out she was a killer, Regan thought. To think that *she* had written the letters, hacked up the doll, and left the mangled cassette. Talk about being out of control.

Luke and Nora were down at the other end of the table with Louisa and Herbert. No doubt, Louisa and her computer were heroes, Regan thought. If she hadn't stopped me with that letter from the Web, it would have been curtains for Brigid. Louisa was thrilled that she'd received several offers for her as-yet unwritten story about her exciting week in the Hamptons.

Pammy, Peace Man, Bettina, and the egg-loving stalker, Horace Helm, all were behind bars, where they had quite a different view from the one they had enjoyed the week before at the Chappy Compound. The two high school kids who'd tried to steal the fiddle were locked up as well.

Only Horace Helm was worth pitying. Regan was surprised to find out the reason he first had ended up in jail—stealing chickens. If nothing else, he's a practical kind of guy, she thought.

Regan looked over at Chappy. Thanks to the generosity of Brigid and Malachy, Chappy and Duke were not sharing the fate of the other criminals. As a matter of fact, Brigid had struck a deal.

"I've talked this over with Malachy," Brigid had said. "This fiddle has certainly been wonderful, but it's also caused me a lot of problems. Seeing as I've certainly faced death, more than once, we're both starting to believe in its curse. We think it should go back to Ireland where it belongs. So I won't press charges, Chappy, if you fund the building of a music school in the West of Ireland. The fiddle will remain where there'll be no curse on it! It will be brought out each year for the top student to play. That way its music will play on and the young musicians will get a chance to share in its luck. And of course the school will be named after Malachy."

"Anything!" Chappy had cried. "Anything!"

Brigid had told Duke that she wanted him to do community service in New York City in the fall. He was sitting across the table next to Angela, who, when she'd found out about the celebratory party, had managed to get herself invited.

Who knows? Regan thought. Maybe those two will be good for each other.

They'd all been to the taping of Conan O'Brien's show and in the morning had listened to Brigid on Imus's radio program. Imus had teased her about the lengths she'd go to get a boyfriend. "You had this Pammy woman thrown in jail?" he'd said.

Malachy was seated with Hank and Teddy, enjoying a rousing discussion of country music. Kit was sitting near Regan and Brad and Chuck from the radio station. Brigid had wanted them along, and they'd been thrilled.

"We feel like we're a part of Brigid's adventures in the Hamptons," Chuck said.

"That's right, partner," Brad agreed.

Finally, Ned and Claudia were sitting near Chappy. Because Ned had moved that fateful couch, Chappy's life had been saved. Now she could hear Ned saying for the umpteenth time, "If it hadn't been for the practice of feng shui, that door would never have been partially open and Tootsie wouldn't have been barking and . . ."

Tootsie was out in the limo on Second Avenue waiting for the proverbial doggie bag.

The restaurant was bustling, filled with celebrities, many of whom stopped at their table, offering congratulations to Brigid and the band. Nora and Luke had been there many times over the years for dinner and book parties and were glad to be back. Elaine had added to the festivities by sending over champagne.

To think that that fiddle is what brought us all together! Regan thought. In one way or another! It might have a curse on it when it's in this country, but it definitely did us at least some good. Especially Chappy. It was a blessing for him. If he hadn't stolen it, Bettina might have succeeded in doing him in.

Chappy cleared his throat. "If you don't mind, everyone, I would like to make a toast."

They all turned and looked at him. He held up his glass. "I want to make a toast to Brigid. First of all, to err is human, to forgive divine. And Brigid is divine."

"Hear! Hear!" they murmured.

"And," Chappy continued, "I want to take this opportunity to invite everyone back to the Chappy Compound next Fourth of July for the opening of Chappy's Theatre by the Sea. . . ."

God help us, Regan thought.

Chappy turned to Brigid. "If I promised to practice every day for the next year, would you come back and play onstage with me just once?" he asked.

Brigid smiled and raised her glass. "What do you think, Regan? Does that sound safe to you?"

Not for the audience, Regan thought. She laughed. "We'll all be sitting in the front row!"